a PJ Sugar novel

Tyndale House Publishers, Inc., Carol Stream, Illinois

Susan May WARREN

Unfortunately, PJ's reputation precedes her . . .

Nothing but Trouble

Visit Tyndale's exciting Web site at www.tyndale.com

Visit Susan May Warren's Web site at www.susanmaywarren.com

TYNDALE and Tyndale's quill logo are registered trademarks of Tyndale House Publishers, Inc.

Nothing but Trouble

Edited by Sarah Mason

Scripture taken from the HOLY BIBLE, NEW INTERNATIONAL VERSION®. NIV®. Copyright © 1973, 1978, 1984 by International Bible Society. Used by permission of Zondervan. All rights reserved.

Library of Congress Cataloging-in-Publication Data

Warren, Susan, date.
    Nothing but trouble : a PJ Sugar novel / Susan May Warren.
        p. cm.
    ISBN: 978-1-4143-1312-2 (pbk.)
1. Murder—Investigation—Fiction.   I. Title.
    PS3623.A865N68 2008
    813'.6—dc22   2008040511

Printed in the United States of America

15   14   13   12   11   10   09

7   6   5   4   3   2   1

For Your glory, Lord

Acknowledgments

A book never makes it to the light of day without encouragers and people who believe in the story cheering it on and being willing to invest their wisdom in the process. I need to thank so many for believing in this book and for their hard work in bringing it to life:

Steve Laube, my agent hero, for sweeping me up off the floor, dusting off my hope, and helping me get excited about writing again.

Karen Watson, who understands PJ so well, for every ounce of encouragement and vision you've given this project. Thank you from the bottom of my heart.

Stephanie Broene, for pressing on to help me find the right titles and cover. Your willingness to brainstorm and keep thinking outside the box is such a blessing.

Sarah Mason, who knew just how to polish PJ's rough edges. I'm so blessed to work with you.

Ellen Tarver, my secret weapon, who puts up with my angst and knows how to counsel a crazy writer.

Christine Lynxwiler, Susan Downs, and Tracey Bateman, who believed with me and encouraged me that yes, eventually PJ would find a voice. Thank you for your dear friendship that makes me a better person as well as a writer!

Rachel Hauck, who never failed to pick up the phone, who listened to my woes and helped me unravel my story scene by scene. Your turn.

Paula and Steve Geertsen, forever friends who so long ago gave me the inspiration for PJ and who never fail in encouraging me and our family in our crazy pursuits. We're so proud of you and love you dearly.

Julie and Jim Williams, who delight my heart with their sweet children, and who patiently answered every single crazy cop question and taught me how to shoot. You rock!

To all the crazy, messy, wonderful friends in my life—this book is for us.

Chapter ONE

PJ Sugar would never escape trouble. Clearly she couldn't shake free of it—regardless of how far and fast she ran. It had followed her from Minnesota to South Dakota to Colorado to Montana, down the shore to California, and finally over to Melbourne Beach, Florida, where it rose with teeth to consume what should have been the most perfect night of her life.

She stood on the shore, her toes mortared into the creamy white sand, the waves licking up to her ankles and, with a cry that sounded more like frustration than fury, threw her linen espadrille with her best underhand pitch. It sailed high, cutting through the burning sky, disappeared briefly in the purple haze of night, then splashed into the ocean.

Gone. Along with her future.

A seagull soared low, screaming, pondering the morsel it may have missed.

"PJ, come back inside." Matthew's voice sounded behind

her as he trekked out onto the beach, kicking sand into his loafers, looking piqued as the wind raked fingers through his brown, thinning hair, snagged his tie, and noosed it around his neck. He dangled her oversize canvas purse from his hand, as if it might be a bomb.

Ten feet away, he held it out to her like a carrot. "They haven't even brought out the crab legs yet. You love those."

"Oh, sure I do. Right along with brussels sprouts and pickled herring." She'd been so soundly ensconced in happily-ever-after land she'd failed to see that the man she wanted to marry didn't even know she hated crab legs.

Pretty much all shellfish.

Thanks to the fact that she was allergic to it.

Matthew lowered the purse, as if her words stung him. "Really?"

PJ shook her head, her mouth half-open, not even sure where to start. Behind them, calypso music drifted out of Dungarees Restaurant, festive themes for happy couples. Twinkle lights stringing along the thatched roof overhung the porch, and the piquant smell lifting off the grills on the patio snarled her empty stomach. Maybe she should go back inside, pick up the wicker chair she'd knocked over.

He owed her dinner, at least.

She stood her ground, forcing him to march her belongings across the sand.

"Here's your, uh . . . suitcase." He held it out to her, letting go before she had her hand on it. It dropped with the weight of an anvil onto the glossy sand.

"Hey, that's my personal survival kit—show some respect." She scooped it up, realizing she'd been entirely too civil during his execution of their relationship. "You never know when you're going to need something." Laugh all he wanted—if a gal was going to haul around a purse, it should be filled with all things handy. Tape to shut someone's mouth, for example. Or a flashlight to guide her way home across a black expanse of shore.

"Sorry." He stuck his hands into the pockets of his khakis, his sports coat like a warning flag as it whipped around him. "C'mon, PJ, come back inside. Please. It's cold out here."

"Seriously? Because ten minutes ago you were telling me how I wasn't the girl for you. How, after nearly a year of dating, on a night when I expected—" Nope, she wasn't going there. Wasn't going to give him the slightest satisfying hint that she might have come to dinner tonight hoping—convinced, even—that he'd actually take a knee and put words to what she thought she'd seen in his eyes. Devotion. Commitment.

How could she have cajoled herself into believing that perfect Matthew Buchanan, church singles group leader and seminary student, might see a pastor's wife in her?

Maybe she wasn't exactly the picture of a pastor's wife, with her curves, dark red hair, too many freckles spraying her nose as if she were still fifteen. She'd never considered herself refined, more on the cute side, her height conspiring against her hopes of being willowy and elegant. But her eyes were pretty—green, and honest, if maybe too wide in her face. And she'd cleaned up over the years. Even if Matthew didn't think her beautiful, couldn't he see past her rough edges to the woman she longed to be—a friend of Jesus, a woman of principle, a servant of grace? a girl who'd finally outrun her mistakes?

Apparently not.

She should be flinging herself into the surf right behind her espadrille.

"Expecting what, PJ?" Matthew had a faraway, even stricken, look in those previously warm eyes.

PJ couldn't believe she was actually answering him and in a tone that betrayed her disappointment. "I just thought we were heading somewhere."

"Like the missions trip to Haiti? You wanted to go on that with me?"

She stared at the place between his eyes, pretty sure she still had her shortstop aim. Her grip tightened on the other espadrille. "No," she said slowly, crisply. "Not the missions trip."

"Oh." Wonder of wonders, he got it then, his face falling as he replayed his rejection. "I'm sorry. It just isn't working for me."

What did that mean exactly? Wasn't working? Like she might be a cog that fouled up his perfect image? Clearly he'd forgotten the depths from which he'd climbed. Especially since, in her recent memory, he'd been a Budweiser-drinking surfer.

"You said that." PJ hauled her bag up to her shoulder and curled her arms around her waist as her sundress twisted through her legs. She turned away, watching the ocean darken with its mystery. She never really swam in the ocean, just waded. The riptides and the unknown predators that lurked below the surface scared her. She tasted the salt in the cool spray that misted the air, heard hunger in the waves as they chewed the sand around her feet. She sometimes wondered what lay beyond the shore, in the uncharted depths of the sea.

And if she'd ever have the courage to find out.

"It's just that, I want to be a pastor, and . . . ," Matthew said, his voice closer to her.

"And?" She wrapped her arms tighter around herself, fighting a shiver.

"You're just not pastor's wife material."

PJ refused to let his epitaph show on her face and found a voice that didn't betray her. "Do you remember the last time we were out on the beach together?"

"What? Uh . . . no . . . wait—a couple weeks ago, we got ice cream on the pier."

PJ closed her eyes. "That wasn't with me."

Silence. She didn't temper it.

"Then, no."

"It was the night of the sea turtles. Remember, we had to use flashlights because they made all the residents along the shore turn off their outside lights? We had our arms woven together to keep from losing each other. I remember wondering if it was possible to read your thoughts, because I couldn't see your face."

"We nearly walked on a sea turtle coming to shore," Matthew said, reminiscence in his tone. She glanced at him, and something like pain or concern emerged on his face, edged in the shadow of whiskers.

PJ turned away, back to the ocean. "I kept thinking—that turtle mama's going to bury her babies onshore and never see them again. She was going to leave them to fend for themselves, to struggle back to the sea, tasty defenseless morsels diving into an ocean where they're the main course."

She stared at her shoe, dangling in her hand. The wind ran

its sticky fingers through her shoulder-length hair, tangling it into a nest. Gooseflesh prickled her skin—she *was* cold and hungry, but she'd wrap herself in seaweed and dig a bunker in the sand before she'd return to the restaurant with Matthew. Probably she could even find something to eat in her so-called suitcase.

"Do you think they made it?" She wasn't sure why she asked, why she prolonged this moment, their last. Probably trying to unravel time, as usual, figure out where it had snarled, turned into a knot.

Matthew dug his foot into the sand, watching it. "If they were supposed to, I guess." He sighed. "Let's go inside, PJ."

PJ ran her eyes over the profile she'd previously—about an hour previously—told herself she loved. His sharp jaw, that lean rectangle frame. Barefoot, she still came to nearly his chin.

She wanted a taller man. "You've got to be kidding."

He frowned.

"I'm not doing this 'let's be friends' thing with you."

"But we were friends before." He reached for her and she dodged him, raising her shoe.

"Back away."

"Whatya gonna do, PJ? Bean me with a shoe?"

"Don't tempt me."

He shook his head. "See, this is why we'd never work out. I need someone who is . . ."

"Perfect? Doesn't show her emotions?"

He raised his shoulder in an annoying shrug. "Pastor's wife material."

Now he was going to get hurt. "Oh, that's rich. Coming from a former surfer with a scar where his eyebrow bar used to be. What happened to 'Ride the waves, PJ, and see where they take you'?"

His eyes darkened. "I've changed."

And apparently she hadn't. "Good-bye, Matthew. And by the way, yes, I hate crab legs. Because I'm *allergic* to them. Pay attention."

She kicked up sand as she marched across the beach, thankful she could see her condo/motel/efficiency—depending on who she talked to—in the distance. She'd give just about anything for her Chuck Taylors to run home in. But she'd dressed to kill, or at least for love, this evening in a floral sundress and new espadrilles that gave her a sort of out-of-body feminine feeling. She needed her Superman pajama pants and a tank top—and fast.

"PJ! Don't run away!" Matthew's voice lifted over the surf.

"Running away is what I do best!" She didn't turn.

"Why do you have to be such a drama queen?"

Okay. That. Was. *It.* She spun around, dropped her bag to the sand, and with everything in her, hurled her other shoe at him, a hard straight shot that any decent first baseman could have nabbed or at least dodged.

His four-letter snarl into the night put the smallest of smiles on her lips as she turned away.

The restless ocean stirred into the sounds of the club music as she hiked up the beach. She clung to the shadows, avoiding the pool of light from houses and condos, restaurants and cafés.

Not pastor's wife material.

She broke into a little jog, hiking up the confining circle of her hem.

Angling up the sand, she hopped over the boardwalk toward

her building. Brine-scented sea grass brushed the walkway, carpeted the trail to the two-story Sandy Acres motel/apartment complex, the half-lit sign now reading only "Sa d Ac es," a term that seemed particularly apropos as she opened the metal gate alone, again.

Around the patio area, rusty pool furniture glimmered under the tinny, buzzing fluorescent lights. A horde of moths flirted with death around the heat of the bulbs; the earthy palmetto smell tangled with the coconut oil smeared onto the deck chairs, tempering the sharp odor of chlorine. Hip-hop thrummed under her downstairs neighbor's door, and wet towels taunted by the wind slapped the metal rail above her as she climbed the stairs to her unit.

Home sweet home.

A temporary home. Three years *could* mean temporary. In fact, until tonight, she'd already been mentally packing, giving away her garage sale wicker and, finally, her Kellogg High School Mavericks sweatshirt. Maybe even Boone's leather jacket, the one she'd stolen the night she left town. It seemed an uneven prize to all he'd cost her.

Her skin prickled as she fought the dead bolt.

Boone had probably forgotten the girl who wound her arms around his waist and dug her face into the leathery pocket between his shoulder blades as he roared them away from Kellogg on his Kawasaki.

Loneliness met her in the silence, the lights between the slats of the blinds striping the bedsheet that cordoned off her so-called bedroom. Her faucet dripped, and she dropped her key onto the counter, surrendering to the habitual attempt to turn it off. Then she *ca-lumped* her bag onto the chair, folded her arms, and stared out the window at the dark, hungry ocean.

Almost without realizing it, she clamped her hand over her left shoulder, high, near the apex, where the word *Boone* marked her in flowery script.

Beep. Behind her, the answering machine beckoned her away from the past and what might have been.

Boone was probably in jail or, worse, reformed and married with children. The great taboo, he wasn't mentioned in her mother's phone calls; his name wasn't scrawled in her letters. She was sure he'd forgotten her, just like everyone else had.

Beep.

Forgotten that she'd left Kellogg, Minnesota, accused of a felony—an accusation too easily pinned on a high school senior whose reputation indicted her without trial. Her only crime had been abysmal judgment in men and allowing her heart to trespass into places her common sense told her not to tread.

A crime, apparently, she kept committing.

Beep.

Forgotten that her mother cut a deal with the director of the country club, one that included a full tank of gas and promises of a new kitchen. Her mother's instructions to her included the phrase "just until things blow over."

Beep.

Perhaps things had blown over long ago. Perhaps she was the one not ready.

Beep!

She pushed the Play button as she opened the freezer. *Please let there be ice—*

"PJ, it's me." Connie. The fact that her sister's attorney-solemn voice tremored made PJ close the freezer door.

"Don't panic." Of course not. Because Connie never called her without some earth-shattering joyful news: *I passed the bar. I bought a house. I'm having a baby. I'm getting married again!*

PJ forced herself to remember that dissecting all that joy was the dark news of husband number one's death. No one, regardless of how successful, thin, wealthy, and smart, deserved to be woken up at 2 a.m. by the police and asked to identify her husband's remains. Or those of his mistress, with whom he'd been traveling when his car went off the road.

Still, PJ *could* hear panic under Connie's voice. Especially when Connie continued, a little too quickly.

"Okay, listen, I know you don't want to hear this, but . . . I need you to come home."

Connie took a breath. And PJ held hers.

"Mom's been in an accident."

Everything went silent—the hip-hop beating the floorboards, the far-off hunger of the ocean, Matthew's criticism in her ear. The years rushed at her like a line drive knocking her off her feet, regrets scattered like dust in her shadow.

Then Connie sighed and hung up. The beep and time signature noted no further messages.

PJ reached for the phone.

✳ ✳ ✳

Connie sounded as if she might be on her fourth cup of coffee in some cement-lined corridor, tapping out the hour in her Jimmy Choos.

"PJ, where have you been? Mom's already had her cast set and is in recovery."

"Please, Connie, not now. Just . . . what happened?" PJ pressed the phone tight to her ear and paced to the window, the ten-year near estrangement with her mother hollowing her out. Had her mother forgotten her silent pledge to carry on, to be waiting if and when PJ summoned the courage to point her car north?

"She fell on the tennis court and broke her ankle."

The window's cool surface broke the sweat across PJ's forehead. Tennis? "For pete's sake, Connie, I thought . . . oh, man . . . Don't call me again."

"PJ!"

"What?"

"Don't you want to know how bad it is?"

PJ sank into a chair. "How bad is it?"

"They casted her ankle; her bones are secured with a pin. She'll be out of the hospital tomorrow. But I need you to come home. I'm getting married in a week, and I need help."

Married. Of *course*. PJ had seen a picture of Sergei, Connie's fiancé, and seriously wondered why a double-degreed lawyer might be marrying her tae kwon do coach. But who was she to question—after all, she, a near felon, had dreamed she might pass as a pastor's wife.

"I thought you two were eloping." PJ had managed to catch her breath and now returned to the freezer, cradled the phone against her shoulder, and dug out the Moose Tracks. As she opened the lid, crystallized edges and the smell of freezer burn elicited only a slight hesitation. She lifted a spoon from the dish drainer cup in the sink.

"We were flying down to Cancún, but Sergei's parents couldn't get a visa for Mexico, so I planned a little soiree at the country club. But the thing is, I have vacation time coming, and if I don't use it, I'll lose it. So we need to get away now if we want a honeymoon, and Mom certainly can't watch David while she's in a cast. I need you, Peej."

PJ leaned a hip against the counter and cleaned the sides of the carton, the chocolate swirls melting against the roof of her mouth—sweet with only an edge of bitter.

"So let me get this straight—it's okay that you weren't going to invite me to the sunny sands of Mexico to watch you tie the knot with Mr. Muscle, but you want me to leave my life and return home at your whim?" She kept her eyes averted from the threadbare wicker and the chipped Formica table and stomped the floor once, real loud, hoping the boyz in the hood might hear her over the rap.

On the other end of the phone, Connie's voice wadded into a small, tight ball. "I know how you feel about Kellogg and Boone and especially Mom, and frankly I don't blame you. I've even tried to respect your decision. But it's time to come home. You have family here. I need you. David needs you. . . ."

PJ tossed the empty container into the sink, licked off the spoon. Down the street, a car peeled out in a hurry, and a dog barked in disapproval.

"You know how I feel? Really? Because you got to stay, Connie. After graduation, you went on to college, to a life. I left town right after the ceremony, a Tupperware bowl of fruit on the seat beside me, praying my ancient VW Bug would make it to the South Dakota border. I've spent the past ten years wandering from one tank of gas to the next, trying to figure out where I should land. You lived the life Mom dreamed for you—"

"You lived the life you dreamed for yourself."

PJ flinched, Connie's voice sharper than she remembered. She stared out the window, wondering if Matthew still stood on the beach, a hand to his bruised head. "Is that what you seriously believe?"

Silence on the other end made PJ rub her fingers into her eyes. Connie had become an unlikely ally over the past ten years, mediating between PJ and their mother, once in a while sending her enough to cover her rent. However, it still wasn't so easy to share the limelight with the sister who was wanted.

As opposed to being the one left on the proverbial doorstep. Being adopted sounded so endearing to everyone but the adoptee. The fact that Connie had been born just a few months later, close enough to share the same classes in school, constantly earning better grades and more awards, only served as a constant reminder that PJ hadn't been good enough, even from birth.

"I'm sorry," PJ said, letting a sigh leak out. "I've had a rough night."

"Then come home, PJ. If only for a couple weeks. Or longer. You can stay with me until you find your own place."

"Did you ask Mom?" PJ winced, hating the question and that she didn't yank it back. Hadn't she learned anything?

"I asked. Even if Mom won't admit it, she needs you."

PJ stood at her screen door, staring out at the now starsprinkled night glistening on the rippled landscape. The Milky Way streamed across the sky, heading north.

"Please?" Admittedly, it was the closest to pleading she'd ever heard from Connie. "I need you."

"How long before your wedding?"

"Six days. Sunday at two."

PJ hung up without promises and walked back outside, over the boardwalk to the beach. The wind had chased the clouds, and a diamond chip moon hung in the sky, surrounded by the jewels of the night, brilliant and close enough to wrap her fingers around. She pressed her bare feet into the sand, then lifted them out, listening to the water slurp, then fill the imprints. Finally, she stared out again at the ocean and wondered how many turtles really made it back to the sea.

Chapter TWO

Whoever said you can never go home again probably hailed from Kellogg, Minnesota, population 2,317.

PJ passed the carved Welcome to Kellogg sign, noting that they'd installed a small placard at the bottom listing the population, wondering if they'd change it should she decide to sink down roots.

Or just how soon the law would appear to run her out of town.

So maybe she felt a bit punchy, twenty-six hours on the road stiffening her brain and her muscles, combined with the wild spree of hope that had caused her to ditch her life—what was left of it, at least—in Florida and head north.

She turned down the country hee-hawing from her radio, still hearing the three little words that had kept her VW Bug's gas pedal to the floor through Atlanta, Nashville, Peoria, Madison, and finally around 694 north, skirting Minneapolis, and then west, around Lake Minnetonka.

Straight into Kellogg.

"I need you."

It scared her how much she clung to those words.

PJ unlatched her hands from the leather steering wheel, flexing her fingers, stretching her neck, hoping to release her bunched muscles. She'd wedged a box of books, shoes, and mementos into the seat behind her and shoved her duffel, filled with only the clothes she really liked, into the trunk.

She'd left the sundress behind.

And the garage sale furniture had been destined for abandonment all along. Her landlord even gave her back her security deposit, thankful for a furnished apartment to rent.

Anytime now, the voice of sanity could kick back in: *PJ, what are you doing?*

Rolling down her window, PJ stuck out her elbow and took a deep breath, the smell of summer stirring in the minty grass, the lilacs hanging from plump trees. Kellogg's Main Street bordered Lake Minnetonka, now dark against the mid-afternoon sun, hazy and fierce behind anemic clouds. Lazy sailboats, moored at the yacht club and out in the harbor, gleamed bright and enchanting, whispering promises of wind-blown hair and a sultry tan as they bobbed like swans in the water. Sunday afternoon sun worshipers lay on the coarse sandy beach, others in blue and white loungers, floppy hats pulled low over sunglasses.

PJ had spent too many high school summers dividing her time between the beach and the country club pool, her legs sticky with coconut oil, hoping Boone might motor by or, better yet, hijack his parents' ski boat and woo her into spending the afternoon skiing on the foamy waves.

Leave it to her fickle heart to trail back to Boone's memory like a homing pigeon.

She breathed in the spice of garlic and smoking wood chips, courtesy of the grills off Sunsets Supper Club's veranda just beyond the beachfront. In the lane next to her, a convertible of laughing, muscle-shirted boys turned up their radio. Rap music spilled out, and they jackhammered their way past closed storefronts displaying preppy fashions meant for leisure. PJ barely touched the gas, noting the new volleyball pit outside Hal's Pizzeria and Bar; a sign over the outside stage advertised a jazz festival. Last time she'd seen a band at Hal's, it had been Ricky Merkel's punk band.

On the boardwalk that stretched along the beach like a border, the occasional couple strolled hand in hand. Frisbees winged on the breeze across lawns dotted with picnickers.

Like an old friend, a lusty wind reached out, tangling her hair into a knotty, carefree mess.

She had the urge to toe off her flip-flops and drive barefoot as she turned off Main at the theater, driving past the redbrick high school, then out to the country club, with its neat hedges, its white terraces, the tidy golf course. Before she could stop herself, her gaze swept the employee parking lot for his Kawasaki.

Boone's voice, low and angry, came back to her: *"You'll be back someday. And maybe I won't be here."*

Oh, she dearly hoped so.

The new kitchen wing, now nearly ten years old, jutted out past the old foundation. It felt too much like visiting a war monument. She had the urge to stand over it, say a little prayer for lives lost.

Namely, hers.

She pulled up at the far end of the parking lot, cataloging the changes. The weathered, white-tiled pool boasted a new slide and, on the high dive that had once trapped her at the pinnacle, a fresh coat of paint. A crisp white flag fluttered on the tenth green, in plain sight to anyone who might be looking.

She hadn't really noticed that before and for a second nearly put her car into reverse. But it wasn't likely that she'd see old Ben Murphy or Ernie Hoffman again, was it? Or that they'd still remember finding her on prom night entangled with Boone on the smooth putting green blanket?

Maybe there were some images a person simply couldn't purge. She certainly had a few.

Behind her, a guest slammed the door to her silver BMW, balancing in her arms a gift wrapped in pink. PJ glanced in the rearview mirror. Why hadn't she stopped outside town to change? Instead she had to show up smelling like she'd spent a week under a bridge, her red—no, auburn—hair greasy, in frayed jeans, a tank, and flip-flops.

"Oh, boy . . ." She sat in the car, hands wrapped around the steering wheel, debate gluing her to the seat. "Oh . . . boy."

Maybe it wouldn't be as bad as she thought. So what if Connie was on her *second* husband, while PJ couldn't even snag the first? No one in Kellogg knew that she'd job-hopped her way around the nation, had more forwarding mail addresses than a sailor. She could pretend . . . well, she was done pretending.

Maybe it was time to find the real PJ, the one she could live with long term. The one who didn't have to be pastor's wife material but wasn't the messy PJ she'd left behind, either.

Besides, Connie, or maybe her mother, *did* need her.

"Don't even think about coming back here, PJ Sugar. We'll arrest you on sight." PJ closed her eyes against Director Buckam's warning in her ears. Just because she'd been banned from the country club premises ten years ago didn't mean they'd recognize her today. She'd changed her hair color, for one. And this time she wasn't wearing silk—or rather, *not* wearing it.

"Therefore if anyone is in Christ, he is a new creation; the old has gone, the new has come!"

Right. She'd memorized that verse first after finding Jesus and salvation on the boardwalk in California. It felt easier to believe then, and especially when she packed up and moved to Florida. Now, however, was when she needed it.

Yes, the new and improved PJ Sugar.

Her cute little lime green Bug looked pedestrian and forlorn as she grabbed her bag off the front seat, shut the door, and climbed the broad, white steps, pushing open the door to enter the grand foyer of the club. Polished wood, worked leather, Turkish wool rugs—the smells of tradition rushed back to her. She smelled Sunday lunches on the veranda and Saturday morning swimming lessons, heard the slap of wet feet running through the main hall from the locker rooms, and felt anew the air-conditioning prickling her skin before she hit the humidity of the summer. She could almost see Boone in his caddie uniform, his wide shoulders under the green polo shirt grooming him into the preppy boy his father hoped to create. How one could hide behind the aspirations of an ambitious parent.

Voices lifting from the anteroom startled PJ to the present. She crept toward the fireplace room overlooking the golf course and Connie's wedding reception area. Fifty friends, she'd said on the phone, a small get-together to celebrate the day. Had Connie dared jot her name on the guest list?

She stopped just outside the door, spotting her mother, her leg in a cast and propped up in her wheelchair, her voice commanding as she engineered the silver and black decorations.

PJ blinked and time fell away. Slim Elizabeth Sugar, directing the caterers at her and Connie's graduation party, her regal pearls at her neck, her dark mahogany hair piled into a tight chignon. Blue and gold streamers had surrounded the graduation pictures on either end of a long table. How she hated that her mother had picked the eleven-by-seventeen shot of her in the pink angora sweater. But had she ever really had a choice?

A carved watermelon fruit bowl, croissants, a three-tiered marmalade cake with sugared orange curls twisting from the top crowned the table, all under an eight-foot sign: "Congratulations, PJ and Constance."

Sisters from different mothers. In every way.

"PJ!"

Her sister's voice fast-forwarded time, and her mother aged, with shorter hair, her face lined and, remarkably, even thinner, her bones sharp through a pair of classic black pants and a periwinkle silk shirt. She still wore the pearls at her neck.

Funny thing about regret. Now that it had climbed up from the hard places PJ had stored it, she couldn't swallow it back down. It lodged in her throat, thick and choking off her air.

Connie handed off a box of corsages to the florist and rushed to PJ. "When did you get here?" She pulled PJ tight against her skinny, French-manicured self, every inch the groomed woman she appeared in the Internet photo for her firm. Poised, her dark hair pinned back, with their father's deep green eyes, wearing a pressed linen suit that looked as fresh as when she'd put it on. True Sugars didn't let anyone see them sweat.

"Just now," PJ managed. "Nice decorations."

"You're tan."

PJ could have hugged her again for not mentioning the chipped fuchsia toenail polish, her ratty attire, the rather unsavory aroma she emanated. "Life on the beach, Sis."

"And you colored your hair." Connie reached out and fingered PJ's shoulder-length cut. "I liked it long and blonde."

Yeah, well, some things had to change. "You look great. Sergei's a lucky man."

"He loves me *and* David," Connie said, her eyes saying more. "You need to get cleaned up—the wedding's in an hour. Nothing like getting here *early*? So as to not worry the bride?"

"You know me—I live for drama." But behind her words, she heard Matthew's voice. "Well, not so much anymore."

"Right." Connie gave her a peck. "I brought you a dress. It's black; I hope that's okay. And some heels, like you asked. They're in the Chip Hill room—you remember."

"You look like you've been driving a truck."

PJ didn't even have to turn. "Thanks, Mom."

"I'm kidding, PJ. Come here."

PJ simply stared at the woman wheeling toward her. Extending her hands to her. Pulling her into her arms.

"I'm so glad you're home."

For a second she didn't move, didn't know how to. *Glad . . . ?*

But then she leaned into the words, wrapping her arms around her mom, pulling her close, feeling the bones that seemed sharper. Still, she breathed deep, smelling the Chanel on her skin. Reorienting. Capturing.

Yearning.

Her mother pulled away from her too soon. "The important thing is that you made it. And you still have time to change."

* * *

Her mother, or perhaps Connie, still had impeccable taste. Bouquets of fragrant gardenias framed the small platform where Connie and Sergei took their vows. Silver and black silk ribbons anchored the serving table, accentuated by the white-gloved servers carrying trays of salmon canapés and caviar on ice. An acoustic guitar player seated on a high barstool hidden discreetly to the side of the head table played unobtrusive, delicate tones. PJ watched as one polished, degreed lawyer friend after another stood and offered congratulations. When she finally raised her glass, her words seemed hollow, unattached to the bride.

Still, Connie beamed at her and raised her glass in approval.

"Isn't she gorgeous?" A thin, elegantly coiffed associate asked as PJ helped herself to another canapé.

PJ watched as Connie, in her off-the-shoulder satin, diamonds dripping from her ears, floated seamlessly from one guest to the next. "Absolutely."

"I just can't understand what she sees in . . . him." The associate raised her eyebrow as if PJ should know exactly to whom she referred.

"Hey, Sergei's a great guy." Oh, she hoped. "And he loves her." Connie had said as much. "Besides, little Davy needs a dad."

"Whatever. Everyone knows she's marrying him for what's under his tuxedo."

PJ's mouth opened, and she cast a furtive look for her mother or any of the country club regulars. Yes, it was true that Sergei probably had the build of one of the surfers from Cocoa Beach, with the accompanying working-English vocabulary. However, Connie had enough words for both of them, and opposites attracted, right?

Besides, the way Sergei's gaze caressed Connie walking down the aisle, the way he locked his eyes with hers during his vows, as if seeing in her something that no one else could see and with her he might find the secrets he'd been searching for all his life . . . well, PJ might pour out eternal promises too.

And she'd bet that Sergei didn't use words like *not working*. Or even *pastor's wife material*, although if anyone could qualify, it would be Connie.

PJ downed her punch, reached for another, and wandered over to her mother, greeting guests by the door.

"Nice ceremony," PJ commented, her best attempt at a "Hi, I'm here, it's just us, what do we say now" kind of statement.

Elizabeth smiled at her.

PJ categorized it as more of a zippered, tight-lipped grimace. "What?"

"Nothing. Of course it was nice."

Raucous laughter lifted from one of the far corners of the room. PJ's gaze darted to a group of what she could only peg as Sergei's contingency. Internationals, earmarked by their dark dress pants, European-cut shirts, squared-off shoes, and hair either tied back or cut high and tight and severe. A regular mafioso clan, right here in River City.

"It's the Russians," Elizabeth said as if reading PJ's mind.

"You make it sound like they're invading us."

Elizabeth gave a wave of her hand. "Thankfully they only have a three-month visa."

"The entire lot is here for three months?"

"No, no. Most of them live here. Just Boris and Vera are here on a visa." She nodded toward a duo sitting at a table not far from the commotion. "Sergei's parents."

Boris had cloned himself in Sergei—thick arms, narrow hips in an oddly fitting suit. His wife, Vera, had squeezed her body into a black cocktail dress that in earlier years might have been banned on country club premises.

PJ glanced back at her mother, who wore an expression that suggested she had eaten some bad salmon. "They can't be that bad."

Elizabeth raised a groomed brow. "Just you wait. They don't speak English."

"Oh no, the Russians are taking over the world."

"Mark my words, PJ, this is just the beginning."

PJ shot a look at Connie, hanging on beautiful Sergei's arm, laughing, her eyes shining. "I certainly hope so."

Her mother rolled away as PJ finished her salmon canapé, ditched her plate, and went after the strawberry white cake. She took a piece and moored herself in a corner while her mother made the rounds, greeting guests with a smoothness bred straight from the House of Windsor. No one would have known that she'd once been a Mulligan, raised on a farm outside a smudge on the map in southern Minnesota before meeting Carl Sugar at Wheaton College and marrying well. She refused to allow his investment firm to drop his name, even a dozen years after his death.

Her mother knew the value of a good investment.

An hour later, while working on her second plate of cake, PJ decided that she'd imagined her own mythology. Three hours at the Kellogg Country Club, and she had yet to hear a police siren, see bright whirling bubble lights, or even hear one snide comment about illicit activities on nearby putting greens.

Maybe she could, indeed, return a new creation.

She tugged at the clinging black sheath dress Connie had bought for her, eased out of the high pumps that tore at her feet, resisting the urge to dig her flip-flops from her purse. She hoped Davy liked the beach. . . .

"Are you sure it's a good idea for PJ to keep him while you're on your honeymoon?" The voice, spoken too brightly for her to ignore, rose from behind her, where Connie had clumped with Sergei and, of course, her champion at arms, Elizabeth Sugar.

"I am perfectly capable of taking care of him, Connie."

Him being, of course, Davy, Connie's four-year-old dark-headed son, formerly slicked up for his parade down the aisle, smiling like an imp for the photographer. Now he sprawled on the floor, rumpling his suit and tie. He'd wedged the ring pillow he'd carried for his mother under his shirt, occasionally beating his chest like Tarzan.

Hey, cool idea.

"PJ's just . . . She's not . . ."

"I'm standing right here, Mom," PJ muttered as she watched

Davy draw his tuxedoed arm across his gooey brown mouth, leaving a trail of glistening chocolate from his pillage of the mints table.

"PJ barely knows David," Elizabeth said as if she hadn't heard PJ.

Maybe her mom had a point. . . . But PJ knew Connie would rally, years of courtroom experience in her corner.

"So she's not auntie of the year."

PJ wanted to raise her hand, call an objection. She did send presents twice a year. And called on his birthday.

"PJ is an adult. She's not likely to burn anything down again."

Oh, good one, Connie. Bring that up. Still, the realization that Connie believed in her despite her past and seriously intended to make good on her request for PJ to watch Davy while she and Sergei escaped to Mexico drowned any words PJ might raise about her innocence.

Besides, apparently she *was* invisible.

Her mother lowered her voice, as if PJ couldn't hear her from twelve inches away. "PJ doesn't know the first thing about kids—" okay, she was right about that—"she doesn't even like kids—" not entirely true, she just didn't like runny snot—"and besides, I'm just in the wheelchair for today. I do have crutches."

"Two weeks with a four-year-old. How hard could that be?" PJ wasn't sure why she'd decided to wage a defense. Her mother made some good points. However . . . *"I need you."* The words had taken over her brain, giving her mouth its own mind.

"Exactly." Connie smiled at her gorilla-impersonating son,

so much unadulterated love in her eyes. PJ's throat thickened. What must it be like to be that adored?

She dumped the unfinished cake onto a table and wiped her mouth with a napkin. "Listen, Connie. Mom. I've worked as a counselor at a wilderness camp, fed gorillas at the San Diego Zoo, jumped from tall buildings as a stunt girl, waited tables, driven dump trucks, cleaned motel rooms, changed oil, apprenticed as a locksmith, been a ski instructor, herded cattle, and even worked on a carpentry crew. I think I can figure out how to make macaroni and cheese, keep Davy fully clothed, and tuck him into bed at night. I'll even read him a story."

"He likes *Horton Hears a Who!*" Connie offered.

"Me too. We'll get along famously." PJ gave her mother a grin, all teeth.

Behind his grandmother, Davy stuck out his chocolate-slathered tongue at PJ.

"Well . . ."

"The truth is, I didn't exactly bring a wedding gift."

Besides, how else would she prove that she intended to . . . stay? The word wedged itself into the middle of her chest like a bubble, so fragile that if she moved too fast, it might pop. But the minute she'd touched her brakes inside the Kellogg city limits, the hope had expanded, taking up too much room inside her.

She *would* start over. For the final time. Connie wasn't the only Sugar girl who wanted a career, a house on the hill, and a man with great shoulders. She just happened to be the one who got them.

"Fine," Elizabeth said, her mouth again that tight zipper.

PJ stifled the urge to wince. Instead she produced a smile

that would have made her eleventh-grade theater teacher cheer. *Please don't pop the bubble, Mom.*

Thankfully, Elizabeth Sugar would rather have her head shaved in public than air her dirty tennis shorts to the world. PJ breathed relief as her mother rolled away.

"David will be so thrilled." Connie's expression screamed victory. PJ shot another look at Davy, now pulling off his socks. "He's really looking forward to your visit."

Oh yeah, he was doing a regular Irish jig.

"You're a lifesaver." Connie brushed her lips against PJ's cheek.

A lifesaver. Yep, that was her, in a nutshell.

Connie finally disappeared into an anteroom and then, ready to depart for her honeymoon, made her entrance to the crowd assembled on the veranda. She towed little Davy by the hand toward PJ, who smiled like Barney and crouched before her new charge.

"So, you're Davy. I'm your auntie PJ."

Davy winged her hard, right on the top of her shoulder.

"David, that wasn't nice. You apologize to Auntie PJ."

"I don't like BJ!" He turned and buried his face in his mother's pressed pants.

"He's a little upset about us leaving."

No, really? PJ stood and congratulated herself when she spied his foot moving and managed to dodge a snap kick to her ankle. "Are you . . . sure you should leave?"

"He'll be fine." Connie crouched before Davy and held him at arm's length. But her mouth trembled. "You and PJ are going to have lots of fun, David. I promise." She pulled him to herself and held tight, whispering in his ear.

"Um . . . Mom moves pretty fast in her—"

Connie's sharp look cut her off and she pursed her lips tight.

PJ blew out a breath and, slipping out of her heels, knelt behind Davy. Then, taking his arms, she transferred his death clench from Connie's neck to hers.

Davy leaned back and roared, struggling, kicking. Connie stood, her hand pressed to her mouth in horror.

"Go now," PJ said quietly, matching his hold, trying not to wince for Connie's sake.

Connie wiped her cheeks. "Okay, listen; he starts summer preschool tomorrow at Fellows Academy. His uniform's pressed and in the closet."

Uniform? For preschool? "No, not Fellows, Connie . . ."

"Stop right there." Connie leveled her a look that she could have learned only from the master. Or maybe on cross-examination. "He's been on the waiting list for three years. It's very important he is there on time, pressed, combed, and smiling." She reached out to run a hand over Davy's head, then pulled back. "Please, PJ."

PJ should have guessed that Connie would be well on her way to grooming Davy for his future. A true Kellogg Sugar.

"Pressed. Combed. Smiling. Got it."

But Connie stood frozen, staring at her son as if seeing him for the first or, perhaps the last, time. Was she remembering that night when her first husband pulled away, waved to her from the driveway, and betrayed her in every way possible?

PJ touched her arm. "He'll be fine. I promise, you won't come home to a son malnourished, ignorant, and hunted by the local law. I will drive him to preschool, bathe him regularly, feed him nutritious suppers, and read him stories. Horton, remember?"

"Horton." Connie swallowed back the pain on her face. "I owe you."

"No. . . . We're just getting started with my payback. Go. Be married." She winked and Connie grinned big.

Sergei was leaning against their gold Lexus, arms folded across that mountainous chest. "Zank you, Peezhay."

So he had some issues with the English language. He clearly adored Connie. And the accent could turn any girl to butter.

He adjusted his Ray-Bans and waved as the crowd delivered their bubbles. He opened the car door for Connie to climb in, then went around to the driver's side.

Connie leaned out the window. "Oh, by the way, Sergei's parents are staying at the house while we're away. Sergei's cousin Igor lives in town—he'll chauffeur them if they need anything. Just make sure that Boris doesn't do any sunbathing." She waved as Sergei pulled away.

Sunbathing?

Davy kicked out of PJ's arms, landing with a thud on her bare feet. "Mommy!" Before she could grab him, Davy raced after them, arms flailing, screaming.

Yes, they were going to have so much fun.

"Davy, come back!" PJ ran down the stairs, cringing as he threw himself onto the pavement. Of course, her mother watched from the porch, wearing a pained expression.

"No, don't . . ." Standing over the thrashing boy, she didn't know where to start. Pick him up? Rub his back? Put something between his teeth? "Davy, c'mon . . ."

The crowd began to shift away as if embarrassed by the spectacle.

"Okay, fine, Mom. Come and help me then." When PJ didn't hear movement, she looked up at her mother, who remained on the porch, shaking her head.

"PJ, actually, I think this will be good for you."

"What does that mean? That's not fair. You know him better—"

Her expression must have betrayed her frustration, because her mother's eyes softened. "Please try and . . . and . . . well, I'm sure you'll do just fine. Just don't get . . . into . . . trouble."

Why did she always feel twelve years old around her? "Mom—"

"Let me know when you're ready to go." She rolled herself into the club.

Davy, dirty, rumpled, and noisy, pitched and frothed on the pavement. Connie's friends had deserted her, probably heading back inside to finish off the canapés.

PJ knelt beside Davy. Maybe she should just hike him over her shoulder, fireman style.

Please, God . . .

A shadow tented over her. "David, do you want some ice cream?"

PJ stared openmouthed at her rescuer, at the unexpected smile surrounded by white whiskers against his dark skin. "Mr. Hoffman."

"I figured you'd show your face back here again."

The past flickered in his eyes, and PJ stilled. *Please . . .*

"It's just a shame that it took you ten years."

PJ could have kissed him. Especially when he held out his

hand, his dark eyes kinder than she remembered when she'd tried to sort out the dates of the Spanish Inquisition and the Crusades, and especially when she'd tried to spit out an explanation so many years ago on just about this very spot.

His gaze scanned her, however briefly, up and down, as if trying to find the girl he knew. Did he see past the PJ that was to the PJ she'd become? the one who longed for redemption, to know how to pick up Davy and hold him close, to be something in his world, in Connie's world . . . frankly, the world at large?

"I see you still have that tattoo."

"Oh." Well, she was wearing a sleeveless dress. She stopped just short of moving her hand to cover it.

He snickered, shaking his head. "Same old PJ."

"Same old Mr. Hoffman," she said back, and he guffawed.

"C'mon, David." Hoffman held out his hand. "Let's get some ice cream."

"He's had tons of chocolate. I don't think ice cream's going to—"

Davy instantly stopped crying. He poked his little tearstained, belligerent face out of his arms and grinned at his benefactor. Perfect. Leaping up, he dove into Hoffman's arms, clinging to his neck.

"Oh!" Hoffman said, and a flash of what looked like pain shadowed his face.

"Are you okay?" PJ eased her nephew off Hoffman, setting Davy down on the sidewalk. She slipped her hand into his, and he promptly leaned down and bit it.

Hoffman nodded, limping toward the poolside deck. "Bad back."

"I'm sorry." PJ switched hands, and Davy landed a fist on her wrist, then went limp. She swooped him up, aware of eyes on her as they struggled their way to the pool.

Davy braced his hands on her shoulders, pushing away with every ounce of his four-year-old power. "I want my mommy!"

"Me too, pal."

"He surely has Sugar in him," Hoffman said.

That wasn't fair. To her knowledge, she'd never bodily harmed anyone. Well, with the exception of that time she'd caught Boone hitting on Angie St. John, but really, it had been mostly words thrown, not fists.

Hoffman must have read her face. "I mean that he doesn't give up." He clamped his hand on her shoulder, warm, welcoming. "Glad you're back. I hope you're sticking around."

PJ had no words as Davy finally struggled out of her arms, landed on the pool deck, and raced for the ice-cream stand. She collapsed into a deck chair.

"Ernie—I need to talk to you."

PJ looked up, and everything stilled as she watched Ben Murphy stride across the lawn toward the pool area. *Oh no, oh no . . . former math teacher and prom chaperone at ten o'clock.*

Really, she had to stop thinking that the past happened yesterday. These people had moved on, and so must she.

"Say hi to PJ," Hoffman said to Murphy, digging out his wallet. He wore a dangerous smile that PJ could have done without.

Murphy stopped as if running into plate glass. "PJ . . . Sugar?"

PJ lifted her hand, waved it like a leaf in the wind. But the scene resonated in his eyes—the fire lashing the dark sky, the scream of the sirens, Boone's breath on her skin a second before Mr. Murphy and company motored up on a golf cart.

She dropped her hand back into her lap.

Murphy had recovered his gait and gave her a small shake of his head as he passed her and joined Hoffman at the ice-cream stand.

PJ sat there tasting yesterday like tar in her mouth.

Davy returned, slurping a single dip chocolate ice-cream cone. Chocolate dripped from his chin. Hoffman followed, having dispensed with Murphy, and lifted Davy onto a chair next to PJ. He pressed his hands against the small of his back and stretched.

"How'd you do that?"

He winked. "Sometimes you just got to give 'em a little sugar."

PJ wasn't sure Kellogg could handle any more Sugar.

"You!" The voice came from the wraparound veranda overlooking the patio. Hoffman looked up and PJ jerked, turning. She'd known her luck wouldn't hold. But no, a man she didn't recognize leaped the banister, landing hard on the cement, right beside a row of teakwood deck chairs.

She stood and backed away as he strode toward her.

"Where've you been?" Tall, with the build of a sailor, he wore the white uniform of one of the waiters or maybe a spa attendant, anger riddling his face. "You don't return phone calls anymore?" His glare landed beyond her.

Oh. He was after *Hoffman*. PJ glanced back at her history teacher and could have sworn he'd turned a little pale. Chatter poolside stopped, all eyes on the ruckus.

A morbid relief that she wasn't the cause of the commotion

rooted her to her spot, one hand reaching out for Davy as the man advanced on Hoffman.

"Where's my money, huh? She's going to find out; you know that, right?"

Hoffman raised his hands, surrender-like.

PJ rounded. "Hey!" she yelled.

But the man never slowed, pushing past the deck chairs and arrowing straight for Hoffman, palm out, and thumping Hoffman hard in the center of the chest.

The history teacher flew back into the pool. Water bulleted PJ and Davy and splattered the deck like gunfire.

Davy dropped his cone and wailed.

PJ stood stock-still as the man dove in after Hoffman.

She'd just known, if she returned to Kellogg, she wouldn't escape the bright lights and sirens.

Chapter **THREE**

"Well, if it isn't NBT. I should have figured I'd find you here."

PJ didn't have to turn from her crouched position on the wet deck around the pool to recognize Director Buckam's voice. She heard the derision in the nickname he'd bestowed upon her—Nothing but Trouble—as if he'd sworn out the restraining order yesterday.

She finished wiping Davy's face, sighing. "Hey, I'm just here because my sister got married. I'm leaving right now. And I really don't think that's fair—"

"Sure it is. Because whenever there's trouble, you're not far away," Buckam said, apparently not pulling any punches.

Davy wiggled away from her grasp and she took another swipe at him, hoping to vanquish one foe before she faced another.

"I think that you should check your facts because it was *your* son—"

But it wasn't Director Buckam. And it seemed cosmically unfair that she might be in Kellogg only five hours and thirty-six minutes before Daniel "Boone" Buckam walked back into her life.

He stood over her, hands on his narrow hips, the dark silhouette of a superhero, complete with broad shoulders framed against the late afternoon sun and the barest hint of a smug smile on his clean-shaven face. Probably she should be glad she couldn't see his eyes behind those dark sunglasses. Her gaze dropped to the dark weapon slung in an arm holster under his suit coat and the shiny silver badge on his belt.

Look who'd cleaned up his act.

"Boone."

"Oh, PJ." He said it softly, like he'd been holding his breath for years and only her name came out on exhale. He shook his head, taking off his sunglasses, unleashing now the full power of those pale blue eyes on her. "PJ Sugar." This time her name emerged with a singsong lilt, flecked with danger, the same tone he used when she'd met him behind the garage after sneaking out of the house years ago. "I knew you'd come back."

"You knew nothing of the sort." The edge in her voice, laced with more desperation than she would have liked, surprised even her as she shot to her feet. She reached for Davy, who twisted away from her, licking his hands. "I . . . My sister got married and I'm watching Davy while she's on her honeymoon. Otherwise, I'd be back in . . . where I lived. *Live*."

Boone's eyes connected with hers with the power to part her lies and zero in on the truth, and for a long moment he just grinned.

Then he laughed low, and she felt it rumbling right below her breastbone.

Until that very moment, she'd thought she might someday be able to find a cure for this dark hold he had on her heart. To inoculate herself from his charm and expunge the memories of being the center of his world.

Apparently, however, there was no Boone antidote. Every cell in her body revived, alive, tingling, remembering his smell on a crisp fall day as she dug herself into the cleft of his embrace, his leather jacket cool against her cheek, his arms the one safe place to hide.

And to prove it, her gaze went straight to his left hand. His *ringless* left hand.

Her hands shook as she reached out to grab Davy's before he could flee. "I'm not back for you," she said, wishing her voice could work with her a little. "In fact I'm hoping that maybe we could just ignore each other."

"You've always been a little tough to ignore, Peej."

"Don't *Peej* me. I've moved on. I mean, it's been ten years, Boone. Good grief, don't look at me like you've been staring at the horizon all this time, waiting for me to appear."

"Feels like it." But he continued to smile, unfazed.

"I'm serious." She put everything she hoped she believed in her expression. "I'm just here to babysit. I don't want any . . . trouble." She managed to avoid Davy's kick, all the while staring at Boone.

Stop staring at Boone.

"NBT, I think you need to wake up and smell the chlorine." His smile broadened, teased, as he glanced at a sopping wet Hoffman and his assailant, now subdued by a couple of Connie's lawyer pals who had taken to the pool after the duo, pulling them out before Hoffman got more than a mouthful of water. Another cop, one PJ didn't recognize, was cuffing the attacker. "What do you know about Jack Wilkes going after Ernie?"

PJ's mouth opened. "You aren't seriously blaming me for this. I don't even know Jack . . ."

"Wilkes. Really? You've never met Trudi's husband?"

Trudi . . . her best friend from school, cohort in the Great Shaving Cream Incident? The one PJ left crying on her front steps, afraid she might be pregnant with Greg Morris's baby? "Trudi is still around?"

"And married to Slugger over there." Boone twirled his sunglasses between two fingers. "Haven't you kept in touch with anyone?"

PJ had no words for that. She'd been . . . Well, after being the girl whose reputation preceded her, it didn't take much to find a delicious freedom in reinventing herself all over the globe. Or at least North America.

"No one I wanted to keep in touch with," she said tightly.

"Hmm . . . maybe there were people who wanted to keep in touch with you." He gave her a look up and down that left no question as to his meaning.

He hadn't changed one arrogant bit.

Except for the suit coat. And his freshly barbered dark blond hair, so short she had the urge to touch it, compare it to the long curls that once ran through her fingers like ribbons. The slightest fragrance of cologne lifted off him, evidencing a man instead of a ruddy high school boy. Okay, so he'd changed *a lot*.

But only in a way that could mean trouble. For she knew

what Boone did to her. She had the scars—and a tattoo—to prove it.

"Boone, I'm not the same person who left Kellogg. I'm . . . different."

"I'm sure you are." He gave her a look that, in a different time and place, would turn her common sense to a puddle of desire, and shortly thereafter, she'd be climbing onto the back of his motorcycle.

Run. The smart side of her brain fairly screamed it.

No. She wasn't going to leave town because of Boone—or his lies—again. Ever.

"Since when did you become a cop—if that's what you are?" It seemed that Connie or even her mother might have given her the slightest heads-up on that piece of trivia.

His face shadowed, a darkness that she didn't recognize, but he chased it away with a shrug. "Decided it was time to pick a side."

"You look good in a suit. What are you, undercover?"

"Detective." But her words seemed to rock him for just a second, as if he hadn't expected anything but claws from her. His smile dimmed, his voice low. "Okay, I just need to know. Not a Christmas card, not a birthday greeting—you erased yourself off the planet and out of . . . everyone's life. And now you're here, as if blown in by the wind. Why, PJ, *why* didn't you come back sooner?"

Like on strings, PJ's eyes traveled to the tenth green, reviving a memory that produced some heat against her cheeks. "You know why."

He looked away, and in the silence that stretched between them, she heard the regrets that neither wanted to voice.

Finally Boone said, "Time heals all wounds." It came out softly and with what sounded like hope in his tone.

"Some wounds can never heal." PJ pulled Davy across the patio toward the country club.

She hadn't expected Boone to follow her to the gate. He stood there, catching it as it swung shut behind her. "It'll be different this time, Peej. I promise."

She didn't turn at his words and managed to coerce Davy up the stairs and into the building before her vision glossed over.

Her mother sat in her wheelchair, saying good-bye to the last of the guests.

"I don't know where Connie lives. Can you give me directions?" PJ said, steeling her voice as she freed Davy to scavenge the debris of the mint table. The last thing she needed was for her mother to see her with Boone.

Besides, she hadn't returned for Boone. And there would be no "this time."

Elizabeth said nothing, her brow puckered, her eyes searching. Then, "You can follow me."

"You're driving, Mom? Are you sure—?"

"My Mercedes can practically drive itself. And my doctor said I could. You don't expect me to sit at home for six weeks, do you?"

Clearly PJ had lost her mind. She opened her mouth to admit this.

"Besides, it's my left ankle, and I don't have a . . . *manual.* I suppose you still have a Volkswagen?"

She said it like she always had . . . as if PJ had brought home a mule to park in their driveway.

"I've upgraded, but I'll always be a Bug girl." PJ didn't exactly mean it like that, but still, she didn't appreciate her mother's expression.

"I'm sure you will." Elizabeth rolled away.

PJ retrieved her traveling clothes and cornered Davy, then followed her mother from the building. Elizabeth ditched the wheelchair for a set of crutches, and by the time PJ strapped Davy into the car seat Connie had transferred to her backseat, her mother had pulled up in her silver Mercedes.

It was then that Boone turned from the crime scene, his pale gaze on PJ.

She didn't look back as she peeled away, even when his words rebounded in her head: *"It'll be different this time, Peej. I promise."*

✳ ✳ ✳

PJ glanced at Davy in the rearview mirror. He'd flattened his hands over his ears, his eyes clenched tight, his breath ballooning his cheeks as his face reddened.

"Davy, are you okay? Davy?"

He didn't react, as if he'd gone deaf also.

Could a child self-suffocate? "Stop it, Davy!"

He let his breath go and gulped in another.

"Don't die on me, okay?"

He stuck out his tongue at her.

She ignored him, following her mother through town, passing the old neighborhoods. Trudi had lived on the "other" side of town—near the high school. So Trudi had married after all. To a man with self-control issues, no less.

PJ's first clear impression of Jack—in his sopping wet uniform, water turning his black shoes squeaky, his blond hair standing in spikes—dredged up memories of Trudi's high school squeeze, a wide receiver who'd caught passes from more than just the quarterback. How many times had Trudi ended up on PJ's back porch, her face in her hands, swearing to dump Greg?

If anyone could convict PJ for not keeping in touch, it might be Trudi. She dearly hoped that the behavior she'd seen didn't follow Jack home.

PJ wondered where Trudi lived now as she followed her mother's shiny sedan up a curve of shoreline that rose to a bluff overlooking Kellogg.

They veered west into the Chapel Hills neighborhood, and PJ tapped her brakes as they passed her old house. She noted a fresh coat of paint on the front porch columns, the hydrangeas grown halfway to her old bedroom window. The trellis had vanished—better late than never. Still, the house looked unaged, a time capsule for everything she'd thought she'd be as she lay huddled under the floral sheets, watching the fingers of the oak tree in the front yard reach past the eyelet curtains into her bedroom, crawl along her baby blue carpet, up the cotton candy pink walls. She'd watched the shadows, longing for daylight and to be the princess that belonged in such a room.

Elizabeth had probably long since redecorated.

They wound through elegant neighborhoods. PJ riffled through her sister's history, remembering how, shortly after Connie found Burke in that compromising embrace with his law clerk, she'd dumped her condo overlooking downtown

Minneapolis's Loring Park. She'd cashed Burke's life insurance check as well as his parents' inheritance and moved the thirty miles back to Kellogg, settling in a fifty-three-hundred-square-foot Craftsman home, built at the height of the roaring twenties, with ten-foot ceilings and a maid's quarters.

Connie had written to her, sent her pictures. Still, PJ hadn't expected this much grandeur. The house, situated on nearly a half acre of groomed landscape, sat back from the street, an island of grace with its dark cream siding, milky white porch columns, and rich mahogany door. Three floors, two chimneys, and a third-story dormer window overlooked a front walk lined with hostas. Two lilac trees, heavy with flowers, flanked the row of purple viburnum and dwarfed cedar trees on either side of the wide steps. They led to a porch adorned with potted impatiens and a white rocking chair.

If PJ had a choice, she would have picked exactly the same house. She and Connie at least shared tastes, if not incomes.

PJ tapped her brakes as she pulled into Connie's driveway. She half expected to see the Great Gatsby stroll out on the porch, lean against the white columns, and stare down at her with prejudice.

For a second, she longed for her floral sheets.

Davy was out of his car seat before she could put the car in park. She reached over and released the door, and he pitched out.

While he ran up the steps, PJ retrieved her duffel bag from the trunk. She stopped for a moment, watching her mother pry herself out of her car, hopping to grab her crutches from the backseat. "You need some help, Mom?"

Elizabeth ignored her.

PJ wondered if her mother would start holding her breath too.

She climbed the stairs, old phone conversations playing in her mind—Connie's rants as she supervised a battalion of subcontractors who restored the home to its natural hand-scrolled oak trim and wood floors, installed replica period light fixtures, and turned the tiled fireplaces to gas.

PJ opened the door to the scent of lemony wax and oil, the floor groaning as she stepped inside, cutting into the hushed reverence.

All her earthly belongings made a thump as she dropped the bag.

"Are you sure you'll be okay here?" her mother said, clunking up the steps.

"I think I'll manage."

"You won't have to clean. Your sister has a service—comes in once a week—and a lawn company too."

Of course she did.

"And the Russians are in the old maid's quarters off the back of the house. So you and Davy will have the upstairs."

"I'm not even going to ask whose idea it was to put them in the servant's quarters. Really, Mom?"

"It's a very nice room. And it has its own bathroom. Remember, PJ, your sister has gone to a lot of work. The stained glass window is original, and she shopped for weeks before she found the right tile—had it imported from a store in New York that specializes in historical restorations—"

"I'll try to keep from breaking anything."

Elizabeth sighed. Then she lowered her voice and glanced behind her. "What about the Russians?"

"Seriously, it's not the 1950s. Joe McCarthy is dead."

Elizabeth didn't even blink.

"I think we can take 'em, despite all their propaganda—"

"For pete's sake, PJ, you know what I mean." She gave a head bob toward the couple now climbing out of a green Taurus. Vera gave a tug on her dress, the neckline having migrated south.

Their driver left them the second they had their doors shut.

"I guess I'll just feed them and tuck them into bed."

Elizabeth rolled her eyes. "They don't speak any English. I mentioned that, didn't I?"

"Listen, I spent a summer as a cook at a camp in Seattle. They had a couple weeks of Russian-only immersion. I'll remember the basics. But do you know why Connie told me not to let them sunbathe?"

Elizabeth raised her plucked eyebrows, and PJ could nearly see her contemplating the images. Then she shrugged. "Call me if you need anything."

The world would ice over before PJ lifted the phone.

"Thanks, Mom."

"And by the way, be sure and stop by. I need your help with something."

Her mother's words, like magnetic shavings, found those Connie had uttered, the ones that had propelled her home. *"Even if she can't admit it, she needs you."*

PJ leaned against the door, watching her mother navigate down the stairs and out to the car, then cast another look at the Russians. They seemed content out on the lawn, so she dragged her duffel up the stairs, surmising the location of the bedrooms. She found Davy sitting cross-legged on the floor in his room, working a PlayStation controller, eyes glued to his thirty-two-inch flat-screen TV. On the screen, a skateboarder did a beautiful flip.

"Davy?"

Deaf again.

Connie had turned two of the bedrooms into her own private suite. PJ stood at the lip of the master, briefly contemplating commandeering the room for her stay. Navy brocade curtains fell ceiling to floor, pooling on the white carpet, and overstuffed pillows avalanched across the top of the king-size bed. A bouquet of fresh flowers adorned a round cherrywood table with silk-seated chairs pushed up to it, and upon a matching chaise longue in front of the window, a copy of *The Purpose Driven Life* lay upside down.

Perhaps Connie had already found it.

PJ edged away from the oasis and found the next available room, this one smaller. It appeared straight out of a Craftsman catalog, a milk-glass overhead fixture pooling light onto the pink chenille coverlet spread over the wide-slat double bed and white-on-white embroidered curtains at the window. Side tables held more milk-glass lamps, and a lowboy armoire with a mirror completed the Craftsman theme. The room came equipped with its own bathroom, vintage in pink tile and a freestanding scrolled sink.

The room—the entire house—bespoke Connie's order, her coordination. Her neatly attired life.

PJ changed into her Superman lounge pants and a tank, then after another check on Davy, found the kitchen.

On the granite counter lay a tome titled, simply, "David."

Just the first page had PJ searching the freezer for ice cream.

> *Dear PJ, I know that David is in safe hands!*
> *Thank you for coming home to look after*
> *him. Please make yourself comfortable. I have*
> *suspended the cleaning service for my time*
> *away, but I know you won't make much of a*
> *mess. Attached is a list of instructions that will*
> *assist you in taking care of David. Sergei didn't*
> *have time to go to the bank before we left, so*
> *if you incur any expenses, we'll reimburse you.*
> *Thank you again!*
>
> *Love, Connie*

> *1. David is allergic to peanuts. Please check all*
> *ingredients on prepackaged food.*
>
> *2. David spends thirty minutes each morning*
> *on one of his preschool Pilates tapes while his*
> *breakfast is cooking. You'll find the selection*
> *on the shelves over his desk.*
>
> *3. Menus are attached. Please uphold the rules*
> *on good manners during mealtime. No*
> *chewing with open mouth, no speaking with*
> *mouth full, napkin on lap.*
>
> *4. David is to be in bed precisely at 7:30 p.m.*
> *No snacks after dinner, please.*

> *5. Please limit his PlayStation game playing to*
> *thirty minutes per day.*

Page 2 listed his favorite outfits, additional no-no foods, acceptable programming.

No wonder Connie had left PJ, a woman with no visible parenting skills, with her precious son. PJ didn't have to think really. Just follow the rules.

Connie, of all people, should have known better.

But PJ had made promises. And this time—for two weeks at least—she could keep them.

Especially if she wanted to stick around. Maybe even make her mother proud.

Yeah, right. Perhaps she should keep her expectations within reason.

Rummaging through the refrigerator, she found some lemonade, added ice cubes, and wandered around until she discovered the back porch. Overstuffed rattan chairs, a hammock, and an indoor fountain—an island getaway in the middle of Minnesota, all enclosed by enough screen to keep out the rain forest. On the lawn, past the grilling deck, was a fortress of outdoor fun—swings, rings, two slides, a bridge, a climbing net, a sandbox, and even a netted trampoline.

Indeed, Connie had invested that life insurance well. PJ raised her glass to her as she eased into the hammock and closed her eyes.

"Welcome back, PJ."

Boone walked into her thoughts like he'd been waiting in the wings for his cue. He didn't in the least resemble the man at the clubhouse, the one with the taunting smile and risky prophecies. This Boone, the apparition born from the persuasions of her fickle heart, she liked.

And in her daydreams, at least, he couldn't betray her.

He leaned against the doorframe, thumbs hanging on his belt loops, wearing his cutoff Kellogg High School Mavericks sweatshirt, his biceps thick after a summer caddying at the club. *"I thought you'd never get back."*

She looked up at him, smiled. *"Really? You missed me?"*

Swaggering toward her, he held her gaze with way too much sweet mischief in his eyes. *"Of course. We have some unfinished business."* He knelt beside her, running his hand through her hair. *"You changed it. But it's cute."*

Then, before she could respond, he leaned close and—

No. Her eyes opened, and she held the sweating glass to her forehead.

Less than a week ago, she'd been hoping to be Mrs. Matthew Buchanan.

PJ got up, the tile cold and bracing on her bare feet. If she was honest, she would have to agree that even Matthew couldn't stir her like Boone had.

"It'll be different this time, Peej. I promise."

She walked to the screen and stared up at the sky, now streaked with the straining of twilight. "I do want it to be different, Lord. Except—"

Glass breaking in the kitchen spun her. She put down her lemonade, imagining Davy on the counter, pulling antique crystal from the shelves. "Davy, if you just ask, I'll get you a—"

Boris crouched in the kitchen, sweeping up glass, wearing a pair of skintight workout pants that stopped PJ short and forced her to avert her eyes. "Uh—"

He looked up and said something in Russian.

I broke the towel?

A close enough translation.

"Da," PJ said, trying to come up with the words for *Please stay out of the kitchen.*

Especially when she spied his after-wedding snack. She peered closer, just to confirm—yes, a plate of raw bacon.

Boris finished sweeping the glass, dumping the shards of Connie's precious, probably antique, crystal into the garbage can beneath the sink. Which suggested that he might have practiced this a few times.

PJ pressed her hand to her stomach as Boris took out another glass and poured himself lemonade. Then he sat down at the table with his bacon.

She couldn't help it—she watched with a sort of morbid stare-at-the-accident fascination as he slobbered the bacon down.

"No! I want my mommy!"

Mommy. Oh yeah, that was her cue. PJ raced up the stairs.

Vera sat on the bedroom floor, sumo wrestling Davy into his jammies. Was it past seven thirty already?

"Let Grandma draw," Vera said, to PJ's closest guess.

Grandma Vera looked like she might be able to take on a Siberian tiger and win, with her wide workman's hands and a grim set to her mouth that screamed *nyet* to quitting.

PJ approached with caution.

Davy launched himself into her arms.

"Shh." She smoothed his hair. Perhaps she *could* figure out this auntie thing. The future strobed in her mind—playing baseball on the beach, swinging on his swing set, licking the beaters from the chocolate chip cookie dough . . .

Davy looked up, met her eyes. She saw in his the burble in time, the hiccup between rescue and realization. Then, *This is not my mother.*

"Davy . . ."

His face crumpled even as his little body stiffened.

"Davy—it's okay."

Too late. Davy's mouth opened and released a wail so wrenching it tore something from PJ's heart. His grief drifted out through the screened windows and into the early summer night.

Oh, please, Lord. The prayer emerged as a moan as PJ attempted to dress the flailing child.

She could feed hungry gorillas, even muscle a motorcycle through a motocross track. Certainly she could dress a four-year-old in a pair of Spider-Man pajamas.

Vera, beside her, barraged him with Russian, which, judging by the tone, might be criticism or platitudes. Come to think of it, she might have been talking to PJ.

PJ finally resorted to Hoffman's Method of Persuasion. "Davy, if you get dressed, Auntie PJ will give you a cookie." She could recognize an emergency when it unraveled in front of her. Oh no, did Connie even have any cookies? Thankfully she had some in her canvas bag, comfort food purchased at a truck stop in Peoria.

Davy stilled, eyes huge and watery, and tugged on his pants.

Three crushed Oreos and some eight books later, he went to sleep, black crumbs ringing his mouth. PJ slouched on the opposite side of his room against the closet, surrounded by Mike Mulligan and Horton, the hall light a portal to sanity.

Davy sighed. Sweetly. As if he might be dreaming of sugary, drippy treats.

She snuck back to his bed. Sweat slicked his hair, and he gripped a ratty blue bear, his mouth half-open, drool forming at the edge. His chest rose and fell, and rising from him, almost in defiance, was the scent of freshly washed pajamas. It evoked memories of a homemade flannel nightgown under floral sheets.

She brushed his hair back, listening to the chirrup of crickets outside the window. By now, Connie would be on her flight to her happily ever after with Sergei.

And PJ had been left in charge.

"Please, God, please help me not to mess this up."

PJ listened, but in the dark quiet of the house, no voice rose to reassure her.

Chapter FOUR

PJ should have figured that Connie would enroll her son in Fellows. Probably the moment the two little pink lines appeared.

She pulled her VW neatly between a Beemer and a Jag and stared at the red and gold sign perched on the lush green lawn of Fellows Early Education Academy. She could nearly smell the air of importance in the elegant building with its redbrick attire, gold-trimmed windows, and manicured front garden, the sprinkler shooting out with a rhythmic whisper of respect.

"You about ready, champ?"

Behind her, Davy sat in a slouch, in no apparent hurry to unbuckle his seat belt. Even the prospect of clobbering her with his shiny new Spider-Man lunch box held no appeal apparently, although he'd tried twice while she'd loaded him into the car. He had connected with the leather briefcase he'd dragged out of his closet and glued to his chubby little hand.

She recognized the late Burke's initials on the brass monogram plate on top and decided to let Davy cling to his persona. He did look lawyerly in his blue jacket, pressed white shirt, long shorts, and black wingtips.

She turned in her seat. "Okay, I know you're less than thrilled, and frankly, I'm pretty sure you'd get just as good an education with a day at the beach, counting scoopfuls of sand, but your mom really wants you to go here, and she's probably right. . . ."

Davy wiped his nose with the back of his pressed arm. He looked about how PJ felt—rumpled and angry. Never mind that she'd pulled up to the school in her Superman pants, tee, and flip-flops—thanks to Davy's ever-so-cooperative spirit as she wrestled him into his uniform. And just because she'd started the morning unproductively by burning the oatmeal didn't mean he had to spit it down his shirt. Twice. She'd finally returned to his room to fetch a new oxford and discovered that he'd unloaded his toy chest and created a traffic jam of bulldozers, Hot Wheels race cars, school buses, and a slew of hit-and-run stuffed animals in time to the cadence of his Pilates instructor's smooth, calming tones. She didn't blame him.

She was stopping by the store to buy a shipping container of cereal on the way home. Mostly because, after returning with said clean shirt, she'd had to plea-bargain Davy down to two more Oreos she'd unearthed in her bag in exchange for two minutes of stiff-armed calm.

"I'm not going." He blew up his cheeks, holding his breath, little blue eyes glaring at her.

"C'mon, Davy, you have to go to school." She got out, pulled her front seat forward, and reached to unlock his buckle. He gave her a kick, but she pushed his leg away and pulled him from the car.

"No! No!"

"Davy, please. Your mom really wants you to Go. To. School!"

Davy had gone limp, a dead carcass impression right there in the grease-stained parking lot. "I don't wanna go!"

"Get up, David. You have to go to school."

"Nyet!"

Thank you so much, Babushka Vera, for that language lesson.

"Don't you want to go and learn how to read?"

"I know how to read." He yanked his hand from hers, crossing his arms over his chest and locking his hands in his armpits.

Sure, Connie, he'll love Fellows. PJ could hardly hold him back. She stared down at him, breathing out long breaths.

Probably, under all that dark curly hair, Davy was cute. Loveable. Especially with that spray of freckles over his nose, crinkling when he smiled. Surely, lined up with a battalion of other tots in blue knickers and jackets with the Fellows crest on the pocket, he would be downright pinchworthy.

Surely.

"Yes, I *know* you can read. You corrected me twice last night, remember?" He probably had the book memorized. He *must* have had the book memorized.

He glowered at her.

"Don't you want to make friends and meet your teacher?"

"No." He rolled over, burying his face in the pavement. PJ

hooked him around the waist and hauled him to the curb. He'd soiled his white shirt. She made it to the grass—the *wet* grass—and deposited him.

Singing filtered out of the building. Happy preschoolers learning the Fellows Academy song.

"They'll probably have snacks," PJ said, crouching beside him, hating how she'd become a weak and pitiful briber.

Davy lifted his head.

PJ nodded vigorously, held up a finger, crossed her heart, and determined to arm the teacher with a year's supply of Ho Hos if it came to it.

Davy narrowed his eyes as if trying to decide if she would lie to him. Then, pouting, he stood and marched toward the school.

PJ retrieved his briefcase and lunch box and slunk in behind him. *I'm sorry, Connie.*

A hall monitor, wearing a ladies version of the Fellows uniform—blue skirt, blue jacket, and white oxford that washed out her already sunless expression—stopped them. "Where do you think you're going?"

Davy ignored her—PJ was starting to appreciate his selective hearing—and followed the singing.

"I'm with him. Note the new uniform."

"You're late." Hall Monitor wore a helmet of thin, cropped black hair and clasped her hands behind her back as if she'd graduated top in her class at West Point. She regarded PJ in her civilian clothes, aka Superman pants. "We don't tolerate lateness."

"Of course you don't—" PJ noted the woman's name on the pin hooked to her chest—"Mrs. Nicholson."

"Ms."

"Ms. Nicholson. Listen, we're really sorry, and we promise not to let it happen again." PJ moved forward, but the woman took defensive action and stepped in for the block. Beyond them, Davy opened the door to a room and disappeared.

"We allow three tardies, Miss . . . ?"

"Sugar." What if Davy went in the wrong room? She perked her ears for howling. "We had a rough first day. I'm sure you can understand."

No movement. PJ cut her gaze back to the woman/prison guard. "It won't happen again."

When PJ was about ten years old, she'd accidentally backed into a door at the school after troop meeting, breaking it with her, well, backside. Sometimes her scouting leader came to her in nightmares, wearing the exact dubious look Ms. Nicholson was wearing now.

PJ held up three fingers, as she had so long ago. "I promise."

"And maybe tomorrow, you could make sure you're fully dressed?"

PJ opened her mouth, words forming. Bad, non-Sugar words. But Connie appeared in her brain, pleading. *"He's been on the waiting list for three years. It's very important he is there on time, pressed, combed, and smiling."*

"Right. Fully dressed." She brushed past Ms. Nicholson, flip-flopping toward the room Davy had entered.

Davy sat with the other preschoolers in a circle on the floor, the model child. He even smiled up at the teacher, a woman also dressed in the Fellows dress blues. She knelt on a red carpet, her knees just touching the edge. An alphabet chart hung at one end of the board, a numbers chart at the other. A giant world map stretched across the back wall.

Desks, tiny desks made for Oompa-Loompas, queued up front to back on each side of the thick, square red carpet.

Boris and Vera would be right at home.

PJ eased in, eliciting the attention of other parents stationed around the room, most in suit coats and business attire. So, she could see the hall monitor's point about attention to clothing choices. Still, she was here for Davy. She could endure some staring.

Davy clapped with the other children, learning the Fellows song. See, he *was* cute.

Just not when he looked at PJ.

"Aren't they adorable?" This from a woman leaning next to her. Her straight, buttery hair looked freshly colored, and a white jacket over black dress pants suggested either a working mom or someone who knew the importance of being *fully dressed* for orientation at Fellows.

"Very," PJ said, smiling back.

"Macey Harrison," the woman said, holding out her groomed hand. "And you are?"

PJ took her hand. "Davy's nanny." *That one was for you, Connie.*

She slipped out during the Pledge of Allegiance, followed by a stream of other parents.

Pulling into the Red Owl Grocery Store, she took in the updated rides outside the door, remembering the days when she'd begged her mother for the quarter it took to make them move. She brushed her fingers over the head of the dolphin on her way in, wondering if she should fulfill a childhood dream and "waste" her quarter on a carnival ride.

She grabbed a cart, calculating what it might take to

fill Connie's coffers, and tooled down the aisles. She didn't really remember anything beyond the chip and pop aisle and was delighted to discover a deli section with Thai food. She ordered a container of Thai noodles, then began her quest for non-peanut items and somewhat healthy foods. Where exactly were the healthy foods?

"I can't believe it . . . PJ Sugar." The voice behind her said it slowly, drawing out the syllables as if each word, even each letter, had its own devout relevance.

PJ closed her eyes, savoring for just a second everything that cadence dredged up. Painted toenails under a hot sun, slumber parties on the screened porch, two girls spinning stories under quilted blankets, eating Cap'n Crunch out of the box, giggling behind their wrist corsages as Greg and Boone swaggered over from the punch table.

"Trudi Lindstrom." PJ turned and couldn't believe how little time had changed her best friend. Her hair was still big—huge in fact—and long and curled with an iron. An oversize tee bagged at her waist, bearing the words *Born to Shop* over a chest she certainly didn't have her senior year. Her face down to her feet suggested a rich, artificial tan, as if she still kept her weekly appointment down at the Surf and Spin Laundry and Tanning Bed.

Trudi smiled at PJ as if she had a secret, one that couldn't wait until Monday morning homeroom. "I can't believe it's you. I just can't believe it! When did you get back?"

"Just yesterday. I'm babysitting my nephew while my sister's on her honeymoon." PJ moved into Trudi's embrace, holding tight. As she pulled away, her gaze fell on Trudi's diamond. "Wow, that's a stone. I heard you got married."

She peered into Trudi's hazel eyes, searching for pain as Trudi waggled her finger. "Two years now. He's a physical therapist and a massage therapist. He works out of our house, as well as a couple other places."

Like the Kellogg Country Club? PJ wrestled out a tight smile.

"And we have a son." She beamed, pulling out a picture. "Isn't he a doll? He's Jack Junior, but we call him Chip. He's just a delight."

PJ took the snapshot. "He's a cutie." A year old, bald, and drooling onto a blanket.

"Yeah. Mike's so glad to have a baby brother."

Mike. The word dropped between them like a sack of flour. *Thud.* PJ's air supply cut off with the rising poof of dust. "Mike. So you *were* . . ."

"Yeah. Pregnant. With Greg's baby. Thankfully Jack's a great dad. We're so lucky."

Lucky. And she said it without a hint of shadow in her voice. So maybe she didn't have to pull Trudi into a corner, ask her hard questions in low tones. "How is Greg?"

"Last I heard, he was in Stillwater, doing time for a nasty barroom brawl."

"Oh." PJ handed her back the picture, noticing the rhinestones glued to the pink polish on Trudi's nails. "Listen, Trudi, I'm so sorry that I didn't keep in touch. I . . . should have."

Trudi said nothing, peering over her shoulder at the contents of PJ's basket. "Where are the Cheetos?"

PJ smiled.

"And the Cap'n Crunch?" Trudi matched her smile, gentle, the past sweet inside it.

"I can't wait to meet Mike," PJ said softly.

"And Jack. He's the greatest guy. Kind and handsome."

She might be ready to give the guy another chance. "I'm looking forward to it."

They rolled their carts toward the produce section. PJ picked up some apples and a container of caramel sauce. Fruit. Davy should have some fruit. "What are you doing these days?"

"I run a day care out of my home. It's attached to Jack's office." Trudi reached for a bunch of bananas. "Jack's watching the kids right now. I've gotta get back with our morning snack."

Then she looked at PJ with an expression PJ should have expected from a woman who knew her secrets. At least the ones that had piled up until she left town ten years ago. "Does Boone know you're back?"

PJ hooked her foot on the edge of the cart. "I, uh . . . ran into him, yeah."

"Did you see that he's a cop?"

"I saw the badge."

"A *cop*. Chew on that for a while." Trudi shook her head. "If that isn't something for a high school reunion reality show, I'm not sure what is. But he does a good job, and people like him."

PJ closed her mouth at that. Of course they did. Boone had a charm that could noodle anyone's common sense.

"So, are you sticking around?" Trudi said it casually, the way she might ask if they could hang out later.

"I . . . have to find a job, I guess."

"What do you do? Maybe I know someone."

Anything? PJ shook her head, not sure how to answer that

question as they wheeled toward checkout. "I don't know what I'm looking for yet."

Trudi said nothing as she dug into her purse, handed the checker her cash card, then pressed a business card into PJ's hand. "Call me."

Peppermint Fence Day Care. The flip side listed Jack's Physical and Massage Therapy phone numbers.

"Cute," PJ said.

"I'm sorry, but it was declined." The checker handed Trudi back her card.

"What? No, that can't be right."

"I tried it twice. Do you have another method of payment?"

"No . . . I . . ."

"Here." PJ handed over a twenty. "It's probably just a glitch at the bank."

Trudi took her bagged groceries. "I don't know what to say. Thanks, PJ."

"Don't say anything—it's the least I can do."

"I'll pay you back."

"Don't you dare." PJ paid for her groceries and followed Trudi from the store.

The sun had crested the lake, fingers of gold gilding the tops of the cars in the parking lot, turning the tar to onyx. A family of ducks waddled across the lot. The scent of freshly mowed lawn lazed out into the breeze.

Trudi one-armed her around the neck. "You look great, by the way. The old PJ, only better."

PJ let those words syrup through her, slow and sweet, as she pulled up to Connie's house and wrangled the two bags of groceries out of the car. She waved to the postman approaching Connie's box in his little truck. One arm hung out the window and he waved back. He looked like he should be slinging ale in some greasy pub rather than delivering the mail, with his combed-back dark hair and the well-muscled arm that PJ noticed as he gathered up the mail.

The last mailman she remembered had been about eighty-five and went by the name Oscar. As in . . . Grouch.

"You new here?" he asked as he handed her the mail.

"Yes . . . and no."

"Name's Colin." Then he winked and pulled away.

She lifted her hand in a wave, then sifted through the stack of bills and magazines, walking across the long, soft grass to the front porch. The sun kissed her shoulders, and with the birds chirruping in the oak hovering over the side of the house, she could feel the beach wooing her.

Or rather, a trip to her mother's.

Only the hum of the refrigerator cut through the quiet of the house. PJ was putting away the ice cream when she heard shouting from somewhere beyond the family room. Russian-ish shouting.

She rushed to Connie's home office, a room outfitted for a contemporary Connie, with a mahogany desk, rich red walls, a leather sofa, and a sleek wide-screened laptop computer atop the L-shaped desk. It smelled of power. Of smarts. Of money.

"What are you doing?" She found Sergei's parents leaning over Connie's laptop, Boris gesturing at the screen. Vera clamped his arm, clearly in an effort to calm him.

"What?" PJ scrolled for the equivalent in Russian. *"Shto? Shto?"*

Please, don't let them have crashed the computer. She circled the desk and spied a Russian site. From the layout, it looked like an auction page.

"What are you buying?"

Boris stood, slamming the desk chair back on its rollers, and brushed past her, raving.

Her Russian wasn't as good as she hoped, because PJ netted absolutely nothing from the barrage spilling forth. Which was probably good because she remembered hearing something about Russians having more swear words than Americans.

"What?" She schooled her voice low and calm, like she had when talking to an irate German Shepherd during the short-lived days of her paper route.

Vera looked at her and began to explain.

PJ recognized a less than helpful "gift, Ukraine, Sergei."

Boris, however, had already tugged out his Russian-English dictionary and was paging through it. A tight hush fell between them. PJ wondered if this might have been how the White House felt during the Bay of Pigs.

Then Boris ran his finger down the page, stopped, looked up at PJ, and grinned. *"Keed."*

What?

He looked at Vera and nodded. *"Keed."*

Kid? They were trying to buy a kid?

"I think you should stay off the Internet." PJ reached over and closed the screen.

Boris's smile faded.

Yes, those were probably curse words PJ heard on her way out of the room.

✳ ✳ ✳

PJ had just turned eight the first time she left home. She remembered the crisp air redolent with decaying loam, pumpkins with saggy eyes peering out from doorsteps, and cornstalks hung from front porches, tied with baling twine. Auburn leaves crunched under her feet, and a slight northern wind bullied the cowboy hat she'd pulled over her jacket hood as she hustled down the road, kicking stones before her with red galoshes. She balanced a stick over her shoulder, and a handkerchief tied to the end held a soggy peanut butter and grape jelly sandwich and a few stolen peanut butter cookies. Enough to get her through the night, during which a wagon train headed west would find her and collect her for their journey to the Oregon Trail and the Little House on the Prairie. And should they happen to run into any renegade outlaws, she knew just how to handle them—with her six-gun cap shooter tied to her leg.

PJ traced her first escape route as she drove toward her mother's home, remembering how big the hill had seemed, how cold and ominous the pond, dotted with shiny oak leaves. She'd reached the railroad tracks crossing Chapel Hills when her father pulled up in his '85 Jaguar, a sleek green lizard, rolled down the window, and stuck his elbow out. He looked regal with his thick black hair, those rich green eyes, a grey worsted wool suit against a black tie. "It's gonna get cold, PJ," he said. "And your mother has stew on."

PJ still made a face, even in her memories.

He had laughed. "All good cowgirls eat stew."

PJ remembered the way she crawled into the car, sliding on the sleek leather seats, smelling his cologne. He wouldn't be home long—probably had a meeting to attend somewhere—yet for that moment, he'd been her champion.

She still missed him most in the fall. "Your cowgirl finally left town, Daddy."

Pulling up to the house, PJ let her VW idle in the driveway, noting the differences in the colonial. The basketball hoop had vanished, along with the cherry tree in the front yard. The evergreens loomed dark green and shaggy along the side of the property—at least they blocked the view of the Haugens' modern monstrosity, as her mother called it. Art deco—giant glass blocks on end or even on their points. PJ always wondered what it might be like to live in that crystal palace, all that light shining in, the sound of rain splattering against the glass.

"PJ, I see you sitting out there!"

Her mother had appeared at the door, just an outline through the screen of the mudroom entryway.

PJ got out, stepping over a few loose bricks on the cobblestone sidewalk.

Elizabeth held the door open for her. "Seems like ages."

"It *has* been ages," PJ said, noting the wide-leg capris that did nothing to camouflage her mother's cast.

"Well, you're here now, and I'm so glad, because I have a little project for you." She patted PJ on the shoulder. "I'm glad you wore your cleaning clothes."

No, she'd worn her best plaid shorts and her favorite green tee.

"Don't forget to take off your shoes."

PJ shook off her flip-flops and followed her mother through the house, albeit slowly, thanks to the crutches that did wonders for slowing her down. "You got granite countertops."

"Of course."

"And took out the screened porch."

"I know. I wanted a room we could use all year round."

We. PJ didn't ask who that might be since, to her knowledge, her mother lived here alone. Indeed, a CSI specialist moving through the house might find scant evidence *anyone* lived here. Not a dish in the sink, a magnet on the fridge. A freshly shaken chenille carpet under the honey oak table—now how did her mother do that? Even the pillows in the family room lay plumped and undisturbed on a set of bourbon brown leather furniture.

"You finally recarpeted the family room."

"Twice, actually."

PJ dreaded what she might see as they climbed the stairs. Five bedrooms for four people—she always wondered why her mother never filled them. Had been afraid to ask. She noticed her mother's door remained shut. But the guest bedrooms hosted new wallpaper, pillowy comforters, fresh flowers on the cherry bedside tables.

"You running a B and B, Mom?"

Elizabeth frowned at her. "What?"

PJ peeked into Connie's room. Once blue with buds of bachelor buttons in a high border of wallpaper, now the walls were creamy white with green ivy twining the windowsills and down the edge of the closet. "If not, then you should be."

"Sometimes I just don't understand you." Elizabeth stopped outside PJ's old bedroom door, hand on the knob. "Now, I don't want you to be distressed by what you see. I just didn't know what to do."

"What did you do, put a match to the room?" Yet an unfamiliar nostalgia cottoned her chest, and with everything inside her, she longed for pink and eyelet.

"For crying out loud, PJ." Elizabeth opened the door.

PJ stood still, that cotton expanding to fill her throat, cutting off her breathing.

Preserved. Nearly to the hour she left it so long ago. Her mother had made the bed, pulled up the floral sheets and matching bedspread military tight. The clothes from her graduation party—a white sleeveless top, a pair of dress pants—lay folded on her desk chair.

The calendar read May 29.

Her clock flashed 12:00 a.m., a power outage fatality.

The room even smelled like the high school girl she remembered, as if she'd misted her Clinique Happy just moments ago. She advanced slowly onto the pink rug, staring at her softball trophies, her letter jacket slung over the bubble spindle of her bed frame, wallet senior pictures of her friends—a big one of Trudi—lined up in a row on her tall dresser.

Her prom dress hung limp in the open closet. PJ hooked her toes around the white stilettos she'd worn and wiggled one on, rising suddenly on one foot. "Back then, I could nearly look Boo—"

Her mother's eyes sharpened.

"Nothing." She shook off the shoe, and it hit the back of the closet. "I can't believe you haven't touched this room. After all these years."

Elizabeth ran her hand over the floral bedding, as if smoothing out the ripples of time. PJ had a picture, fast and stinging, of her mother standing right there, staring out the window, breathing in the lingering fragrances PJ left behind.

"I'm sorry that I . . . that it took me so long to come back, Mom."

Elizabeth sighed, adjusted the pink pom-pommed pillow on the bed. "I need to remodel this room. So, could you clean your stuff out?"

With everything inside her, PJ wanted to close the three feet between them, to pull her mother against her. To remind her of the little girl who baked her a cake for her birthday and carried it home from Trudi's house on her bicycle.

But that wasn't the Sugar way.

PJ ran her fingertips over the gold mock Oscar she'd won in theater class. "All my stuff?"

Elizabeth smiled as if PJ might be the maid who'd just comprehended her English instructions. "Yes. All of it. Before you leave town again."

"Sure, Mom."

The phone rang.

"I can get it."

"No, you stay here and get started." Elizabeth eased by her on her crutches.

PJ reached out and steadied herself on the bed, her bones suddenly brittle. *"Before you leave town again."* Because one never knew when she might have to leave town.

Clearly her mother was planning on it.

She walked over to the bookcase and pulled out a Nancy Drew book. *The Secret of the Old Clock.* She blew the dust from the worn pages. How she'd loved mysteries, fancied herself as Nancy, the supersleuth. She put the book on her desk, her hand dropping to the top drawer, her thumb running over the pewter pull.

She opened it. And sure enough, her prom pictures lay on top.

Her finger traced Boone's smile.

"Oh no."

Her mother's voice traveled through the halls from her bedroom. Something in it made PJ turn, close the drawer, step out into the hall.

"That's just terrible."

PJ moved closer to the bedroom door, spying her mother through the crack. She'd sunk down onto the bed—a burgundy tapestry comforter PJ didn't recognize—shaking her head. "Of course. Thanks for calling." She hung up the phone, her shoulders slumping.

"What is it, Mom?" PJ opened the door, noticing her father's pictures neatly lined up on her mother's chest of drawers.

"I can't believe it. Right here in Kellogg. Oh." Her hand covered her mouth.

"You're scaring me a little. Is it Connie? Sergei?"

Elizabeth shook her head. "It's just horrible. Ernie Hoffman's been murdered."

Chapter *FIVE*

Somewhere in the back of her mind, she knew it was a dream. Still, it felt real, nearly like a memory. PJ clutched her history book to her chest, the spiral-bound notebook catching on the straps of her camo-patterned tank. "Boone, stop it, I'm late for class."

Across from her, over Boone's shoulder, a poster announced the upcoming prom in silver glitter and blue swirls. The early smells of summer leaked in through the open windows, the redolence of freedom and the fragrance of warm grass on bare feet. Students filled the halls, the roar and laughter backdropping Boone's murmurs against her neck.

"Boone!"

Of course, he didn't listen, never did. He stood firm, bracing one hand over her shoulder, against the lockers, while the other caught in her long blonde hair. PJ looked down, watching it twine through his fingertips. "Hoffman will kill me. Again."

"Peej, it's gorgeous outside. I just got the bike out. How can you even think of being inside on a day like today?" He stepped back, arms wide, his smile every inch trouble, eyes twinkling, his bronze hair already kissed by the sun. "Skip school with me."

Indeed, heat had slithered into the hallways on rays of summer sun. From far away, the school buzzer sounded.

"I'm late." The words resounded outside her body, as if someone else might be reminding her of the PJ she knew she should be, the PJ who should fight to extricate herself from Boone's magnetic pull. She managed to turn away, and as she did, the hallway bowed, as if made of gelatin. She took another step; it wobbled, and she ricocheted off the lockers.

Boone's hand closed around her arm.

"I'm late!" Did she yank her arm away? The floor now sucked at her feet, and she pulled each step out with a slurping sound. Sweat slicked her forehead, dripped off her brow.

The buzzer sounded again.

"I'm late!" She threw herself into Hoffman's classroom, landing hard on her knees. Her books bounced against her stomach, ripping at her breath.

"No! No! No!"

Mr. Hoffman stood over her, his mouth open—the words must be coming from him, but his lips didn't move—his dark eyes wide upon her. As she stared at him, his eyes filled and he began to cry, thick crimson tears that dribbled down his chin and splashed on the black-and-white tiled floor, over her books, pooling at her knees.

PJ held out her palm. No, not tears. Blood.

She screamed, thrashed awake, and sat up fast. The force

slammed her against the little assailant sitting on her knees, bouncing. They smacked foreheads and he rolled off the bed and landed on the floor.

"Ow!"

Davy wailed, staring at her like she'd tried to murder him. He scrambled to his feet and ran. "I hate you! I hate you!"

PJ held her hand to her forehead, trying to sort dream from reality.

Her white curtains hung limp in the windless morning. Sweat dribbled down between her shoulder blades. A bird chir-ruped, *late, late, late*.

Her breathing motored to idle. A dream. Just a dream brought on by shock.

Next to her, on the bedside table, her radio buzzed. She slapped at it and realized she must have done that in her early morning daze because it read half-past the hour.

Awww.... "Davy! We're late!"

Throwing off her comforter, she ran to his room. He crouched before his PlayStation, still sniffing. He cut his eyes to her with a look that read betrayal. Tears dribbled down his cheeks.

It hit her then. He'd been on her bed. Trying to wake her? "Davy . . . are you okay?" She knelt beside him, reached out to push away his hair, survey the bump. He jerked away. "Was I having a bad dream?"

He wiped his snotty nose on the sleeve of his pajamas.

"Were you trying to wake me up, buddy?"

Slowly he put down his controller, drew up his legs tight against his chest, and locked his arms around them. He nod-ded without meeting her eyes.

PJ sat back on the floor next to him and touched his ankle. "No oatmeal this morning for heroes. How about some Cap'n Crunch?"

He picked up the controller, gave another swipe across his nose, and nodded.

"Listen—let's race. Get dressed and the first one downstairs wins."

His thumbs continued pounding at the buttons. But his eyes caught hers. PJ slid her feet underneath her, poised like a runner. "Ready. Set . . ."

He sprang to his feet and ran to his clothes, neatly laid out the night before.

PJ took off for her room.

Davy beat her downstairs (but only because she stood in her doorway waiting) and she poured him a bowl of cereal. She made coffee, leaning a hip against the counter as she watched him, his hair still wrecked from sleep, a line of milk drizzling down his chin. He occasionally looked up, then, as if caught stealing something, sank his face back into the bowl.

PJ packed his lunch box with a cheese sandwich and a Rice Krispies Treat and herded him out of the house. He kicked her only once, as she helped him into the car. The sprinklers showered her windshield as she pulled into the loading zone.

"That's two tardies, Miss Sugar."

"Yeah, but note the missing Superman pants," PJ said, giving Ms. Nicholson a wink as Davy ran past them to class without a good-bye.

At least they'd avoided the pre-school sumo wrestling today. Behind Davy's anger, the stolen looks, the kicks to her shin, she'd recognized something vaguely familiar. Panic, maybe.

Or even desperation. She couldn't put her finger on it, but it niggled at her, right alongside her thoughts of Boone, her mother, and of course, poor Ernie Hoffman.

The sun blasted out of the sky, hot and stinging, as she drove home from Fellows. She made the mistake of angling around the beach, and an old hunger stirred inside. First thing on the agenda for the morning—a tan. Then maybe she'd have the internal fortification to return to her mother's and begin the Great Sort. She still didn't know what to do with the feelings evoked by seeing the pristine, almost mausoleum condition of her room.

And after her nightmare, she needed to dig her toes into the warm sanity of the coarse Kellogg beach and lie with her eyes closed, letting her brain stop its crazy whirring.

She'd circled the question all night—obviously long enough to let it embed her dreams: who would have killed good old Ernie Hoffman? The man didn't have a mean mitochondria in his body, as evidenced not only by his generosity of spirit at her return but his kindness the night of the fire.

No, Hoffman wasn't a person with a black book of enemies.

PJ flinched as she recalled the conversation with her mother yesterday after Elizabeth had told her the news.

"Ernie Hoffman, my old history teacher?" PJ had hung on the door, absorbing her mother's words. "When? How?"

"Today, apparently. His daughter-in-law found him. And—" Elizabeth lowered her voice—"his neck was broken."

"Are there any suspects, any clues?"

"I don't know, PJ; I'm not a detective." Her mother shook her head.

And that's when things turned south, thanks to PJ's sudden inability to keep a secret. "I saw him yesterday at the wedding. Did you hear about Jack Wilkes shoving him into the country club pool?"

Her mother hadn't blinked, hadn't moved at the name.

"Jack Wilkes is Trudi's husband."

"Your . . . friend Trudi, from high school?" She said it like she might be talking about a fatal disease, with the accompanying expression.

"Yes, Mom, *that* Trudi."

Elizabeth had risen, smoothed her pants. "Well, that explains it, then. I always knew she was trouble." She'd brushed past a speechless PJ and gone back to work.

Tried and convicted by Elizabeth Sugar.

Yes, definitely, PJ needed the beach and soon.

She arrived home and sprang up the stairs, donned her swimsuit and grabbed her towel, Connie's daily edition of the *Kellogg Press*, and a highlighter.

She fully planned on being gainfully employed by the time Connie returned. Employed and perhaps not homeless.

She did a quick but less than committed search through the house for the internationals. The house was blessedly quiet.

Shoving a lawn chair into the backseat of the Bug, she left the house and in moments pulled up to the Kellogg beach. It couldn't be called large—more of a strip of sand and grass fortified by two tall lifeguard stands—white skeletons against the pale sky—and a still-closed snack stand. Behind the beach, cordoned off by a small bridge, an inlet blanketed by lily pads, corralled kayaks, canoes, and skiffs tethered to stakes and buoys.

PJ parked her car and pulled out her paraphernalia, then stood at the edge of the sand and took in the panorama of memories, from early childhood swimming lessons to middle school mortification to high school mischief.

And of course, nearly every one of those memories included Boone.

She picked a spot near the middle, free from shadows, unfolded her lawn chair, whipped off her T-shirt, and lathered on the coconut suntan oil.

There was little in the way of options in the employment ads. Waitstaff at Sunsets Supper Club and a cook at Hal's Pizzeria. Security person needed at the bank and a home health aid listing.

She sighed, closing the paper. Frankly she'd easily qualify for any of those jobs—she'd worked for six months as a reception-ist in a swank Vegas spa. And with her stint as a stunt girl and her spotty knowledge of tae kwon do, she could probably land the bank position. But most likely, she'd find herself listing off the daily specials and filling cocktail orders at Sunsets.

Joe would probably still take her on. He'd liked her even after she dumped the roasted chicken with gravy into Craig Shuman's lap. Didn't even bat an eye when she pointed out that Craig deserved it.

She leaned back, closed her eyes, and let the sun caress her face. A lazy day was spooling out before her, and for the first time in over a decade, calm seeped into her bones, and finally she could breathe, could allow the wind into her lungs slowly. No more gulping, as if running hard behind the pack.

Home sweet home.

"I thought I'd find you here."

The voice carried the sultry tone of a thousand memories, none of which she wanted to infect her beautiful day. "Go away."

"Can't. I'm on official business."

PJ opened her eyes. Boone stood over her, his dark shadow cutting across her legs. He looked on the job in a blue dress shirt that probably turned his blue eyes into lethal weapons. The silver badge on his belt glinted shiny and bright like a medal. As usual, just seeing him curled a wave of emotion through her, not all of it painful. Someday her heart and her head were just going to have to learn to communicate.

"Are you stalking me?" PJ pushed up on one elbow.

"I might start."

"Hey. Eyes up here, pal." She grabbed her shirt and draped it over her.

He smiled. "Miss me?"

She leaned out of his shadow and cupped her hand to shade her vision. "What's your name again?"

"Lieutenant Buckam to you, ma'am."

PJ laughed and then cringed. She had to be tougher than this. "You're cutting off my sun. Now I'm going to have a stripe." She lay back down, closing her eyes to his imposing drama. "Really, go away."

"Can't do that."

"Are you on beach patrol or something? bothering the locals?" She waved her hand at him, dismissing. "Fetch me a lemonade, then."

He stood there, saying nothing. She peeked open an eye just in time to see him slip on his silver sunglasses. They hid his eyes and elicited the smallest burst of rebellious disappointment.

Oh, she was *such* a slower learner.

"Put some clothes on. I can't bring you down to the station like that. The guys won't be able to keep their eyes in their heads."

"Hah! Like I'm going *anywhere* with you. Besides, are you *arresting* me?" She let out a laugh that was part disbelief, part righteous anger. "That's uncannily perfect. I'd bet you'd just love to put handcuffs on me. Better yet, march me right out of town."

She didn't know when her tone had changed from humor to hurt, but there it hung between them, their past, bruised and bleeding.

PJ looked away, clenching her jaw, blinking, refusing to cushion the silence.

Boone stood above her, his chest rising once, twice. "The last thing I want to do is run you out of town. Or arrest you."

His words were a splinter, driving through the hard places to the tender flesh beneath.

"But I do have to ask you to come down to the station with me because . . . we have a problem."

"I'm pretty sure there's a statute of limitations on—"

"No, I'm not talking about the incident at the country club *or* Hinton's pontoon boat."

Oh yeah. She'd forgotten about the time they'd *borrowed* her neighbor's pontoon boat.

"Why bother me, then?"

Boone held out his hand to help her up.

She ignored his help and stood, then took off her sunglasses and pulled her T-shirt over her head. It stuck to her skin.

He folded up her chair and draped her towel over his shoulder. "It's about your . . . uh . . . houseguest."

✳ ✳ ✳

Public lewdness?

PJ stared at the charge sheet, then back at Boone. He cracked a mocking smile and she teetered one nerve short of decking him. "Oh, this is fun for you, isn't it? Just a laugh fest."

"Well . . . maybe. I mean, don't you think it's just a little ironic? Especially for me, a guy who knows your history. What is this, something that runs in your family?"

"Hush up. I'm sure they still have your records somewhere." PJ glowered at him, as if she just might sprint past him into the files and dig up his rap sheet.

Still, being here at the police station, with its cool marble, the wanted pictures wallpapering the bulletin board, the phone jangling behind the glass partition, gave her the smallest of chills. Or maybe it was standing in her swimsuit, smelling of coconut, her skin prickling against the full blast of the air conditioner.

She certainly didn't appreciate the look Rosie the desk clerk gave her as Boone escorted her in, his hand cupping her elbow, as if she might be the suspect.

Boone closed his mouth, but a ghost of a smirk remained.

"He's not family." PJ peered past Boone to Boris, wearing a towel—and little else—and sitting on a chair in Boone's office, his bare feet planted. "Can't you give him your jacket or some pants or something?"

Boone raised an eyebrow as if she'd asked him to hand over the keys to his motorcycle—did he still have a motorcycle?— or perhaps his beloved Mustang convertible.

"He looks cold."

"He should. He's in his birthday suit."

"Maybe he was hot. It's a hot day out."

"Is that your excuse?" Boone ran those pale eyes over her again and she tugged at the bottom of her T-shirt.

"How much for bail?"

Boris lifted his head, as though just hearing her voice, his chiseled face stony, revealing nothing. She guessed that he'd already revealed too much for the day. Oh, she shouldn't be laughing. This cut way too close to her own greatest fears.

"He's not officially arrested yet." Boone lowered his voice to gossip level. "Actually this is the third time we've hauled him in. I think Mrs. Cartwright must be standing at her bathroom window, her thumb poised over the speed dial to the station. The guy was still chanting when we got there. Hadn't even gotten to the baptism part."

"Baptism?" PJ's voice matched Boone's, and Rosie shot them a look. *Yeah, look out, Kellogg. Boone and PJ are up to their old tricks—someone get a fire extinguisher.* She resisted the urge to stick out her tongue.

She could admit, however, that the old electricity sizzled just under her skin, especially when Boone bent close and whispered into her ear, jump-starting her heartbeat.

"After the first arrest I went online, did a little research. Evidently there's a Russian religion that requires all their members to douse themselves with cold water every morning—"

"In the nude?" PJ valiantly attempted to purge from her mind any accompanying mental picture.

Boone raised his eyebrows.

PJ stepped away, crossing her arms. "I don't know Mrs. Cartwright yet, but I'm thinking I'm going to have to make a neighborly visit with homemade cookies. Seriously, though, don't we have some privacy in our own backyard?"

"Maybe you can put up a little beach umbrella?"

"Oh, very helpful." PJ ran a hand around the back of her neck, squeezed a tight muscle. Her skin felt hot and greasy from the sun. "Is he under arrest? Do I have to post bail?" Restocking Connie's barren pantry had taken her pocket cash, and she was still waiting on her final check from the Shrimp Shack. If bail was more than $37.53, then Boris was going to have a nice long sit in the pokey.

Maybe, however, jail was the safest place for him.

"No, you can take him home. Just no . . ."

"Sunbathing?"

Boone nodded, too much humor in his eyes for her good as he opened the door for Boris. PJ averted her gaze as the man strutted past her, his chin up. Oy, as Vera would say.

"By the way, he seemed pretty upset when we brought him in. Kept repeating the word *kid*. . . . Is David okay?"

PJ stared at him, shaken as much by his tone as his question. "Yeah. I mean . . . how do you know Davy?"

Boone's eyes gentled. "I was on duty when they found your sister's husband."

Oh. The cold floor radiated through her flip-flops as she stood there, contemplating all she'd missed. "Boris was surfing the net last night. . . . I thought he was looking to buy . . ." Her own stupidity grabbed her around the throat, tightening it. "Obviously he wanted a present for Davy. I guess I owe him an apology."

She turned to go, but Boone reached out. His touch on her arm sent a jolt of warmth, a hot mix of danger and exhilaration she thought she'd left in the corridors of Kellogg High.

"I'm going to call you, you know."

She swallowed, caught in Boone's heartbreaking expression. Her lips parted to say no, but nothing emerged.

PJ shook herself free and ran out after Boris.

∗ ∗ ∗

Cheese Nips could be counted as grains and proteins. At least that's what PJ told herself as Davy turned his nose up at the chicken nuggets she heated for him. She'd managed to negotiate three into his stomach before ransoming the crackers into his possession. He grabbed the box and sat down on the floor.

"I know your mother doesn't let you eat like this, Davy. We're going to have to come to some understanding here." She could be speaking through a wall of ten-inch glass for all the acknowledgment he gave. She had held on to a vibrant hope that they experienced a breakthrough that morning. Not only had she awakened some sort of affection from him—after all, he'd been trying to rouse her from her nightmare when she bashed him in the head—but they'd gone the entire ride to school without him screaming once.

But he'd kicked her twice when she picked him up at Fellows, once in front of Ms. Nicholson, who did nothing to hide her smirk. And when he arrived home, he tossed the contents of his briefcase on the floor of the front room, stomping on the Rice Krispies Treat that PJ had packed him for lunch. She spent a half hour digging marshmallow from the carpet.

She had to wonder what had happened. Yes, she'd been slightly late picking him up, what with paging through a

Russian dictionary for a good portion of the afternoon, spelling out rules in Cyrillic for Boris and Vera. Starting with no landlocked skinny-dipping.

Seemed like a simple request.

Still, fifteen minutes late wasn't an eternity. Wasn't worth being kicked in the shins. Twice.

She'd found Davy in his classroom playing with building blocks. He'd made a castle with a moat, and she'd crouched behind him, watching him stack one block on top of another. He wore a slight smile, as if he might be daydreaming, and with the late afternoon sun caressing his curls, his uniform rumpled, he looked like every other four-year-old tot. Any moment he might see her, grin, and launch into her arms.

She'd held her breath, afraid to move.

When he eventually spotted her, he gave his castle a destructive kick before he trudged out of the room.

He'd refused to remove his uniform for dinner.

PJ lowered herself next to him. "Whatcha doin', pal?" He'd taken a sheet of paper from his briefcase and now ran a red crayon over it in wide, violent sweeps that caught on the edges and striped the travertine tile floor. PJ reached for the sheet, but he snatched it from her.

"Mine!"

She quickly backed off. "No problem. Just wanted to help."

He smoothed the paper, pursed his little lips, and resumed his coloring attack on the paper.

She peered over his shoulder and grimaced. Math problems. Or rather, connect the dots. "Is that for school, Davy?"

He said nothing as his red crayon demolished the paper.

"Buddy, listen, I'm not any good at math either. English,

drama, journalism—I get those. Imagination skills. Math is all about rules and logic, and frankly I'm just not a logic girl. I dig the red scribbling. But that's probably your homework, so what do you say you start at the one . . ."

He threw the crayon. It exploded against the dishwasher.

Outside, the smell of grilling burgers laced the air, and warblers sang in an evening serenade.

PJ blew out a breath. *Help me here, Lord.* "Hey, wanna go to the beach?" After all, she hadn't exactly completed her tan.

Davy looked up, as if she might be speaking French.

"The beach? Sand, sunshine?"

A slow smile creased his face, the same smile she'd seen that morning. *There you are, little man.*

Abandoning his crayons, he leaped to his feet and disappeared up the stairs. PJ cleaned up the crayons, and moments later he returned, his swimsuit lumpy and backward over his suit pants, his shirt and tie untucked, his black socks shoved into a pair of swim shoes. He picked up his briefcase and walked over to PJ.

She resisted the urge to duck. "Okay, pal, I can work with that."

She grabbed her keys off the counter, and just like that, a memory ricocheted off her. Standing at the window, watching it pour down rain, muddying the backyard, her umbrella open over her head, red galoshes on her feet. And her mother putting away the contents of their picnic basket.

PJ braced her hand on the cool granite counter. The Como Zoo. Mom had promised, just PJ and her. PJ had watched her dreams dissolve with the tears sliding down the glass door.

Davy stared at her, wearing that same mysterious, stolen

look he'd given her this morning over his Cap'n Crunch. As if she could see something inside him he wasn't quite ready to reveal.

She fought the crazy urge to reach down and lock him in an embrace. She'd collected enough bruises for one day.

Grabbing her towel, she banged out the front door, Davy on her heels, and nearly knocked over the key-jangling, dark-eyed Russian standing on the stoop. Freshly barbered, with high cheekbones, he wore a silk shirt open to the third button and enough cologne to qualify for a biological weapon.

PJ took a step back. "Can I help you?"

"Boris ee Vera," he growled.

Ah, Cousin Igor. She should have guessed. She moved aside, and he brushed past her like she might be the doorman.

For Connie's sake, she would not leap to any conclusions.

The sun hung low, dipping into the waves, glazing the advance of twilight with hues of gold and bronze as they motored down to the beach. PJ ran a hand through her hair, letting it tangle, supposing the beach escape might be an old habit returning from dormancy—as a teen, when math or other problems seemed overwhelming, she'd floored it straight to the cool sand and easy lapping waves of the beach, where her mind cleansed, her thoughts calmed. With the expanse of freedom spread out before her, the parameters pushing against her seemed less suffocating.

It didn't help that Connie had embraced math with the passion of a true Sugar, the family legacy filled with CPAs, nurses, doctors, and investment bankers.

Davy piled out of the car and skipped across the parking lot, swinging his briefcase. PJ followed with two towels and a lawn chair. Squeals of laughter preceded little bodies running across the beach. A kite floated overhead, its tail friendly in the wind.

"PJ!"

The voice lifted above the laughter, followed by a hand waving furiously over the encampment of families on beach towels.

"Trudi!" Next to her, Jack—now dry and less menacing when not throwing old men into the pool—sat on the beach blanket, cradling a baby in a water diaper. The baby—Chip, PJ assumed—tossed sand into the air by pudgy handfuls, laughing as it rained down on his head. Jack didn't look in the least riled by the grit in his hair.

PJ called to Davy, and they navigated their way to Trudi's blanket.

"Hey," PJ said. Jack showed no hint of recognition. So this was what it felt like to be on the other side of gossip.

"This is Jack." Trudi gestured to her husband. He seemed nice. Innocuous. Sandy blond hair, brown eyes, an easy smile.

Not in the least a wife-bashing, country club–brawling attacker of history teachers.

Or a murderer. The fact that Hoffman now lay in the Kellogg morgue seared her brain like a brand, and she nearly yanked her hand from his strong grip. "He . . . hello, I'm PJ."

"The infamous PJ Sugar. Nice to finally meet the other half of the Trudi and PJ duo." His words were accompanied by a warm grin.

"Hey now, I think I get to tell my side of the story. Except, I want to meet Mike—is he here?"

"Summer camp for the week." Trudi picked up baby Chip,

wiping sand from his hair. He toddled off toward Davy and sat next to him, patting his briefcase. "He goes every year to play football. He's hoping to play for the Vikings."

PJ smiled, the words *like father, like son* on her lips, but she caught them. Probably Greg Morris was the last person Trudi wanted her son to emulate.

Trudi leaned back against Jack, and they appeared so happily-ever-after that something painful twisted inside PJ. Trudi, more than any of them, deserved to be happy. Few beyond PJ knew the challenges she'd lived through at home, with her agoraphobic mother, her workaholic father.

PJ would do nearly anything to revisit those years and rewrite them with a heroine who knew how to be a true friend.

"So, let's hear your side," Jack said. "All I know is that the country club caught fire—"

"I didn't set it."

Trudi jumped in. "She has to start at the beginning. With Boone."

"How long do you think we have, Trudi?"

Trudi laughed.

PJ spread out her towel, sat down, stretched out her legs. "There are some men who should have the word *trouble* tattooed on their foreheads. Boone Buckam is one of them."

PJ glanced at Jack, again searching for a sign of recognition. Jack's gaze was affixed to his son, now scooping up more sand.

"Anyway, I met him in fifth grade, and he just wouldn't leave me alone."

"Really, that's how you're going to put it?" Trudi laughed. "Try, PJ and Boone were made for each other. Both were bred to be straight A Ivy Leaguers, with scholarships. But the minute they got together, it was like the entire world lit up. Bang. Flames—"

"Do you have to use that metaphor, Trudi? Flames? Really?"

Trudi grinned. "Absolutely. It was like they each saw that little smoldering fire deep inside and knew exactly the kind of fuel to throw on it."

"Seriously, enough with the fire."

"PJ wasn't necessarily a bad girl—it was more all good fun than real danger. Like the time we filled the phys ed teacher's car with toilet paper. And TP'd all the football players' houses."

"And wrote the school fight song in shaving cream on the side of the building."

Trudi put her fingers to her lips. "That wasn't me, remember?"

"Trudi's right. I was just trying to have fun. But it didn't help that I skipped a few classes."

"You failed gym, sweetie."

"It was first hour—it interfered with my donut run."

She got a laugh out of Jack.

"My reputation preceded me and eventually convicted me. On prom night, the kitchen wing of the country club caught fire. Unfortunately, I'd been seen with a cigarette by the back door near the trash, where it started. The fact is, it was Boone's—but a few of his drunken friends pointed the finger at me, and Boone . . . well, he had a scholarship to protect."

"And it wasn't like Director Buckam—Boone's father—would have let his own son take the rap for it anyway." Trudi clearly remembered that night as well as PJ. "I'll never forget the look on your face as they hauled you away in your prom dress."

"You spent prom night in jail?" Jack looked genuinely sympathetic. "That's the saddest thing I've ever heard."

"Yeah, well, I could have used your defense when my mother showed up at 2 a.m. She'd woken our family lawyer, and they went behind closed doors with Director Buckam. The next thing I know, he's dropping the charges in exchange for a terse agreement that I leave town after graduation."

"I always wondered why you didn't fight it, PJ." Trudi handed a teething ring to Chip.

"Maybe a part of me wanted to leave. I could just imagine the court battle—it would be, at the very least, ugly. Besides, my mother had already handed over a fat check to the country club director—"

"I think Roger Buckam just wanted you away from his golden son." Trudi touched PJ's arm, something firm and true inside those hazel eyes. PJ leaned into them like a beggar. "But more people knew the truth than you think. Word on the street was that PJ took the rap for someone else. Someone like Boone."

PJ blinked, breaking her gaze away, looking at the sun now half-gone, an orange shimmer gulped by the hunger of the night.

"Innocent until proven guilty," Jack said.

"Except in Kellogg." The words in PJ's throat scraped it raw, and she swallowed against a fresh, unexpected pain.

"So, PJ and her prom night live in infamy," Jack said.

Oh, he had no idea. The fire was just the public part of the night's infernos. PJ drew in the sand.

"I think it takes a lot of guts for her to come back."

PJ lifted her eyes in time to see Trudi's wink.

Jack murmured something, pressed a kiss to his wife's head.

PJ resisted the impulse to fill the silence with words that might diminish everything Trudi had just given her.

"Isn't that cute," Trudi said softly, finally. "David is reading to Chip."

PJ glanced at Davy. He held a book open on his lap while Chip sat in rapt attention. "*The Little Rabbit Who Wanted Red Wings*. I love that story. Always wanted a pair of red wings."

"I thought the moral of the story was to be who you were created to be," Jack said.

"Yeah, that too." PJ leaned back, putting her arm over her eyes.

"You know, if I'd known you were coming back to town, I would have made sure Jack's cousin was around. He's single."

PJ shook her head. "Thanks, Trudi, but the last thing I need in my life at the moment is romance. I have to find a job, not to mention a place to live."

"And what about Boone?"

What about Boone? So what if he could still turn her to liquid with a look. She refused to be that girl. She was a new creation. Not Boone's girl. "What about Boone? This isn't high school anymore."

"So you're sticking around after Connie comes home?"

PJ lifted her arm, squaring with Trudi's gaze. The warmth in her eyes prompted her to shrug, add a smile.

For today, that would have to be enough.

Chapter **SIX**

"Can you believe I kept all this junk?" PJ dumped the top drawer of her desk onto the floral bedspread. Out tumbled pencils and paper clips, senior pictures, dried nail polish, an old tube of pink lipstick, a dog-eared book—*The Littlest Horse Thieves*, a story she'd always somehow identified with—and an envelope.

Elizabeth turned from where she'd decided to dust the dresser, a soiled rag in her hand. "It was your room, PJ. I tried not to interfere."

PJ opened her mouth, a retort balling on her tongue. Did her mother have some kind of memory loss? What about the time she'd stood over her for an entire weekend like a prison warden and made her sort through every sheet of paper in her desk, try on every T-shirt for size? Her mother had done everything to this room but move in. Even the wall color had been Elizabeth's choice.

PJ closed her mouth, picked up the envelope, and dumped the contents on the bed. Tiny, slick-backed patterned shapes mounded on the comforter. "My Girl Scout badges." She picked one up. "Oh, look, my safety award badge."

Elizabeth reached out for it, and PJ handed it over. Outside, the sun winked at her, beckoning, the breeze warm and sweet through the bedroom window. When her mother had called this morning, PJ had agreed to one hour of cleaning and sorting.

One had run into three, with most of her clothing now boxed up in the give-to-charity pile. She still had to go through the boxes of memorabilia in the closet.

Thankfully she had to pick Davy up from school in an hour. And of course, it was important to be on time.

Her mother ran her thumb over the tiny green triangle, something distant in her eyes.

"I don't think I ever did all the requirements for this badge." PJ sorted through the pile. She never did get her sewing badge—hence why the badges had never been sewn onto her sash.

"Oh, I think so. Remember the car safety instructions? and the family fire exit plan?" Elizabeth smiled, as if reliving the day PJ plotted out the house exits and made them rehearse their escape, complete with waking from a "sound sleep" in their beds. "Remember how your father pretended to snore?"

PJ let that memory seep into her, seeing her father lying on his bed, still in his suit; Connie in her room; PJ, the fire marshal, feigning sleep in her own, one hand on the fire alarm buzzer. When she pushed it, they all came alive—except her father, who pretended to sleep through the alarm.

If Mrs. Johnson, her troop leader, had only known that they'd failed miserably, thanks to her father's playacting and the fact that he grabbed both her and Connie and held them down, tickling them until they all died of asphyxiation, if not giggles.

PJ ran a finger under her eye. "Yeah, he never did take the safety badge seriously."

"I'd say that probably neither did Mrs. Johnson, the way she acted when you broke the school door."

"You remember that?" PJ glanced at her mother, who handed back the badge and began wiping out the inside of a dresser drawer.

"Of course. I showed up at school, and there you were, sitting on the steps sobbing, Mrs. Johnson standing over you, screaming."

"I couldn't believe that I'd broken the door. We were just playing—tag, I think—and I slammed the glass door and tried to hold it shut with my . . . my . . ."

"Your backside." Elizabeth looked up, something unreadable in her eyes.

"Yeah. After that everyone called me . . ."

"Iron Bum."

PJ stared at her. "You knew?"

Elizabeth pushed in the dresser drawer. Its pewter handles rattled. "I was so angry with Mrs. Johnson for screaming at you. You were simply white with fear. She made it seem like you did it on purpose, when everyone knew perfectly well that Jaycee Cummings and Shelley Mortinsen were chasing you through the building. She and I had it out the next day. I told her she should never have blamed it on you." She turned back to her work, scrubbing out another drawer.

"I didn't know you did that, Mom."

Elizabeth didn't look at her, simply closed the next drawer.

"Sometimes, someone just needs a champion. Don't forget those boxes under your bed."

PJ slipped the badges back into the envelope. "I think I'll sew these onto a sash after all."

✳ ✳ ✳

PJ ripped the pink slip into tiny squares and dropped it into the trash under the sink. A warning. In *preschool*.

As if she tried to be late.

Did they not know the time it took to wrestle her guilt, oatmeal pot in hand, before she surrendered to a box of Lucky Charms? And the hunt for Davy's uniform consumed at least half the morning.

Where was the grace?

She picked up Davy's half-eaten hamburger and slid it into the disposal. He grinned at her, the frosting from an oatmeal cookie wedged in his teeth.

Roughage. That's what she would call it.

She rinsed off the dish and slid it into the dishwasher, drying her hands before her finger hovered over the blinking red light of the answering machine.

It was probably a message for Connie. From her office.

It could, however, be Boone, making good on his threat.

Or maybe it *was* Connie, calling from a beach in Mexico.

Except what if it was Boone, leaving a little verbal bomb to terrorize her night? She hadn't heard a word from him since yesterday, and she'd routed the urge to call him when Boris met her this morning armed with a towel and a bucket of water. She'd have to check some of her translations on her list of rules.

In the next room, under the soft twilight hues turning the office crimson, Boris sat at Connie's computer, surfing. He'd bargained away his religious freedom for an hour on Connie's computer.

She turned away from the answering machine. "How about some milk, little man?"

Davy nodded and she poured a cup and handed it over. He made a mustache.

She stared hard at the blinking light, gulped a breath, and pressed.

"Hey, PJ, it's Joe, down at Sunsets Supper Club. Yeah, we have an opening. Come by tomorrow morning, and we'll see if your old uniform still fits." Joe's message ended on a hard laugh, and PJ hit Delete before it could turn over to the time/date stamp.

Last night's survey of her George Washingtons trumped the pride that wanted to waggle its impertinent head.

Besides, maybe she *could* still fit into the uniform.

She slid onto a stool next to Davy. "You have a field trip tomorrow."

"I don't like field trips. They make us be quiet."

"I couldn't agree more, kid. But the good news is that you won't have to be quiet at the museum. Ask lots and lots and lots of questions. Really, lots."

The phone jangled. PJ's hand hovered over it only a moment before she picked it up. Just conjuring him in her mind didn't mean she had the ability to make Boone materialize on the other end. "Hello?"

"Hello, this is Fellows Academy. We're looking for David Morton."

She wanted to bang her head against the ash cupboards.

"Davy's, uh . . . occupied." And four. Did they not have that fact somewhere in their records?

"Can you tell him he has a book overdue?"

"What's the title?"

"I'm sorry, ma'am; I'm not allowed to tell you."

"What?" She handed Davy a napkin.

"Ma'am?"

So maybe her tone had been a bit strident. She lowered her voice. "How am I supposed to know what book to bring back if you're not allowed to tell me the title?"

"It's David's book."

"He's four—you do know this, right?" She put her hand over the mouthpiece. "Davy, did you know you have a book out from the library?"

Davy slid down from the high-top stool at the counter and stuck out his tongue.

Apparently it was time to institute Connie's rule about manners.

"He doesn't know where it is. You'll have to clue me in so I can search for it."

"I'm sorry, ma'am; those are our rules."

For a long beat, she just rolled the words around in her head. "What? I'm sorry. . . . I don't understand." PJ retrieved Davy's lunch box and began to clean it out. "Really, just tell me the name of the book; I'll find it."

"It's against our privacy policy to tell you."

PJ listened as, in the next room, Boris let out a stream of Russian. She had the dark urge to hand him the phone.

"Let me get this straight. I, as his guardian, am not allowed to know what my four-year-old is checking out of the library?"

"It's a privacy issue."

"You mean to tell me he could be checking out books about nuclear weapons, or even—" PJ lowered her voice—"other books, and you wouldn't tell me?"

"I'm sorry, Mrs.—"

"Who do you think is going to *pay* for Davy's overdue book? Is he going to cough it up out of his milk money?"

Out of her peripheral vision, PJ spotted Davy climbing the stool again, his eyes darting to her, as if she might not see him inching his way to the oatmeal cookie box. She swiped the box off the counter. "What kind of school is this? The kid is four years old!"

"Hold, please."

Hold?

Davy settled down on the counter, his legs crossed, arms folded, waging a sit-in. "I want a cookie," he said, his little blue eyes fierce. Yeah, well, she wanted a job, a tan, an insight into Boone's brain, a house like Connie's, and perhaps even world peace.

"Mrs. Morton, this is the director of Fellows Academy. What seems to be the problem?" Despite her crisp memory of appearing on the Fellows stoop in her pajamas, PJ didn't appreciate the derision in the director's tone . . . in her *familiar* tone.

Oh no. The voice matched the visual picture of the stout woman who sentried the door every morning. Ms. Nicholson. Perfect. She schooled her voice, extricating from it everything she felt. "Thank you for your help. I'm trying to locate my nephew's library book."

"I hear you have a problem with our privacy policy?"

No, PJ, don't—"I have a problem with your entire school. Just tell me the name of his book, and I'll bring it in."

Silence, and in it PJ heard Connie's pleading: *"Please, PJ, this is important."* But behind that, she saw Davy, his uniform rumpled from yet another round of hide-and-seek (this morning she'd found it wadded in a truck under the bed). Nearly a week into summer and the kid hadn't a bit of a tan, not one decent stubbed toe.

"Perhaps tomorrow, if you can make it on *time*, we could have a chat in my office—"

"Sometimes, someone just needs a champion."

"Davy is a little kid. He should be at the beach, swimming or chasing frogs or burying his aunt in the sand, not spending his summer doing math problems. He won't be there tomorrow . . . or ever, until you reveal to me the title of this contraband book he's been hiding!"

"I'm sorry, but that won't be possible."

The words formed in her throat, like the roll of a wave on the ocean crashing to shore, disseminating sand castles and dragging back to the cold depths all the pieces of shell, now broken and lost. She could hear a faint *Stop!* Knew she should close her mouth before her words swept her out on a riptide to a place of no return.

But she'd never been proficient at *stop*.

"It's schools like yours that make people believe they're more or . . . or *less* than they are. I wouldn't send Davy back there if you fell at my feet and begged!"

"Which we most certainly will not do. Call me when you find the book."

Click.

Click? PJ stared at the phone, her heartbeat pelleting her throat.

Click?

Davy stood on the counter and, with a look she couldn't place, began to peel off his uniform.

✳ ✳ ✳

Trudi's day care, Peppermint Fence, encapsulated PJ's wildest five-year-old daydreams. The backyard, through the black chain-link fence, declared a moratorium on tidiness, with toys strewn from one side to the other. A jungle gym pinnacled the center of the yard, complete with safety netting, two towers, a sandbox, a swing set, and a sprinkler tree under which a group of youngsters frolicked as PJ pulled up.

For a long moment, she wished she could whip off her dress pants and white cotton blouse—she knew her old Shrimp Shack uniform would come in handy—and join them in abandon. Maybe she'd forget that she'd managed to evict Davy from his five-star school in the space of three days.

"We've already filled David's spot." The words dug into PJ's brain and lodged there like a pike, dissecting her hopes of a victorious stint as Davy's caretaker.

Who was she trying to kid? She hadn't a prayer of competing with Connie. And after tearing apart Davy's room, searching even between the mattresses for the renegade library book, she simply hadn't possessed the internal fortitude to call her mother and ask her to watch Davy while she interviewed at Sunsets. Between the expulsion from school and her old high school job prospect, PJ wasn't sure where to start that priceless conversation.

Besides, at least here at Peppermint Fence, Davy would have fun, albeit illiterate fun. Connie would return to a fat, happy, academically stunted son.

Trudi stepped out from the shade, carrying a tray of what looked like Dixie cups and graham crackers, looking very motherly in a pair of Bermuda shorts and a pink sleeveless T-shirt. She set the tray on a little tykes-size table and turned, as if she could sense PJ in the parking lot, deliberating.

No doubt a skill Trudi had honed long ago.

"What are you doing here?" She said it in a welcome tone, one filled with surprise. It mustered PJ's courage to slide out of the car and open the door for her uniformed little future tycoon in the backseat. She should have brought him a change of clothes, but she'd dressed him with hope. And apparently, naiveté.

"Help." PJ gave Trudi a quick rundown. "Can you just watch him while I interview with Joe?"

"Seriously? Sunsets Supper Club? I thought you hated that place."

"I hate starvation worse. And I have a couple Russians living with me that will feed me scary things like fried liver if I don't bring home my own bacon. Besides, if I hope to stick around . . ."

Trudi reached for Davy's hand. "Come with me, pal."

He yanked his hand away and looked up at PJ with what could only be the eyes of a death row prisoner about to meet his fate.

"You'll have fun, Davy. I promise." PJ gave him a little nudge toward the Dixie cups and graham crackers.

"Let's just sign a couple papers, and we're all set," Trudi said. Davy drank down one cup, threw it to the ground, and then ran to the sandbox. He was digging his way to Taiwan when PJ left.

Sunsets Supper Club had never been high elegance, with its long ramp leading to the front door, the dark wood paneling, the wide window advertising the weekly specials. Now the early seventies decor would be called retro. Still, the place bore hints of updates—gleaming hardwood had replaced the thinned brown carpet, and the menus were linen-bound instead of in the previous red plastic folders. PJ spotted an earlier version of herself in one of the summer staff photos. She'd worn her hair pulled back then, and from this vantage, had on way too much makeup.

The vacancy at the hostess stand gave her opportunity to peruse the new menu. They'd added a few Caesar or club wraps to the usual surf and turf platter.

"PJ Sugar!" Joe hadn't changed much in ten years—short, slightly balding, and missing a right incisor. He still wore Hawaiian shirts over khaki pants, and he greeted PJ with a hug like she might be his long-lost daughter.

PJ found herself holding on far longer than she planned.

"I didn't expect you to dress up to interview for a waitress gig," Joe said. "Are you sure this is what you want?"

"Just till I get on my feet." PJ followed him through the restaurant. She didn't have the heart to tell him that until last night's conversation with Director Nicholson, she'd planned on showing up in her shorts, a T-shirt, and flip-flops.

"How long are you back for?" Joe settled himself on one of the chairs at a white-linened table.

PJ straightened a place setting, not sure how to answer.

Joe finally nodded, gathering in her silence. "I'm going to need at least the summer. Can you promise me that?"

Did she want a job she had in high school?

Better question—did she want to eat? Because once Connie discovered Davy's truancy, she just might be out on the street. "Yes," she said, sliding the word from her constricting throat before it got stuck. "The summer. But I can't start until after Connie gets back from her honeymoon."

"Give me a call then, and we'll see what we can do."

She took her time tooling back to Trudi's, unable to shake the sound of defeat dragging behind her like shackles. So much for breaking free, starting over.

She couldn't bear to pass Fellows, with its manicured lawns, the shaved shrubbery along the walk, the fragrant, pristine gardens, and turned instead onto a side street. She recognized it as the route to the old VFW, the *other* country club in town.

Except the square, brown brick building no longer stood in the lot, replaced instead by a new building, shiny and white, with a three-story steeple. PJ tapped her brakes long enough to read the sign on the outside—Kellogg Praise and Worship Center.

Her Bug nearly pulled in on its own.

PJ sat in the parking lot, hands tight on the steering wheel, once again hearing Matthew's pronouncement like a gavel upon her soul: *"You're not pastor's wife material."*

She found herself climbing out. The cool air prickled her skin under her shirt as she entered with a swoosh of air into the quiet building. The place felt . . . large. Looming double doors led to a dark sanctuary; a hall extended to room after Sunday school room, the smell of new carpet embedded in the walls. A bulletin board by the door white-lettered the weekly events. She noted the time of the service, then wandered to a reception desk and picked up a brochure detailing women's events.

For the first time in over a week, she didn't hear the ghosts, didn't feel her past sneaking up behind her, ready to lunge over her shoulder.

She closed her eyes and drew a deep, fragranced breath.

Sunday's bulletins lay stacked on the table and she picked one up, read the order of service, the message title, and the text for the week. Taken from 1 Peter, the first chapter, the words were written in italics at the bottom: *To God's elect, strangers in the world, scattered . . . who have been chosen according to the foreknowledge of God the Father . . .*

She didn't read more. She knew just how it felt to be a stranger, to be scattered in home and purpose. Except she didn't feel at all chosen—well, maybe chosen for trouble. Chosen to mess up people's lives, starting with Davy and Connie.

The trapped air of sanctity swelled over her as she crept inside the dark sanctuary, dim light streaming in through the window-paneled doors. She guessed it must hold over five hundred people. A muted spotlight up front hued a dark drum set, a baby grand piano.

She sat in a pew, closed her eyes, and tried to hear the beat, the tones of a praise song, but all that thrummed under her skin was the dormant rhythm of a peace she had once, briefly, known.

She hadn't even thought about attending church in Kellogg. But maybe here in Kellogg she needed God more than anywhere else on the planet.

She'd learned plenty in the three years since becoming a Christian. Enough to dispel the common myth that Christians always made the right decisions, that they threw off the shame or guilt of bygone mistakes without a backward glance, and most of all, that they didn't, at times, long to fold into the temptations that blinded them before.

Temptations like Boone. Or the urge to pack up her duffel and flee, leaving behind the rubble.

She ran her hand over the sleek wood of the pew, the smoothness soaking through her palm to her veins, her bones, calming the frenzy of her thoughts.

I think I need help. I thought I had changed . . . but it's looking to me like maybe I haven't.

She bent forward and leaned her forehead onto the pew in front of her. Was it possible for a girl to rewrite her past, create a new future?

Lord, help me understand the person I'm supposed to be here.

She sat in the dark, trying to decipher the silences.

As she left the church, a slight breeze scurried through the poplar and oak, and the sweet breath of incoming rain softened the crisp air. Across the street, the savory aroma of hot dogs lifted from the outside grills of the credit union—Customer Appreciation Days written on the blowing sign stretched across the doors. She skirted the temptation to be anonymously appreciated and arrived at Trudi's just in time for an afternoon snack inside the house.

Five children sat at a pint-size table in the center of the room, holding Dixie cups, some wearing red mustaches.

"C'mon in, PJ. We're having fresh-from-the-oven peanut butter cookies." Trudi set down a cookie on Davy's napkin square.

PJ yanked the treat out of Davy's hand seconds before his life flashed before his eyes.

Above his scream, she met Trudi's eyes, shaking. "He's allergic to peanuts."

Trudi set down her tray of cookies. "You forgot to write that on his form."

"Oh . . . I did." PJ collapsed into a toddler chair. "I can't believe I nearly killed the kid." She cupped a hand to her head. "Or maybe I can."

Trudi dug through the cupboard, snagged a box of graham crackers, and handed one to Davy. His screaming silenced. Then she crouched before PJ, as if she might also need a cracker. "Calm down. I've dealt with allergic reactions before. I would have known what to do. But more than that, you were here in time."

"I don't know, Trude. It just seems that . . . trouble seems to follow me. I dodge it. And now I'm back here, the same person I tried to leave behind."

"The same?"

"Joe hired me."

"PJ, you're hardly the same person. For one, you're smarter."

"I got my nephew kicked out of preschool."

"You had to make a stand."

"And I'm all but sitting by the phone. Hoping . . . you know."

"That Boone will call?" Trudi's eyes told PJ exactly how pitiful she'd become.

"I just don't know how things can get worse."

"Hey, Trude." A door opened behind her and Jack poked his head out. "Has the postman been here yet? I'm expecting a package."

"No—"

"That's not all you should be expecting."

The voice came from behind Jack, who turned. PJ groaned. It just wasn't fair that even here, even now—

"Boone, what are you doing here?" Trudi rose as he appeared at the door.

Boone wore an unfamiliar, even dangerous expression, similar to the one he'd worn on Sunday at the club, his eyes unyielding.

His gaze scoured over PJ, unreadable for just a moment before he turned to Jack. "Jack Wilkes, you're under arrest for the murder of Ernie Hoffman."

Chapter SEVEN

Surely there was a wink coming. Something scandalous and Boone-ish. Only PJ didn't like this joke, not at all. What was his problem that he had to skulk around town after her, arresting the people in her vortex? Was he trying to pull the world out from under her? knock her off her feet and hopefully into his arms?

But it had to be a joke. Jack might have had a dark moment last Sunday at the country club, but didn't they all at one time or another? Or more often than they liked . . .

Most of all, something about the way Jack played with Chip and how he adored Trudi told PJ in her bones that he wasn't a killer.

Only Boone didn't wink. Didn't smile.

"Boone—," Jack said.

"You have the right to remain silent," Boone started, and PJ watched in disbelief as he pulled Jack into the office away from the kids, whirled Jack to the wall, and cuffed him, an edge of anger to his movements.

"Boone!"

"Stay out of this, PJ," Boone snapped before he finished Mirandizing Jack.

"You're doing it again; I can't believe it!"

Boone rounded on her, something sharp in his expression. "Doing what? My job?"

PJ took a step toward him, refusing to let the anger pulsing off him intimidate her. "You know what you're doing—accusing someone of something they didn't do."

"You don't know what you're talking about."

"Don't I?"

For a long, brilliant moment, pain filled his eyes, lethal and deep. Well, he wasn't the one who'd been on the wrong end of a false accusation. He didn't seriously think that she'd stand here and watch while he marched Jack—*Trudi's* Jack—off to the slammer, did he?

PJ's voice levered low. "I'm not letting you do this again."

Boone tightened his jaw, and his Adam's apple plunged quick and hard. When he spoke, his voice matched hers—only with an edge of warning that sent a tremor through her. "Stop, before you say something you wish you hadn't."

Oh, she couldn't count the things she wished she'd said. "Just stop for a second, Boone. Think about this." *Please don't wreck another person's life.* "Jack might have been angry with Ernie, but certainly he's not the type to commit murder."

"You don't want to get between me and my job here. You're the one who'll get hurt." Boone's eyes flashed, and for a second she saw him as she always knew he'd be—passionate and resolute, serious and able.

"Oh, I know all about how it feels to get in your way."

He flinched, but she didn't care that she'd hurt him or that she'd let something ugly stir to life and sour in the pit of her stomach.

"Wait—" Trudi lunged toward them as Boone pushed Jack toward the door. "I heard about Ernie." Her voice dropped to a horrified whisper. "But what does Jack have to do with it?"

Boone stopped, glanced back, as though seeing Trudi for the first time. His gaze slid over to PJ, his eyes in hers, as if waiting for her to fill in the blanks even as he spoke to Trudi. "Jack didn't tell you that he attacked Hoffman on Sunday? At the country club?"

PJ tried not to hear accusation, as if for some reason, she should have told Trudi.

Or maybe it was simply guilt, rushing up to knee her in the kidneys.

No. This wasn't her fault.

Trudi turned to Jack, who stared at the floor.

"Yeah," PJ said softly, painfully. "At Connie's wedding. Right after Ernie bought Davy an ice-cream cone."

"You were there?"

PJ didn't even have to nod before the air flushed out of Trudi. She stumbled back against the massage bench set up in the office. "They said he was strangled . . ."

Boone hadn't yet taken his eyes from PJ, and now he sighed, as if by just being here with Jack and Trudi, she'd become part of a world he hadn't invited her into, a side of himself he didn't want her to see.

Perhaps they all just wanted to live in a pocket of time when everything felt whole and fresh and bulletproof. PJ knew, right then, that she did. At least long enough to get her bearings, to figure out who might be telling the truth.

Finally Boone faced Trudi. "He died from a broken neck. Denise, his son Tucker's wife, found him on his massage table at his home Monday afternoon. ME says he'd been dead since that morning."

"What makes you think I'm involved?" Jack had found his voice.

"You have a weekly appointment on Monday mornings, don't you?"

"Yeah. I showed up, but his door was locked. He never answered. I called him but didn't get an answer." Jack looked at Trudi as he spoke, his tone saying so much more than his words. *I didn't do this.*

"According to Ben Murphy, he saw your car there Monday morning."

"Sure, I was there, but like I said, he didn't answer. I did some paperwork in the car and then went on to my next appointment in Edina."

Boone shook his head and gave him a small shove. "Give us your alibi down at the station."

But Jack wouldn't be moved, not yet. He looked at Trudi, and everything in his face made PJ tremble. "I haven't done anything wrong, especially murder someone."

Trudi edged up beside Jack, took his arm.

PJ glanced at the kids. They'd gathered at the entrance to the office and now stood in a clump of wide-eyed horror, glued to the drama. "Why don't you guys go into the next room?"

"We're going to the station," Boone said.

"I was talking to the—"

"I'm not going anywhere," Jack snapped.

"Boone, you're scaring the kids." PJ returned to the day care kids. "C'mon, Davy." But Davy had frozen and apparently lost all feeling in his limbs, because when she reached out to take his hand, he didn't so much as snarl at her.

Clearly all of them had entered the twilight zone.

Trudi covered her mouth, sucking in broken sobs.

"We'll figure this out, honey," Jack said, a second before Boone pushed him out the door.

Trudi crumpled onto the floor next to the door.

PJ's eyes burned as she grabbed the graham cracker box and pushed Play on the DVD player. On the screen Barney began clapping, jumping up and down, delirious over some happy song. PJ felt a little delirious herself, although she felt more like wailing. As if something perfect and wonderful had been torn, ripped to tiny, fraying shreds.

By Boone . . . again.

The kids wandered back into the room and sat down, wooed by Barney and his enthusiasm. PJ returned to the office in time to see Trudi cover her face with her hands, shaking. The sight of her dredged up the too-raw memory of the rainy night she crumpled on the front stoop, eyes puffy, with the dark news that she'd been thrown out of the house by her father. *"I think I'm pregnant."*

PJ stood over her with the fresh realization that once upon a time she'd left Trudi behind to wrestle her troubles on her own as PJ slunk off into the night.

"Do you need a paper bag?" PJ asked in a tone reserved for

a small child. "Maybe you should put your head between your knees?" She got up, went to the small refrigerator in the day care, and pulled out an apple juice.

Trudi rose and followed her, propping herself up against the doorjamb. PJ handed her the juice and Trudi's hand shook as she drank it. Then she leaned her head against the doorjamb, closing her eyes.

Outside, PJ heard Boone's patrol car pull away.

"Remember on Monday, when the grocery store refused my ATM card?" Trudi said, her voice quavering. "I went down to the bank to straighten it out. All our accounts had been drained."

"By whom?"

"I don't know. But Jack wouldn't answer when I asked him about it. He told me . . ." She shook her head as if the words wouldn't fit, as if she wouldn't let them. "It's . . . nothing. I'm sure it's a mistake." Then her voice brightened into something otherworldly, full of pageantry. "Who wants to go outside and play?"

"Trudi."

But she pushed past PJ and tapped the Pause button on the DVD player. Barney froze midclap. "Outside, please, everyone." Trudi's voice screeched, high and on the edge of breaking.

"Trudi—" PJ grasped her arms—"stop. What did Jack tell you?"

She met PJ's eyes, then looked at the floor as the kids scrambled outside. "Just that he'd given Ernie some money to buy something for him—you know, on eBay. But maybe . . . You don't think that Ernie would have stolen . . . No, that's not possible."

"What was he going to buy?"

Trudi shook her head. "He said it was a surprise."

"Yeah. Well, surprise. Listen, you're going down to the police station. Now. I'll stay here."

Trudi's eyes focused, finally, briefly. "With the kids?"

"No, with the sheep. Of course with the kids. Are you okay to drive?"

She nodded, but it was wobbly and reminded PJ too much of their tailgating days. "Maybe I should call someone to drive you?"

"No . . . I'll be okay. I'll take the baby."

Oh, that would be in everyone's best interests.

Trudi stood there too long, however, rooted, and PJ wondered if she'd heard her at all.

"Trudi."

She looked up, and PJ saw her, ten years ago, hair stringy around her wet face, holding herself as her future roared up, dark and ugly before her.

"Don't leave me."

PJ pulled her tight, held her with everything she had inside, and more. "No, Trudi, not this time."

✳ ✳ ✳

"I wanna go home!"

Davy wasn't the only one. For a moment, PJ let him go as he pushed away from their Play-Doh garden, complete with red snakes and green lizards and blue flowers. She smelled like paste, and dough mortared her fingernails.

Two hours. No wonder she hadn't lasted more than two weeks as a camp counselor, preferring instead lifeguarding and nature hikes. The graham crackers had long since run out, and PJ just wanted to climb to the tall tower outside and pull up the gangplank. Clearly she wasn't cut out to entertain preschoolers with grace and charm. Although, until Davy had decided to jump ship, she'd had her little sailors singing right along with Barney.

"Davy, don't you want to play with the Play-Doh? I'll teach you how to make a snake."

"It's yucky. It sticks to my fingers." He made a face. "I want a cookie."

Of course he did. But she'd set a rather deplorable precedent over the past few days and perhaps it was time they all straightened up. "After supper. We have to wait until Daniel and Felicia's mommy arrives; then I'll make you some macaroni."

Davy glared at her. PJ held in a retort to the effect that it was either that or leftover vodka-soaked walleye. Just once, she wanted to see him choke down the alternative.

"Is my mommy going to be here soon?" Felicia, a little girl with golden brown cornrows that must have taken her mother hours of painstaking braiding, stood on her chair, raising her skirt over her head. Showing off her pink My Little Pony underwear.

PJ grabbed for the hem of her dress. "Sit down, honey. And yes." *Please yes*. With the exception of the Hudson twins—Felicia and Daniel—the children had all been picked up within an hour of Jack's arrest, something PJ could only credit to the Kellogg grapevine. How PJ looked forward to telling Trudi that most planned on finding alternative child care.

Just one more minute with Boone, preferably in a closed room without witnesses—that's all PJ wanted.

Four-year-old Daniel sat at the table, his big brown eyes

huge and full of vigor as he pounded his pile of dough to an indiscernible mess.

"And what about Miss Trudi? Will she be back?" Felicia hopped off her chair and twirled in a circle, her sundress flying out around her. She giggled and fell into a heap.

PJ had the inexpressible urge to join her, giggling insanely in a heap. "I hope so."

"Knock, knock!"

The woman accompanying the accented voice was beautiful and dark-skinned, her hair in enviable spirals to her shoulders. She wore hospital scrubs.

"Mama!" Felicia bounced to her feet and sprinted for her mother.

Daniel squeezed his dough between his fingers like the blob.

PJ brushed off her hands. "Hi there. Trudi had an emergency. I'm PJ—Davy's aunt."

"Maxine Hudson. Thank you for staying and watching the kids. I hope everything is okay with Trudi."

PJ opened her mouth, not sure how far the news had traveled. Maybe hearing it from someone in Trudi's corner would be better.

Or not. No matter how "her husband's been arrested" came out, it only sounded dark and painful. "I'm sure she'll be back tomorrow." PJ crouched next to Daniel. "Honey, your mommy's here. Time to clean up."

Daniel smiled at his mom, then started to smash the dough into the container.

"You help too," Maxine said to Felicia.

Oops, PJ's turn. "Davy?" He lay in the fetal position on the floor. "Davy, can you help clean up too?"

"No!"

PJ cleared her throat, Maxine's gaze heavy on her neck. "Davy—"

"Go away!"

"What should we do with these salt-dough hearts?" Maxine asked, transferring her daughter's creations to a cookie tray, neatly deflecting attention from the drama.

"Uh . . . Felicia can keep those to dry off and paint tomorrow."

Maxine carried the tray to the counter and placed it next to the other drying art projects.

PJ turned back to Davy. *Please.*

"Is he okay? Maybe he's just having a hard day."

PJ instantly liked her. Which could be why the words just seemed to spill out, unguarded. "He's tired of me, I think. His mother is on her honeymoon."

"Oh." Maxine lifted Daniel from his chair, brought him to the sink to wash up. "He's new here, right?"

"He is. He was in Fellows, but . . . I thought it was too constricting. So, he's here now." She didn't have to unearth everything for Maxine, who apparently was not only a superb mother but looked good doing it too.

Maxine glanced over her shoulder, and PJ spotted a sisters-in-arms smile. "I looked at Fellows for the twins, but they have so much stress in their lives, I thought another year of playtime instead of preschool might benefit them."

See, she knew she liked this woman.

"I couldn't agree more."

Maxine returned to the table to finish cleaning up. "Are his parents divorced?"

"His dad died a few years ago. His mother is a lawyer."

"I see," she said cryptically, then crossed to Davy and knelt next to him, actually laying her head on the floor so she could look him in the eyes. "Davy, your aunt PJ wants you to help her. Can you be a big boy and get off the floor?"

"No."

Maxine glanced at PJ. She shrugged. Welcome to her world.

"Did you have fun here today, Davy?"

He turned away from Maxine, but undaunted, she climbed over to the other side, smiled at him as if she had his number. "Do you want to come back tomorrow?"

Davy's little lips squished together, resembling a fish. He managed a barely perceptible nod.

"Well, if you want to come back tomorrow, you have to clean up today. Can you help Daniel and Felicia pick up the Play-Doh so it doesn't get yucky?"

PJ held her hopes, or at least her breath, clenched against her chest.

Davy pushed himself off the floor. Walked to the table. Grabbed Play-Doh and shoved it into a container.

Maxine sat up on her knees. "Wow, you're a really good picker upper." She gave a little clap.

He grinned at her, full on, without a hint of extortion in his expression.

"Who are you . . . Supernanny?"

Maxine laughed. "Child Psychology 101. In a previous life, I was a child therapist."

"Oh, that's an unfair advantage, but I'll pick your brain any day."

"You're welcome to it, whatever's left after having twins."
Maxine stood and grabbed Daniel's backpack. She glanced at
Davy and pitched her voice lower. "Must be hard to be alone,
without siblings. I'll bet his mother works a lot. And now that
she's on her honeymoon . . . well, I'll bet the little guy has big
questions." Her voice stayed soft as Davy, Daniel, and Felicia
moved toward the kitchen set to put away toys. "He's probably
afraid you're her replacement."

"He does kick me a lot. And his new grandparents are
staying with us, but they don't speak English. I can see why
that might be frightening. Add to that the fact he's got a new
daddy, and he spent three days in a Fellows straitjacket. I'd be
craving sugar and kicking people too."

"Maybe he just needs to know that you're not going
anywhere."

PJ moved to pack up the blocks and put away the DVDs.
She *had* been essentially dumping him places and throwing
cookies at him since the moment they'd met.

Davy stood at the door waving as Maxine left in her mini-
van with Daniel and Felicia. Outside, the sky had finally given
over to drizzle. A low rumble of thunder rippled through the
early twilight, and across the street, a car—a red Geo—drove
past slowly, then roared away.

"Want to come back here tomorrow, little man?"

Davy didn't answer.

✳ ✳ ✳

"They officially arrested Jack for murder." Trudi's voice
sounded as though it had been through a meat grinder, prob-

ably along with her sanity, after an afternoon at the police station. PJ knew too well how Rosie's scrutiny could chew up a gal's insides. Even when said gal was innocent.

PJ sat on a wicker chair on the screened porch, her legs pulled up, redoing her fuchsia toenail polish, the phone pinned to her shoulder. The wind and rain had dampened the fringes of the patio porch, and moisture glistened on the fronds of a rubber plant in a wicker basket in the corner. A cup of Earl Grey steeped on the glass table next to her. Finally, finally, she'd gotten Davy to sleep, after a round of Horton, *Green Eggs and Ham*, and *Mike Mulligan and His Steam Shovel*.

She had to applaud her talent at the various voices. Maisy, of course, was her best.

"I thought he had an alibi."

"He did—or I thought he did. He had an at-home massage therapy appointment in Edina, but when he arrived, no one was there."

"What happened?"

"He doesn't know. She didn't cancel. The appointment wasn't made through the clinic, just straight to his office at Ovations Spa."

"Did Boone check it out?"

"Boone went to the address, but the woman said she'd never heard of Jack. Jack says he's got the appointment written on his calendar at work, but I've been banned from the spa, and apparently Boone couldn't locate it. Who knows if he even tried to find it."

Trudi hiccuped, the smallest of sighs, her voice watery. "I don't understand it, PJ. He won't even listen to Jack, like he wants Jack to be guilty. I begged him to check out Jack's alibi and he says he will, but . . ."

PJ longed to interject, to assure her that Boone was honest. But her own iffy history with him pressed her to silence. Boone hadn't exactly been honest all those years ago when he'd let the police haul her away.

Even though he and a handful of others knew the truth.

"Boone says that the DA is going to try to deny him bail—that the prosecutor's waiting for him to confess. Jack says he's innocent and that he had no reason to kill Ernie. But you were there—Jack attacked him in broad daylight, and Boone's got about ten witnesses to that fact. Jack says that he and Ernie were just doing some investing. That he panicked and wanted to know where his money was. He said they worked it out. You should have seen him, PJ. I didn't recognize him. My Jack, he . . . he . . ."

PJ listened to her breathing, knew there was more.

"The worst thing is that we can't afford a lawyer. We're in over our heads. All my families, except for the Hudsons, have pulled their kids, and we're overdrawn. They gave Jack a public defender, but the lawyer looks like he's about fourteen. I don't know what to do."

Not for the first time, PJ wished Connie were here. She could take on the case, even just hand out advice.

Nighttime settled its gray swarthy blanket over the yard and the rain had left a residue of chill that prickled PJ's skin.

"I do know one thing: Jack didn't do this. Someone is trying to destroy our lives."

"Who would do that? Do you have enemies?"

"Not a clue, Peej. Jack is well-respected—his patients love

him. They lavish him with gifts—popcorn buckets and plaques and travel books, gift certificates to restaurants. Last year for Christmas one of them even gave him an entire collection of coins from their trip to the Holy Land or Greece or somewhere. There's no reason Jack would . . . that . . .'"

PJ leaned back, letting the breezes harden her polish. Despite the silence on the other end of the phone, she could almost hear Trudi's brain assembling the pieces—Jack and Ernie's poolside brawl, Boone's apparent investigative apathy.

But even PJ couldn't imagine that Jack—the man who'd tickled his baby at the beach, who'd listened to her long, sad tale—could murder sweet old Ernie Hoffman, beloved history teacher. She supposed it could happen—there were plenty of killers living double lives. But she wasn't going to say that aloud.

"Guilty until proven innocent," she said quietly. "Especially in Kellogg."

Trudi sniffed, jagged and sharp.

"Listen, Trude, I believe you. I know Jack's innocent." At least she desperately hoped it. "And I know how it feels to have public opinion crucify you before you've had your day in court."

Only Jack wasn't going to get off with some smooth finagling by his mother and the country club director.

"I guess you do know how it feels to have the town staring at you, accusing you, treating you like a criminal," Trudi said in a tremulous whisper.

Suddenly the words from the crumpled pew bulletin she'd wedged into her purse flashed in her mind: *To God's elect, strangers in the world . . . who have been chosen according to the foreknowledge of God the Father . . ."*

Perhaps God could use her, just a little. In fact, if she stretched her faith, worked out some of the knots, she might even believe that He'd sent her home for this very reason. *Chosen . . .*

"Listen, maybe I could . . . you know, nose around a bit."

"Oh, Peej, Boone wouldn't like that."

She didn't really mean the harsh, cutting burst of laughter. "Seriously? Trudi, I'm not the same girl who lived for Boone's smile. In fact, the guy's got an overinflated sense of self, if you ask me. Listen, I used to work at a spa. Not as a massage therapist or anything, but I know how they work, and maybe I can just . . . you know . . ."

"Are you serious? What if you get caught?"

"I'll make an appointment to get my legs waxed or something. And I'll just slip into Jack's office, nice and quick."

"You'd do that for me?" Trudi asked, her voice soft.

"Yes, I'd do that for you." PJ got up and retrieved a throw blanket from a basket in the corner. "Ever since I've been back, I've felt like . . . like I've been sucked back in time. Like I'm walking around in my old body, but there's this new person inside screaming. However, no matter what I do, she's locked in there, and I'm destined to be the person I left behind."

"For what it's worth, I don't see the person you left behind. But then again, I never saw the person you did."

PJ let those words find her wounds, soothe. "Let's hope the staff at Ovations don't see her either."

"Don't get into trouble."

"Me? Oh, never, Trudi. Never."

Chapter *EIGHT*

PJ slammed the door to her Bug outside Ovations Salon and Spa, a sleek, silver and pink building where once stood a row of pastel bungalows—one the former residence of one of Boone's football teammates—now bulldozed and revitalized into commercial zoning a block behind Main Street. PJ well remembered throwing toilet paper into a tall oak, now replaced by the shiny black sign advertising an escape for the body, mind, and soul.

She just hoped to escape with all three intact. Especially soul. She wasn't really stealing, though—she had Trudi's permission. And everyone who went into a spa hoped to come out someone different, right? Except PJ was going *in* as someone different, thanks to her sister's swank Vittadini shades, her cherry red lipstick, and a creamy two-piece Ann Taylor suit she probably wore when she was pregnant.

Surely Connie would have donated it all for the cause of truth.

"May I help you?" A receptionist the size of a cotton swab, with gleaming gold hair and nails imprinted with pink flowers, smiled at PJ as she entered the cool, perfumed air. Piano music ran its hushed river of calm over the hum of hair dryers and low gossip.

"I have a ten o'clock therapeutic massage with Jack," PJ said, not removing her sunglasses, noting the name, Tami, on the girl's name tag.

Beyond the reception counter a gallery of hairdressers and manicurists groomed the royalty of Kellogg. Beyond that, through an arched doorway, PJ guessed she'd find the therapy rooms. To her left, a nook off the reception counter housed aromatic oils, lotions, shampoos, hydrotherapy salts for sale.

She wondered if they were hiring.

"Jack isn't here," Tami said. "Can I reschedule?"

"He told me his assistant would see me." PJ pulled her glasses down her nose. "I'll wait, thanks."

Tami frowned. "Just a moment." Taking her portable telephone, she unwound herself from her seat and clip-clopped on pink sandals through the gallery, toward the back.

PJ ducked into the supply room off the nook, yanked off the glasses, and affixed a black hair extension she'd picked up at a drugstore that morning. With her hair pulled back in a scarf, the extension snaking down her back, every hint of her red hair vanished. She wiped off her lipstick and pulled on a pair of pink scrubs she'd found at a uniform supply store, yanking them up under her skirt. Securing the skirt into her waistband, she pulled a smock over her jacket and tugged on a sanitary mask—another convenient purchase from the drugstore—clipping it behind her ears and concealing her mouth.

Perhaps Matthew was right—her bag *was* a suitcase.

Stowing her bag behind a carton of conditioner, she grabbed a bottle of massage oil from the shelf and slipped out of the storage room.

PJ brushed past Tami as she headed toward the back. She spied her scanning the reception area with a frown and hid a grin as she slipped into the inner sanctum beyond the arch.

The musical river flowed louder in the back. Three women paged through magazines, having made it past the castle guard and into advanced reception. Well-groomed and prim, one of the ladies looked up at her, and PJ ducked her head as she beelined for Jack's office, right where Trudi said it would be.

PJ dug the key from her pocket. Yes, she had learned to pick a lock when she worked as a locksmith apprentice, but perhaps that would attract some attention.

The key turned. PJ resisted the urge to look over her shoulder as she slid into the office. Furtive looking only created suspicion should someone else be watching, right?

She turned on the light and warmed up the computer as she paged through the Day-Timer on Jack's desk. There, neatly penned in tight handwriting, were his Tuesday appointments. PJ scribbled them all down just to be thorough but circled the telephone and address of his 10 a.m. appointment—Carol Billings.

The computer had just begun to hum when a knock at the door nearly shot her out of her scrubs.

She didn't move, didn't even breathe as she stared at the humming computer. *Hurry, hurry.* According to Trudi, Jack also kept a journal of his daily activities on his computer.

Wouldn't that be worth sticking around to find? Especially if he had something about a missing appointment with Carol Billings?

Another knock.

PJ glanced at the door—*don't look!*—and then, of course, it opened. She froze.

Tami blinked. "I . . . uh . . . I'm sorry. I didn't realize Jack had sent a replacement today. We canceled all his appointments."

PJ waited for her to point a finger—*you, you, the missing redhead!*—but Tami only stared at her, waiting for a response.

God bless her face mask. "Oh. Okay. I guess I'll go home."

"No." Tami looked so apprehensive, PJ squelched the guilty urge to tell her not to worry about the ten o'clock customer who had disappeared in the lobby. "Can you take Denise Hoffman? She has a ten o'clock herbal wrap scheduled, and Marianne is running late."

Denise Hoffman. That name rang alarms in her head, but she couldn't place it. The computer continued to whir.

"I'll put her in the Arizona room."

Swell.

Tami closed the door with a soft click, but PJ's pulse ratcheted up to high.

A wrap?

Would that, by any chance, require her to touch people? Especially their skin?

Maybe she didn't need the computer files. As she stepped out into the hall, the side exit light, the one with the red fire escape handle, neoned.

Right then, Boone's voice kicked in: *"Denise, his son Tucker's wife, found him on his massage table at his home."*

Denise *Hoffman*? Daughter-in-law of the deceased?

PJ found the Arizona room and cracked open the door. There, standing with a towel wrapped around her caramel-colored birthday suit, was her patient.

Recognition hit her like a line drive to the cheap seats. Denise Franklin, homecoming queen and girlfriend to Tucker Hoffman.

Tucker Hoffman, son of Ernie.

And reaching even further back, PJ pinpointed a shady memory of Tucker getting arrested. For assault? Had he done time in juvie hall? Because he'd been two years younger than she was, it was a gauzy memory at best.

Denise shivered. "Could you close the door?"

"Oh, of course." PJ closed the door with a soft click, sealing her fate. Thankfully the stainless steel shelf next to her held a clipboard with the treatment listed. PJ grabbed it, pretending to read, but questions streamed through her mind. When did Denise find Hoffman? Where was the massage table? Where was Tucker when his father was killed? Were he and Denise the sole beneficiaries of the estate?

"I'll be right back," she said, exiting to find the correct body spread. Five minutes later she returned, armed with lemon and sage cream, cellophane, and rubber gloves. Getting a wrap was like having your body buttered, then wrapped tight and left to cook, the herbs seeping into your skin to rejuvenate it.

PJ knelt before Denise, held her breath, scooped out a handful of spread, and began to apply it to her long legs.

Jack had better be innocent.

"Are you related to Ernie Hoffman?" PJ asked, the rest of her body treatment dependent upon Denise's answer.

Denise nodded, her hands still over her upper carriage. PJ noticed a fresh manicure as she glanced up at her, catching her answer.

"I'm sorry for your loss." She finished one leg and moved on to the next. The fragrance of lemon and dusky grass lifted off the cream, and it had the texture of cooked oatmeal. PJ tried not to think about it.

"Thank you," Denise said.

"What a horrible thing to happen."

Denise nodded, then, as if catching herself, said, "Actually, we all knew he was in over his head. Probably a couple of loan sharks after him." She shifted her weight. "I just can't believe he'd get himself in so far."

"Loan sharks? I thought they caught the guy." PJ kept her voice easy.

"I don't know. He had a broken neck, and I found him on his massage table. But the house had been ransacked. I know Jack. I recommended him to my father-in-law." She shook her head. "He's not a killer, and the way Ernie was spending Tucker's inheritance, I have to wonder what really happened."

PJ said nothing.

"He probably lost it gambling. He was always online. I have to admit, I wondered if he had an addiction. I had to beg him to come over on Sundays for dinner. You'd think a widower in his twilight years would want to spend time with his son and grandchildren."

PJ rolled out the cellophane, starting at Denise's ankle and winding her way up her legs. "Was anything stolen?" she asked as she wrapped Denise's thighs together, averting her eyes as much as possible. Perhaps she'd leave the backside for . . . later.

"Who knows? He had a desk safe, and it had been smashed open, but what did he have to steal? He knew the names of all the Roman Caesars and their descendants, but he didn't give a second thought to his own offspring. Or his future." She made a sound that PJ labeled as disgust. "If it wasn't for Tucker bailing him out over and over, he'd have lost his house."

PJ buttered Denise's stomach, which she didn't have to suck in. PJ tried not to hate her for that. Denise had the stomach of a surfer while PJ had been born with a little poochy thing. Still, she had to respect her a little too, because PJ would never stand in the near nude letting someone butter her body just so her skin could be supple.

"Didn't he have a pension from the school?" PJ stood to butter and wrap her upper body.

"Should have. He kept telling Tucker that he had a nest egg." She glanced at PJ, her expression hard. "Yeah, that's right, his nest egg was me and Tucker."

The bitterness in her tone stung PJ, and she frowned.

Denise caught her look. "I'm sorry," she said as she lifted one arm. "It's just that the last time he and Tucker talked, they had a fight. Tucker is so grief-stricken, he hasn't gone out of the house since Monday."

"They had a fight?" PJ wrapped her torso tight, then handed her a Kleenex as tears began to stream down her face. She looked like she needed a hug but, well, she was naked, even if wrapped in cellophane.

"Just that morning. It was horrible. Tucker went over, stood on the front porch as they argued. The entire neighborhood probably heard them. Tucker is horrified that this is his last memory—his dad slamming the door in his face."

"What did they argue about?"

To PJ's surprise, Denise's eyes turned glassy. "We asked him to move in with us. To sell the house and not worry about finances. He refused. It's not like we're made of money—Tucker is a math teacher and a football coach. We barely make ends meet. But with the recession, we were hoping we could pool our resources."

Which begged the question, how did she have the extra cash to get buttered?

PJ eased her onto the table, more questions spinning in her head—or perhaps that was simply the redolence of lemon. Still, if Ernie was bankrupt, why had she seen him hanging out at the golf course? Did Jack suspect him of misinvesting his money? or losing it?

The memory of Ernie's smile and Davy's slurp of an ice-cream cone made PJ's chest tighten. She placed a heated mask over Denise's eyes and turned down the lights. "Someone will be in to check on you in thirty minutes."

PJ slipped out of the room and caught a glance from yet another needy client. Dumping the empty butter dish and cellophane box in the sink, she whipped off the gloves and strode for Jack's office. She printed his journal for last week and tucked it under her shirt. She'd call in a half hour and ask for Denise . . . and someone would find her.

PJ snuck back to the supply room, shucked off the scrubs, grabbed her bag, and exited the spa.

Was Tucker big enough to put his dad in a headlock, maybe accidentally . . . kill him? Could their argument be a motive for murder?

And would Denise Hoffman leave a tip?

❊ ❊ ❊

"What's wrong with you?"

So many options . . . where to start? She was out of maca-roni and cheese. Vera was chopping up what looked like a squid on Connie's countertop. Davy was starting to look like a sausage in his Spider-Man jammies, now covered with choco-late ice cream. And she had yet to find the runaway library book from Fellows.

"You're going to have to be more specific." PJ crossed her arms and leaned against the front door, staring at Boone. He couldn't intimidate her.

Not after she'd spent the morning smearing goo on another woman's body.

"You know what I mean." Boone didn't smile, and the fact that he'd arrived in his street clothes, smelling freshly show-ered like this was an off-duty and personal visit, didn't escape PJ despite his police intimidation tactics—bracing one arm on the doorframe and angling a pair of shades down his nose as he stared at PJ with his cool blue eyes.

"You don't scare me." PJ put a hand to his shirt and pushed against his hard stomach—she well remembered that. "So stop crowding me."

"I'm just getting started if you don't back off."

She wiped her hands on her towel and flipped it over her shoulder. In the background, Davy slurped a Fudgsicle, his reward for finishing his hot dogs and Tater Tots. He'd smiled at her today when she picked him up from Trudi's, although when she went to hug him, he wiggled out of her arms. They'd spent the rest of the afternoon swinging, making sand castles, and playing hide-and-seek. She knew she'd figure out a way to use that play set.

Across the street, a neighbor mowed his lawn in the early evening, the buzzing hum keen accompaniment to the way her pulse seemed to come to life whenever Boone entered her atmosphere.

PJ stepped back from the doorframe. "Let's start over. Hi, Boone. What are you doing here?" She slid him a smile meant to diffuse his dark mood, but she'd obviously lost her powers, because he ignored her and muscled his way into the house. "Come in, please."

"Why do you always have to go looking for trouble?"

Now that wasn't fair. He, in fact, was the one who'd started all this. "I'm not looking for trouble. I'm just trying to be the friend I should have been . . . would like to be."

No, if she were honest, there was more to it. Like proving that Trudi's husband wasn't a murderer and that she wasn't an abysmal judge of character by putting Davy in Trudi's care. Or that she wasn't a giant failure as an aunt for getting him kicked out of Fellows.

Well, there wasn't much hope of changing that. "Besides, is there trouble?" She said it sweetly, batting her eyelashes.

His face was stone. "Trudi seems to think that Ernie Hoffman was killed by his son, Tucker."

"Really? I wonder how she got that idea."

Boone shook his head like he wasn't buying her bluff.

"Okay, okay, so I *might* have suggested something to that effect this afternoon when I dropped by Peppermint Fence to pick up Davy. But, Boone, the poor woman had been on the telephone for most of the day, trying to scrape up 10 percent of the *one-hundred-thousand-dollar minimum bond*—hello, what kind of judge sets that?—for murder. Now Jack's stuck there at least for the entire weekend, if not longer."

"He's a flight risk. We placed him at the scene around the time of death. He had means—a guy who's a physical therapist could certainly break a man's neck. And he had motive—Ernie took his money. We traced a wire transfer from Jack's account to Ernie's the day of the murder that Jack finally admitted knowing about. Which was why he attacked Ernie at the country club. At best, Ernie lost Jack's money. At worst, he stole it."

"I don't think old Mr. H. was a thief. And I can't believe Jack is a killer."

"Why? Because you feel sorry for him?" Boone took off his glasses and shoved them into his pocket. "I'm not the bad guy here."

"Turning over a new leaf?"

"Sometimes, PJ—"

"What, can't take the truth?"

Boone's eyes flashed. "You might not know the entire story; did you ever think of that?"

"I know enough. And unless the bank gives Trudi a second mortgage, Jack's in for a long stay at Kellogg Sing Sing. I hope you're proud of yourself."

"You act as if I'm a vigilante posse. For pete's sake, PJ, I'm a cop. We arrest people."

"That seems to be what you Buckams do best."

Boone gave a quick intake of breath. PJ looked away, running her hands up her arms, now blistered with a chill.

"The thing is, we haven't had a murder in Kellogg since I was in seventh grade."

PJ glanced at his cold expression.

"Until you came to town."

"You don't think I'm responsi—"

"I think you're sticking your nose in where you shouldn't." He leaned close and PJ tried to dismiss the fact that summer air clung to him like sweet cologne. "Guess what, PJ—I actually went to school to become a cop, and I just might know what I'm doing."

He slid a step closer to her, and PJ felt the doorframe needle up her spine. His look softened as he scanned her face. She'd forgotten how handsome he . . . was . . . no, she *hadn't* forgotten, not at all. He still started a smile with a slow curve on one side and had dark lashes that framed those pale blue eyes. PJ drew in a long breath and realized that was a mistake.

"We found our killer. You should be cheering."

"Boone, I just think you should look at Tucker Hoffman. And did you ever get ahold of Carol Billings?" Her voice, however, ended with a tremor that belied her frustration. "I gave the list of Jack's appointments and his journal to Trudi, but—"

Oops. She might have given too much away there. She wanted to slap her forehead, but that would really convict her.

Boone narrowed his eyes slightly, then looked at her lips. "Carol Billings is out of town and has been for two weeks. And, yes, I checked Tucker's alibi. He was teaching summer school all day."

Not all day. After all, he'd had time to stop by and fight with his father. PJ's voice dropped to a whisper. "Don't you think it's weird that Carol would make an appointment during the time she's out of town?"

"She claims she never made the appointment. She was at a

funeral when Jack says he went to her house." Boone touched her face gently with two fingers. "What are you doing back here, anyway?" His voice held the tone that had chased her for a decade, the one that found her in that naive place between asleep and awake. "You shouldn't be here. Not now. Don't you know that when you're around I can't think straight?"

Oh.

When he leaned close, PJ lifted her face, caught in the sweet danger of being in the hot circle of his embrace, churning up unfinished business.

"Aunt PJ!"

Boone jerked away as if he'd been slapped.

"Davy!" She ducked under Boone's arm, her heart nearly cutting off her air, and almost ran to her four-year-old savior. She turned Davy toward the kitchen to wipe the chocolate from his face.

"PJ, listen to me." Boone came up behind her. She caught warning in his voice, even if it still held a tremor of desire. "Just let me do my job. If Jack is innocent, justice will be served."

PJ whirled hard, the emotions in her throat swift and fresh. "Oh yeah, I know all about justice. Like the fact that the man I thought I . . . the man I almost . . . well, the guy who told me that he loved me let the entire town think I burned down the country club, and he didn't say a word to defend me—"

"That's not exactly how—"

"Why didn't you tell them the truth, Boone?" Her voice cracked. "That you were the one who was smoking, not me? That I was waiting for you, like you asked me to while you went and bragged to your football buddies about me and about what we were going to do."

"I wasn't bragging—"

"I don't want to know what you were doing. But you should have stood up for me, told them it wasn't my fault."

"I had my scholarship—"

"You lied to save your own skin."

He flinched. Oh, how she wanted to slap him. And perhaps in a different life, a different time, she would have. Only she wasn't that person anymore. Or was trying not to be.

She schooled her voice, glancing at Davy. "I hope you did well at the university. I never did make it to college."

"That wasn't my fault—"

"Do you seriously think I could have gone to the same school—seen you on campus every day? You were my whole life, Boone. I didn't even apply at any other colleges. And then it was too late."

"You were my life too. You and football. Only you were gone, and I broke my ankle in preseason practice. I never got to play. Ever. I lost my scholarship and joined the army."

That snapped the wind out of her sails. Just long enough for Boone to gather his feet under him.

"You don't know the mess you left behind."

"*I* left behind—"

"Me, Peej. You left me. I wasn't ready to lose you." His voice sounded as if he'd torn it from someplace inside. "Do you have any idea what life was like after you left town? You weren't the only one whose life derailed that night. And I had *more* to prove than you—I still do."

He took a step toward her, but she held up her hand. "Don't—"

His face quivered, emotion flashing across it, but he kept

his voice tight. "I felt sick. I even drove down to your aunt's place in South Dakota once I got the address from your sister, but you'd already left."

"I couldn't stay there."

"But you didn't come back to me either. Sheesh, PJ, I thought . . . yeah, okay, I loved you. And I thought you loved me back. What about this?" He yanked up his shirtsleeve, and the name *PJ* on his shoulder, small and defined, matched the *Boone* on hers. PJ felt the urge to put her hand over it, hide it, or even trace it back into her heart. But she couldn't move. Because everything she'd hoped for—too much, probably—shone right there in his eyes, crisp and brilliant.

He let his shirtsleeve fall. "That meant something to me—everything to me. I was ready to marry you." He shook his head, turning away from her.

She saw herself going up to him, touching his back, calming the fury she saw between his tense shoulder blades.

But she couldn't go back there, not without tripping over all the baggage she'd dragged behind her—and after ten years, she needed a virtual trailer. Most of all, she wasn't the girl he'd chased to South Dakota. And she needed a man who believed in her now.

"I didn't know you did that."

"What, loved you?" His voice hovered just above a whisper.

"Came to South Dakota."

He let a beat pass. "I went to California too. Connie told me you were living on the beach there, and I took one summer . . . and tried to find you."

He turned, his blue eyes in hers.

"No, you didn't."

"Yes, PJ, I did. But you were gone. Again." A muscle pulled in his jaw. "You have no idea how sorry I am. How many nights I tossed away, wishing I could take back that night, wishing you could hear me call, see me looking for you. The best day of my life was when I pulled into the country club on Sunday and saw you standing there, as if you'd never left." He took a step closer to her, and she didn't stop him. "I want you back."

PJ closed her eyes, the words rushing over her like an ocean wave. The floor tilted under her.

"But you and I have nothing to do with Jack. Stay away from my investigation." His breath touched her face.

She opened her eyes. "He's innocent, Boone." But her voice lacked muscle.

"Everything I've uncovered points to Jack."

"But—"

"Hey, I'm a cop. You can trust me."

Oh, how she longed to trust him—especially now, with his heart wide open for her to see his regrets. But something inside tightened down, her scars hardening to close over the tender flesh of her own heart.

He must have seen the doubt in her eyes. "Okay, maybe I should rephrase. What if I say, if you don't trust me, I'll make sure you get more than a suspended sentence this time?"

She tried for a nasty look, but he reached out and ran his hand behind her neck, and it felt so warm and familiar and safe . . .

"Boone, stop," PJ whispered, but it came out against the soft smile curling his lips as he leaned close. Too close. And of course, her heartbeat slammed against the thumb caressing her neck to betray her. "Jack is innocent; I know it."

He gave her a one-eyed wince. "Peej—"

"What if I can prove it?"

"I don't want you to prove it." His lips moved against her neck, a shiver of dormant feelings brushing through her. "Don't you get that part?"

She sighed, put her hands on his chest, and pushed with everything she had inside her, which at the moment, seemed feeble. In fact, she couldn't be sure if she didn't just hang on.

He took a half step back. "All right. I'll dig a little. If you promise to behave. And if Jack Wilkes is innocent . . . I'll . . ." He took her face in his wide, warm hands. "I'll . . . take out an ad and tell Kellogg that you didn't set fire to the country club."

Oh no, he'd made her laugh. In the back of her brain she knew he was just trying to charm her . . . but his eyes were on fire as he drew her to him, angled his head . . .

"What on earth is going on in here?"

This time PJ was the one who jumped. Her mother stood at the front door, her hazel eyes cold as she stared at Boone.

What was her mother doing here? PJ needed some sort of early warning system if her mother was going to suddenly start popping into her life.

Boone took one look at Elizabeth Sugar and let go of PJ as if she might be made of fire. Amazing how fast a nearly thirty-year-old man could morph into a teenager with a look of sheepishness. "Mrs. Sugar—"

"Get out, Boone. Now."

PJ opened her mouth to defend Boone, but her mother's

tone touched something inside her. It sounded just a little like . . . panic.

Boone clenched his jaw tight as he strode out without a word.

Elizabeth's icy look nearly sent PJ racing out behind him. "I can't believe you let him in the house after . . . after . . . Haven't you learned anything?"

"Calm down, Mom. He was just filling me in on Mr. Hoffman's murder. They have Trudi's husband in custody, but I know he's innocent."

"And you're the town crier?"

"What brings you by?" PJ gave her a little hug, still feeling Boone's hands in her hair.

"I don't like that Boone coming around here. He's just going to get you in trouble again."

PJ stared at her mother as she unwrapped her head scarf, pulled off her driving gloves. Get *her* in trouble? And here she'd always figured her mother believed Boone's side of the story. "I know. So, what's up?"

"I brought another box by that I thought you could go through."

PJ peered past her to the driveway. The Mercedes backseat looked piled high with the file boxes from her closet. "I would have come by tomorrow."

"I'm sure you would have," her mom said, not sounding sure at all. She brushed past PJ, into the house. "David? Come give Grandma a hug."

Davy ran to her from the far side of the kitchen, still chocolated.

"So nice that you're remaking friends in town," Elizabeth

said, glancing at PJ. "Although . . . are you sure you want to run around with Trudi again?"

She made it sound like Trudi was stationed on the nearest street corner. "She's married with two kids. And Trudi is about the only friend I have in town."

"What about Kristi Farr? She liked you."

"No, she liked Boone." In fact, ten years clear of Boone's whirlpool of power, she wondered who had been groupies and who had been true friends.

Friends. Friends told each other secrets, their deepest fears. Especially lifelong friends.

Friends like Ben Murphy and Ernie Hoffman, golfing buddies.

"Mom, do you still have Dad's golf clubs in the garage?"

Elizabeth wrung out a washcloth in the sink, then advanced on Davy. "Sure, honey. Why would I give those away?"

Why indeed? PJ didn't answer, just wandered out to the car for the boxes, her mind still trying to wrestle free from Boone's embrace. Across the street, a pizza deliveryman pulled out of a driveway. The sprinkler in the front yard switched on and sprayed the yard.

"He's just going to get you in trouble again."

She had a dark feeling that her mother was, as usual, painfully right.

Chapter NINE

PJ stood on the walkway of the country club, the sun caressing her bare shoulders, her father's clubs hanging over her shoulder.

Summer scented the air—freshly cut grass, hollyhock and hydrangea, chlorine and ice cream. It was too early yet, but soon the grills on the veranda would fire up. Wind chimes tinkled behind children's screams, and splashes in the pool fell like raindrops onto the cement.

Like some sort of lighthouse beacon, her gaze was drawn to the lifeguard stand.

Of course Boone wasn't perched atop it, white sun cream frosting his nose, watching through dark glasses the first graders learning the front crawl. Still, she could see him as clear as yesterday, bronzed head to toe, wearing only the black trunks of the country club lifeguards. He'd been sufficient incentive for PJ to attend every one of her golfing lessons her freshman year of high school.

She liked to think he'd noticed her, even back then.

She dearly hoped no one noticed her today. At least, not the girl under the disguise. She'd done her homework and discovered that Ben Murphy still kept his 10 a.m. Saturday tee time. Pilfering her duffel bag, she found a skort and a sleeveless pink shirt. Trudi managed the wig, thanks to her supply of day care dress-up clothes. PJ found a tube of bright pink lipstick in her bag and, when she swung by her mother's house, loaded in the clubs and unearthed her mother's golf shoes.

She looked like Barbie Goes Golfing.

It hadn't escaped her, however, that she might be tempting fate.

Maybe her good fortune the first time undercover had simply been God on her side because of the righteousness of her quest. After all, the outing at Ovations had been about unearthing information for Trudi.

This was all about Boone.

He already had Jack tried and convicted, although PJ wasn't sure why. But last night as she stared at her ceiling in the darkness, she'd known she couldn't leave Jack's fate to Boone.

"I loved you. And I thought you loved me back."

Yeah, sure he did. PJ had rolled over to her side and dug one fist into her pillow, cupping the other over the small tattoo on her shoulder.

It didn't matter anymore, anyway. She hadn't returned for him.

She did believe one of his declarations—namely if he caught her messing in his investigation, he'd probably make trouble. Like four-cell-walls trouble.

She'd watched the stars fade into the pale morning.

Now, tugging at the wig, she scanned for Director Buckam, then walked down the path around the side of the building, past the shrubbery and the splashing children, to the pro shop located off the patio below.

Her plan was simple: wrangle a tee time out of the pro, then drop back and join Ben's foursome, maybe with some well-placed shots into the rough.

The pro in the shop, a junior Matthew Fox look-alike, was checking out a group, handing them their scorecards, and getting mileage out of his high-wattage smile. She noted his name on his engraved tag—Ryan.

PJ watched him. Yes, she could probably do this job in between her shifts at Sunsets. Maybe she should pick up an application.

As the group filed out, on their way to the first tee, she sashayed up to the counter. "Can I get a tee time?"

Ryan raised an eyebrow. Hey, where was his smile for *her*? Did she look broke?

"Please?"

"We're pretty full today, Miss . . . ?"

"Sukharov. Constance Sukharov."

So she didn't look Russian. Connie wasn't using her new last name at the moment, at least in Minnesota.

He nodded, as if he'd heard the name, and paged through the book on the counter.

PJ picked up a scorecard and a pencil, tucking it behind her ear. "Maybe I could just hook onto another group?"

She heard said group enter, right behind her.

"Hello, Mr. Murphy," Ryan said, looking past her.

Murphy. PJ stilled. *Please, please let this work.*

Ben approached the desk, wearing a healthy retirement tan along with his crisp name-brand golf attire. Two other men followed him in. PJ flashed them all a small, flirty smile.

Not a hint of recognition in Ben's eyes. Maybe he was just used to seeing her disheveled, in silk. What did they say about the unexpected being half of a disguise?

The group registered their tee time.

"I'm so sorry to hear about Mr. Hoffman," Ryan said, handing them pencils and scorecards.

Perfect. They hadn't filled Hoffman's spot yet. "Excuse me, can I ask you fellas a question?" A little Southern could get a girl a long way. "Would you be willing to let me join you? I forgot to make a tee time."

Ben glanced at her, and PJ flashed him another award-winning smile, reminding herself that she was trying to save lives—four lives, to be exact—and a backside. Hers.

"I think that would be fine." Ben flicked a look at his cronies for confirmation.

See, that wasn't so hard.

Except, well, the wig was starting to itch, and she looked like an uncoordinated duck as she swung with her father's too-long clubs, sending her shot into the trees, the sandpit, the rough. By the fourth hole, she knew that Ben and his two cohorts were just looking for a place to dump her body after they gave it a good whack with a nine iron.

Or perhaps that was just Ernie's murder creeping up to haunt her. Still, at the ninth tee, she could hear tightly knotted frustration underneath Ben's patient voice. "Don't be so stiff. Keep your eye on the ball." The other two stood to the side, shaking their heads.

"I'm sorry; I'm sorry—"

"Don't apologize; just swing—ow!" Ben moved away as her club slipped from her hands and bounced off his shoulder.

"Sorry!"

Ben offered a sad smile. "That's okay. You'll get it."

She added another scratch to her card, then ran to keep up as Ben strode down the green. He was in amazingly good shape for a man over sixty. "Thank you for taking me. I'm sorry I'm so horrible."

Ben looked over his shoulder. He wasn't a tall man, but fit, sporting only a small paunch, still graced with a full head of dark hair, now silver at the temples. He toted his golf bag on a cart. "No problem." His smile didn't touch his eyes, however. "Usually we have a fourth, but he's not here today."

There it was, the opening she'd been looking for over the past eight miserable holes. "Is he ill?"

So the question lacked sensitivity. It sounded innocent.

"No." Ben sighed, turned, and waited for PJ to catch up. "He was killed in his home last week."

Hearing him say it made it feel fresh and raw and awful, and she didn't have to fake the horror on her face. "Oh, I'm so sorry." She pitched her voice low. "Do you know anyone who might have wanted to kill him?" Was that too obvious? She didn't think it sounded too obvious, but now it seemed as if every living creature on the golf course stopped, listened, could see right through her disguise to the quivering, nosy outcast of the Kellogg Country Club.

And of course, they were approaching the tenth hole, where Ben might very well figure out who she was when he saw her begin to sweat.

"No. Ernie was a great guy. Loved to give advice and to help people." Ben pulled out a wood, began to polish it. "We loved him." But the way it came out, his voice tight—as if he didn't believe his own words—brought PJ back to that moment when he'd chased down Ernie at the pool.

"Were you close?" She took out her own wood, keeping her voice loose.

Ben shrugged. "We taught at the same high school for thirty years. And golfed together most of that time."

She'd expected a different answer. Something to confirm that Ernie would have unloaded his deepest secrets to Ben.

"I guess with Ernie gone, you won't have to kill your goat, huh, Ben?" one of the other players said, obviously overhearing their conversation. She remembered him as Gary Kolowaski, math teacher, brand-new her junior year. He'd aged long and lanky, a pure Swede with blond hair and blue eyes. He wore knickers and a green sweater, a real old-time professional.

PJ waited for a laugh at his words and even began to start it herself.

They looked at her as if she'd just ridiculed a terminal health report.

Perhaps this was some sort of weird old-man code for golfing or betting.

But Ben nodded, leaning one arm on his cart. "He got the local health department sniffing around my house. You'd think I had predators living in my backyard instead of a few chickens, a pig, and a goat. A guy has the right to do what he wants on his own property." He shook his head. "Putting down Billie is likely to kill Ruthie. I can't do it. I asked Ernie to back off, but he just couldn't leave well enough alone."

PJ stared at him, wading past his tone and his words to the truth. He wasn't kidding . . . the man had a goat in his back-yard. "What did your friend do?"

Ben took a practice swing. "Billie got out a few times, ate his roses and a few other things—"

"The goat ate his entire crop of tomatoes!" Gary said, now laughing, and Ben shot him a dark look.

"Ernie got angry and wrote to the health department." Ben set his feet, lined up the ball with his club. "Problem is, my wife bought that goat for the grandkids, and she loves it like a child. However, since her stroke, even she agrees we can't keep it. But I have to find 'a good home for it.'" He used his fingers to quote, elicited laughter, and even managed a wry smile. "Ernie was always overly protective of his tomatoes." He swung, and the shot cut through the perfect blue sky, straight and true down the fairway.

PJ watched it with a pang of golfer envy. But right behind it pulsed a question—how far would a man go to protect the heart of the woman he loved? PJ analyzed Ben's hands as he packed away his club, then crossed his arms over his chest, watching Gary take his shot. Were those hands strong enough to break a man's neck?

What if a friendly chat turned dark? What if punches were thrown, a simmering anger ignited? What if frustration turned into manslaughter?

PJ excused herself after the ninth hole, with fifteen over par. She should probably clue Boone into another possible suspect—Ben Murphy.

Oh, that would be fun.

Throwing her clubs into the backseat of her VW, she

headed toward the snack stand. Sweat slicked the inside of the wig under the little nylon cap. Nothing would feel more welcome than a splash in the pool, but a lemonade would have to do.

And frankly, she enjoyed the freedom of wandering the Kellogg Country Club grounds in different skin. Without eyes on her, weighing her choices, filling in the gaps of gossip.

She ordered from the snack stand, then took her drink to the veranda, pulling up a chair in the shade.

"Here's to Ernie."

PJ's ears perked up, and from the corner of her eye, she recognized the foursome who'd headed out before her. She bet none of *them* got fifteen over par.

"Ernie knew his coins and his art. I'll miss him for that." This from a lean, well-dressed man who wore his thin hair in a comb-over. PJ watched through her sunglasses as he raised his glass of iced tea to the subject of his commentary.

"You'll miss him for his insider tips, Dennis," commented another man, his large, fleshy back to PJ. She noted one reddened spot right in the back of his balding head. *That* was going to hurt in the middle of the night. "Ernie was a walking encyclopedia of historical knowledge. He should have been a professional numismatist."

Numismati . . . ? Where was a pen when she needed one? PJ slid her chair out, turning her face to the pool as if watching the first graders but tuning her ear to their conversation.

"Did he ever sell all the Nero coins?"

"I don't know." She recognized the thin man's voice. "He said he had a lead. Ernie might have shared his insights, but he kept his investments close to his chest."

Investments? Denise had said he was flat broke.

"I guess a guy just never knows who's watching and when it's over."

With that cryptic statement, the quartet rose and PJ let them escape without pouncing. But it would've been nice to find out what a *numismama* . . . whatever was. Or what sort of investment Ernie had.

Or just why she couldn't get the kink out of her swing.

PJ felt bulletproof. And tan. Even, maybe, a little thinner. Or that could have just been from taking off the wig. She hadn't seriously held out hope that she'd pull it off, believing that she'd been hypnotized by the heady victory at the spa. It went right to her head, fertilizing all those spy-girl wannabe moments. But there she was, supersleuthing her way around Kellogg, digging up questions and gouging semi-size holes in the evidence against Jack.

She dropped the wig and accessories at Trudi's and picked up Davy, getting the sorry lowdown on Jack. He wasn't moving from his cell, and according to Trudi, his defense lawyer had pimples.

Once they were headed home, PJ turned on the radio and glanced at Davy in the rearview mirror. "What do you think, little man? Ready to have some fun this afternoon?"

Davy looked at her and put his hands over his ears.

PJ refused to be discouraged. Summer should be about Fudgsicles in the backyard, bare feet with grass slicking between toes, maybe a sprinkler to run through, or a saggy blow-up pool that contained grass clippings and various action figures.

She sang along to the Beach Boys. "'Little deuce coupe . . .'"

Maybe God did have a reason for her here in Kellogg. Maybe she'd returned just in time.

She pulled up to the house and freed Davy, who ran and banged open the front door, a sufficient announcement to their presence. Still, PJ stood on the stoop just a moment, in case Boris was doing some, uh . . . sunbathing.

She heard nothing.

"Boris? Vera?" So she hadn't exactly kept tabs on them since Connie left—it wasn't like she didn't care. But since the vodka-soaked fish and slimy bacon incidents, she just . . . well, a girl could only turn down the offer of food so long before it became rude. And uncomfortable. And a giant faux pas in foreign policy.

Mostly she just stayed out of their way and hoped they weren't buying stuff on eBay.

Or getting hauled into the local police station.

But perhaps she'd been too rough on the Russians. It couldn't be easy to lose a son to a woman across the ocean. And they had been shopping for a gift for Davy online. That was sweet.

Last night, after her mother left, PJ had sat on the deck, breathing in the fragrance of the flower garden, listening to the crickets begin their nighttime serenade. Boris joined her and they'd sat in silent appreciation. He must have had a green thumb, because he actually got up and surveyed the bleeding heart bush for a long time.

On page two of Connie's instruction manual, she'd listed a

subsection on her garden. Because Connie excelled at everything she put her brain to, she also had a flower garden featured
in a Twin Cities magazine every year. Peonies, delphinium,
lupine, phlox, columbine, lily of the valley, and a hedgerow of
roses. In the back, safely away from the swing set, were two
exotic Japanese crab apple trees that cost a small fortune and
a vibrant bleeding heart bush, already in bloom with hanging
pink buds. But her pride and joy were the gladiolas. Tall as
oboes, with buds running down the shoots, tiny trumpets of
red or yellow or pink, the color of new beginnings. Connie
personally harvested the bulbs every year, and they would be
in full bloom when she returned from her honeymoon.

Thankfully the lawn company tended her garden as well
as her lawn.

"Davy, go get your bathing suit on. I'm going to show you a
fun thing your mommy and I used to do in the summer."

PJ netted a glimmer of a smile from him as he pounded up
the stairs. A few moments later, PJ followed and spied him sitting in his room, working his LEGOs. Clearly they had some
focus issues. She could relate to that—lately her brain felt like a
bad penny movie, jerky images flickering through her thoughts.
Jack's face when he tackled Hoffman at the pool. Denise's glistening eyes while telling her about Ernie's bankruptcy. Boone's
expression, dark with anger and something else as he touched
her face. Ben's smooth swing sending the ball in a perfect arch.
Most of all, she saw herself standing at the country club, facing
her mother as she said, *"I'm so glad you're home."*

She could hear the code—*"Please don't mess up"*—but she
could also choose to hear something else. Sincerity. Grateful-
ness. *"I need you."*

Wouldn't that be something?

She went to her room and rooted through her mound of clothes for her swimsuit top, a pair of shorts, and a baseball hat.

"Auntie PJ, I'm ready!"

PJ poked her head out into the hall just in time to spot Davy wearing his swimsuit, his scuba mask, his fins, a life jacket, and a towel around his neck. "Yes, you are, pal."

They headed down the stairs, through the house, and to the kitchen. "I loved running through the sprinkler when I was a kid, daring myself to dive through the spray, squealing when the cold water hit me. You're in for a treat."

When they walked into the screened-in porch, she heard a groaning, something moaning.

"Boris, are you ok—?" She stopped, her mouth half-open as Davy broke into a wobbly run, threw open the door, and scampered out, his little fins flapping on the deck.

"I love it!" His scream jolted her forward, and she stumbled out onto the deck as he hurled himself at the animal tethered to the fence.

PJ reached for an iron chair to steady herself. She probably needed to put her head between her knees. "Is that a . . . ?"

She couldn't say it.

Where the bleeding heart plant used to be—five feet of delicate grace tended with love by her bereaved sister—stood a goat. Long white beard, stubby horns, beady dark eyes. And littered around their new backyard inhabitant, PJ recognized the remains of the gladiolas.

This couldn't get worse, couldn't get—"Boris! Vera!"

"Mine, mine!"

Davy's voice yanked her back to aunthood. "No, Davy!"

Davy already had the goat in an armlock. Before her eyes was a hazy vision of blood and screams, accusations, and finally her leaving, exhaust in the outline where her happy future had once been.

"Davy, get away from it!" PJ began to peel his arms off the animal, averting her face from the rank, earthy odor.

The screaming started.

And finally out came the Russians. Vera stood on the porch yelling, but Boris leaped the hostas and raced out to the goat. *"Nyet!"*

No what? No, don't touch the goat, or—her preferred choice—maybe a disbelieving no, there was no goat?

Please let this be a nightmare. Maybe she'd gotten hit in the head, and she lay, right now, on the ninth tee, bleeding, her wig askew while her tired threesome waited for Boone's arrival.

No, that would be worse.

But as she stared at Boris and Davy, at Vera waving her hands, everything went eerily silent and she saw a movie scene—a horse's head on a pillow, regards from Vito Corleone, only this note read *Boris Sukharov.*

The goat began to buck, trying to get away. PJ landed in the dirt, pillowing Davy on her stomach. Screaming filled her ears, and she wasn't sure it wasn't coming from her.

"Nilzya!" Boris grabbed the goat and growled at PJ like she'd just terrorized his newborn. She sat up, scooting back, away to safety, Davy pulled tight against her as Boris crouched next to the goat, speaking to it in low, soothing Russian, which sounded way too much like he was clearing his throat of a fur ball.

"I want it! It's mine! Mine!"

"No, Davy." PJ wrapped her arms around his flailing body, trapping him against herself as she found her feet. He'd reached uncharted decibel levels, and when she turned toward the house, PJ was suddenly a filament short of joining him.

Elizabeth Sugar stood on the deck, dressed in her Saturday-afternoon-at-the-club best, her hand to her mouth, the other braced on the same chair PJ had just used for stability.

Like mother, like daughter.

Slowly Elizabeth drew her hand from her mouth and pressed it to her chest as if trying to slow her heart, maybe stave off a cardiac arrest.

"Mom—"

"Oh, PJ, what have you done?"

Chapter TEN

Pizza. PJ needed a deep-dish pepperoni—and fast.

It wasn't completely fair that the second her mother began to question PJ's hold on sanity, she reached for the pizza. Like some sort of Pavlovian conditioning, just a tone of voice made her body crave cheese, pepperoni, and tomato sauce.

Lucky for her, she'd seen a pizza deliveryman outside a neighbor's house just last night. With the goat moving in on the roses and her mother soothing her terrorized nephew, PJ crept into the house and dialed information.

She just about poured her troubles out to the operator, she sounded so friendly. *My mother thinks I'm insane and I have a goat eating my sister's prized garden.* But she could clearly hear the short circuits inside her fraying nerves and limited her request to the number for pizza delivery.

"I'm sorry, but I'm not showing a pizza delivery in your area."

"Are you sure? Did you check all the pizza chains?"

Silence. "No. I'm showing nothing under pizza for your area."

Listen here, sister. "How about delivery anywhere in Kellogg?"

"I have two listings—one for a Hal's, the other Angeno's Pie Palace."

"Angeno's, please." Relief leaked out of PJ even as she pulled open Connie's desk drawer, searching for a scrap of paper. She found a jumble of rubber bands, some dried-out pens, a few bent business cards, and a photo album. Glancing outside, she could see her mother still comforting a crying Davy, and Boris had plopped down on the grass, petting the goat. Vera, thankfully, had stepped in, trying to shoo the animal away from the roses, throwing out feed.

Sure, she'd eat hard barley instead of rose hips if she were a goat.

She took down the number, scratching it on the back of a business card for carpet cleaning, and dialed Angeno's.

"I'm sorry, we don't deliver to the Chapel Hills area." PJ detected just a touch of pride in the girl's voice on the other end. Well.

However, she received the same line from Hal's, and as she put down the telephone, she had the strange impulse to run across the street and ask where they'd ordered their pizza. Because as her mother led Davy into the house, a grim look on her face, PJ knew that frozen just wouldn't do.

She climbed onto a tall leather barstool and leaned her head into her folded arms as Elizabeth and Davy came into the kitchen, Davy dribbling from his nose and eyes.

Elizabeth grabbed a tissue and wiped his entire face. Then she settled Davy in the next room, in front of a Magic School

Bus DVD. "You can dispose of the goat tomorrow while he's at school," she said, returning to the kitchen.

Oh, sure. That would be inconspicuous.

Her mother stared at her a long moment. Then, "What were you thinking?"

"Please, Mom. Take a good look at what's happening out there." PJ gestured to the goat bonding with Boris in the backyard. "It's not my goat. I didn't even know they were getting a goat."

Her mother shook her head, as if seeing a natural wonder. "He sure seems taken with it."

Something to look forward to when she hauled the goat away to the . . . pound? Where did one dispose of a goat? Or rather, put a goat up for adoption?

PJ pressed a hand against her stomach. "Mom, do you know of any pizza places around here that deliver? I can't find one."

Elizabeth raised an eyebrow. Sugars didn't "do" pizza. Another reason she'd left home. "I don't know, PJ. You'll have to check the yellow pages." She went to the French doors and stood there, arms crossed. "I can't believe your sister has only been gone a week. Just wait until Constance sees this."

The tone transported PJ to the days before they moved into the Colonial—maybe third grade—when she made a fort on her sister's lower bunk bed and accidentally started the bedding on fire with a candle. What was a campout without marshmallows? The flames had charred Connie's new satin comforter and pillow sham.

PJ managed a deep, steadying breath. Connie didn't have to know anything. She'd get rid of the goat, beg Davy back into Fellows, somehow scrape up the money to replant the garden—

"I wonder if it's a religious thing," her mother said, still staring at Boris. PJ gave a silent prayer of thanks that at least he was still fully clothed. "You know, I read once that peasants in Russia give livestock as wedding gifts."

PJ narrowed her eyes, trying to laser out of her mother's brain where she might have picked up that tidbit of information. Elizabeth read long literary novels—maybe she'd read Tolstoy or something.

"So you think the goat is a wedding gift?" PJ latched on to this notion with a whitened grip. It was ever-so-much more palatable than a head on a pillow.

Her mother shrugged, and PJ grimaced, remembering Boris and the computer and the lightbulb that had gone on behind his eyes when he pronounced the word *keed*. Oh, a *kid*.

"What's this?" Her mother lifted the photo album from Connie's open desk drawer. She flipped through it. "I remember this."

PJ sidled up to her mother, peered over her shoulder.

Two faces, both tan, the older one wearing a pair of bug-eyed glasses, her hair tied up in a bandanna. The younger wore a swim cap topped with bright orange flowers. They posed before a stunning sand castle, the sun lifting the gold from the chocolate sand.

PJ guessed she might have been about five or six in the picture. "I remember that light blue whale bathing suit."

"Mmm-hmm."

"Where's Connie?"

"She was probably playing with her Barbies under the umbrella. She loved to drag them out to the beach. But she never liked the sunshine like you did."

"Did you make that sand castle?"

"Oh, sweetheart, I was one of the best sand castle–making mothers on the beach." Elizabeth gave her a wink, something soft behind her eyes. "Remember the high dive?"

PJ took the album from her mother, ran her finger over the smile of the five-year-old. "I remember I was scared to death. Connie dared me to climb it, over and over. But every time I got to the top, I stood there, frozen."

"It was the same way at the country club high dive. You couldn't jump. Until you were ten years old. I remember watching you, climbing again and again, and I felt sick, knowing you'd get to the top only to have to climb back down."

PJ closed the album. "I stood there shaking, thinking that the water looked about a million miles below, wanting to throw up." She could hear the jeers of the boys lined up behind her, smell the water, feel the grit of the sandpaper ledge, the slick hot metal of the railing in her whitened grip. Fear soured her throat.

But then . . . then . . . her mother was there. Climbing up past the boys on the ladder, inching out to the edge. Her mother, in her black one-piece with the big red flowers. Her mother, with her hair pinned up, her eyes neatly mascaraed, red lipstick bright under the afternoon sun. Her mother, unpeeling a hand from the railing, lacing it with her own. The voice, soft in her ear: *"That's about enough of this."*

"We did it." PJ said softly. "We jumped off that platform. Together. I remember the fear, wild in my stomach, my scream as I flung myself out into space. I loved it."

"I knew you had it in you. Just needed someone to hold your hand." Her mother regarded her with a smile. She took the album from PJ, put it back in the drawer, closed it.

"Unfortunately you weren't afraid of much after that. I probably started an obsession."

What obsession might that be? Her propensity to fling herself out into the wind, or the primal need to head to the water?

Elizabeth ran her hands up her bare, now goosefleshed arms, looking past PJ, seeing something PJ couldn't place. Then abruptly, she came back to herself. "How about I take you to Sunsets for lunch?"

Sunsets might be nice. PJ thought they might even have a view of the beach from there.

Elizabeth turned off the DVD. "Let's go get some lunch, Davy."

PJ watched her, the way she held out her hand for Davy, again wiping his ruddy, moist face, then plopping a kiss on his clean cheek. She had eased off his swim fins, mask, and towel and now disappeared with him up the stairs.

They descended moments later, Davy dressed in a clean white shirt and a pair of pressed navy shorts. Elizabeth picked up her purse. "Are you going in your bikini?"

"Oh." PJ looked at herself. "Uh, what about Boris and Vera?"

Elizabeth dug out her keys, glanced at the yard. "We'll pick them up a pizza."

Oh, not fair. Only, somehow, PJ wasn't hungry for pizza after all.

✳ ✳ ✳

"It must be hard for him, with his mother gone all the time."

Maxine Hudson's words echoed in PJ's thoughts as she leaned against Davy's doorframe, watching the little guy sleep. He lay on his back, one leg up, the other crossed over it, as if sleep swept in and froze him midmovement. His dark hair fell over his eyes, his lips were slightly askew, and inside that brain she hoped he was dreaming of the sand castle they'd made today.

She still had sand lodged between her toes, and the burn on her shoulders had started to smart, but she had waged a sound rescue of their afternoon, obliterating the image of the goat from his mind, at least briefly.

After lunch at Sunsets she'd packed up Davy's discarded scuba gear and, ignoring the beast in the backyard, trotted down to the beach for some afternoon sun. Instead of opening her beach chair, she'd hunkered down in the sand with Davy.

She couldn't believe it when Maxine showed up to survey their work, along with a small crowd of admirers, other mothers out with their youngsters.

"You've quite a talent." Maxine dropped down beside her. "You should take it on the road."

"Just one of my many skills," PJ said as Davy joined Daniel and Felicia running back and forth into the lake, dragging up globules of sand, plopping them onto the pile, laughing.

"Look at me, Auntie PJ!" Davy screamed, erupting in a sweet high laugh with an explosion of giggles. A wave from a nearby speedboat splashed onto his ankles.

His joy ignited explosions of warmth in her chest.

"Trudi tells me that you and she used to be best friends," Maxine said, lathering sunscreen onto her smooth, dark skin. She wore a lemon yellow one-piece with matching flip-flops and lay back onto a light blue beach mat. She looked like an ad for a beachcomber magazine.

PJ tried to ignore the dry, gritty sand that layered her up to her thighs, the fact that she wore a shapeless muscle shirt cut off at the waist over her swim top and a pair of faded men's swim trunks. They were here to have fun, not look good.

But she hoped that Boone didn't happen by.

Why, oh why, did her thoughts always return to Boone the minute her feet touched sand? Did she not remember their last dangerous conversation?

Yes. Painfully well.

She nodded to Maxine's comment, digging a moat around their castle. "I left town right after high school, but we've caught up in the last week." PJ peered at her through her sunglasses. "I take it you're not from around here?"

"We moved to Kellogg about six years ago. I work at the Hennepin County hospital as a trauma nurse."

Ah. That would explain her calm demeanor and bent toward psychology. PJ's gaze darted toward Maxine's left hand as she shaped the bottom of the sand pile. Davy ran up and dumped more sand on top. "Is your husband a doctor?"

Maxine smiled, and it seemed just cryptic enough to spark curiosity. "He works from home, on his computer." Although PJ didn't know her well—and with the sun in her face, it was hard to tell—she thought she saw something dark cross Maxine's expression, followed by a sigh. But PJ felt it, knew it well. She possessed her own shadows, her own sigh.

"He prefers to stay to himself and only goes out for church."

"Sounds like that might be a challenge."

A muscle twitched on Maxine's face. "We all make our choices and have to live with them."

PJ's stomach hollowed, as if they'd both fallen into a place where neither wanted to go and now gulped for air. *Choices.* That was one word for them.

"How long have you been back in town?" Maxine asked.

"About a week."

"Then you haven't been to the Mall of America new park yet. They just renovated the rides—we're going over there on Saturday. Want to join us?"

PJ could barely think beyond dinnertime. But maybe it would be nice to a have a friend in Kellogg who wasn't attached to the past. "Maybe, yeah."

"Well, for sure we need to get the kids together for a play—"

A scream edged with terror cut off her words. PJ spotted Davy standing hip-deep in the water, arms flailing, eyes closed, as waves, this time from a yacht motoring by, pummeled him chest-high.

"Davy!" PJ jumped to her feet, splashed through the waves, and scooped him up into her arms. He threw his arms around her neck and wrapped his trembling legs around her waist.

"You okay, buddy?"

His face dug into her neck, and he shook his head.

PJ waded farther into the water and lowered herself, bobbing as she held him. "Pal of mine, are you scared of the water?"

He didn't move, his breath rushing in and out, broken. PJ pulled his arms from around her neck. He resisted, but she leaned back to look in his face. "Little man, what's the matter?"

"I . . . I . . ."

"Have you ever been out past your knees?"

He shook his head, and PJ touched her forehead to his. Of course not. Without a father, and with Connie hating water . . .

"I knew you had it in you. Just needed someone to hold your hand."

"Come with me."

"No!"

"Shh. Look at me, Davy."

His wide eyes, big and feverish, latched on to hers.

"Auntie PJ isn't going to let anything happen to you. Hold on to my neck; see, I have my arms around you. Do you feel them?"

He nodded.

"Now, let's just bob. Easy." She stood, and he clung to her like a starfish. But as she moved out into the water, he shook.

"No . . . no . . . no . . ."

"Shh. Look, we're bobbing." She held him tightly to herself and began to move in the water. Up, down, the water splashing over his hips, his back. "I'm not letting you go."

The water lapped at her shoulders, her legs registering the temperature change as she waded deeper, all the while bobbing.

Davy loosened his hold on her neck yet kept his legs vised to her waist. But he looked into her eyes.

And smiled.

PJ grinned at him. "See. We're swimming, aren't we?"

"Swimming!" His smile broke into laughter, his eyes alive.

"And look what a big boy you are, deep in the water!" She turned so he could see the shore. For a second, his grip tightened, and she matched it. "Remember, I'm not letting you go."

He began to wiggle in her arms as she bobbed them, higher, stronger. Then he let go of her neck, splashing the water beside her. It sprayed into their eyes, and she laughed with him.

"Deeper!"

His blue eyes shone and she couldn't help but oblige. They finally returned to shore, laughing.

"He's lucky to have you, PJ," Maxine said as PJ collapsed beside her, wiping her face with a towel. "I think you're just what he needs."

PJ said nothing as she lay back in the sand beside Davy, soaking in all the afternoon offered.

They'd returned home baked, popular, and tired.

After checking under his bed again for the library book—she was seriously starting to doubt Fellows' checkout system—she tiptoed down the stairs, standing barefoot in the screened-in porch, watching the goat lay in a contented white pool of fur just outside the bright rim of porch light. The debris of the gladiolas nested like a bed under its hooves. The crickets were out, and the sky above was dark, moonless.

She was standing in front of the Sub-Zero in the kitchen, attempting to conjure up ice cream when she heard the car drive up.

Oh no, here came trouble.

And trouble looked good. She wasn't used to this tidy, pressed-khaki-and-oxford Boone. But she recognized the swagger as he swung his keys around one finger, not realizing that with every step closer her stomach did another full twirl.

PJ opened the door before he could ring the bell. "Hey," she said, leaning against the doorframe, one arm blocking his entrance.

Boone smiled, every inch of it slow and devastating. As if he knew that, with such little effort, she could imagine herself right back in the circle of trouble with him, picking up where they'd left off. "I just got off work. Thought you might enjoy a walk along the beach." He scanned past her, leaned in, his voice low. "Your mom around?"

"No." She went outside and closed the door, sitting on the steps. Fresh air. She needed fresh, bracing, brain-clearing air.

Boone sat beside her, resting his arms on his knees, twirling those keys.

And probably she should focus on Jack's case. Only.

"Ever heard of a numismatist . . . a guy who collects coins?"

"Sure. My dad collected quarters from every state."

"No. I mean expensive coins."

"Like silver dollars?"

"Maybe like old coins, like during the time of Nero."

"There's such a thing? Don't they belong in museums?"

PJ lifted a shoulder.

"Why do you ask?"

"No reason."

Boone glanced at her, a sideways look that she decided not to oblige. "I checked on Jack," he finally said. "And Tucker, although don't get your hopes up."

But PJ grinned. "Really? Does he have a motive?"

"He might. He was in the bank a couple weeks ago trying to get a loan. They turned him down."

"So you don't think Jack's guilty?"

"I didn't say that, now, did I? Just because I'm asking around doesn't mean I buy your theories."

Uh-oh, she'd stirred the old troublemaker in Boone, the one who argued with her just because he could.

"But you think I might be right. Something inside you feels it."

"I feel something, that's for sure."

Ho-kay. PJ got up and walked out into the cool grass, running it between her toes, cleaning off the sand. The lawn needed cutting and curled around her bare feet.

"Okay." Boone rose from the front steps, hooking his keys into his pocket. "I might have a few questions. Like, there was no sign of a struggle, even though the house was ransacked. So if it was Jack, he would have had to blindside him—Ernie was strong enough to fight back. The ME says that Ernie's neck was broken cleanly but that bruises on his knees indicate that he fell, probably after being killed. If Jack killed him, he'd have to have been on top of him on the table, and Ernie wouldn't have fallen."

In the moonless night and from this distance, she couldn't clearly read Boone's face, especially with his back to the porch light.

"Then there's Jack's confession about why he attacked Ernie at the club."

"Oh?"

"Ancient coins. Ernie bought and sold them on the Internet. He convinced Jack to let him invest his money for him—and Ernie emptied out his bank account."

"Hence Trudi's account being empty."

"Jack was panicked, thought maybe Ernie was taking him for a ride."

"Which gives him motive." She turned, settling herself into the curve of the cottonwood in the front yard. "So he had opportunity and motive . . . but can he break a guy's neck?"

"He's a physical therapist. I'd say . . . yes."

PJ nodded.

She could hear Boone moving silently through the grass like

a panther. She caught the scent of a clean Boone: soap and that aura of fresh air and freedom that had always hypnotized her lifted from him, heady and going right to her common sense.

For a second she didn't care why he was here or even if he believed her. Just that he wanted her back.

Why was it so hard for her to be the girl she longed to be whenever Boone entered her airspace? It was like, despite her best efforts, the old PJ—the nothing-but-trouble PJ—took control of her thoughts, her heart, and made her do things that, in the light of day, she might run from. She didn't want Boone. Really. She wanted a nice guy, the kind who would go to church with her and see in her the woman who longed to live by faith instead of by her passions.

But that kind of guy didn't want her, exhibit A being Matthew "it's not working for me" Buchanan.

Clearly she didn't know what she wanted. Which left her where?

"I can't go for a walk with you, Boone," she said, her voice catching on her own longings. "I have to go back inside. Davy is upstairs."

He closed in on her, his arm touching the branch above her head. "Maybe I could come in."

Yeah, and they both knew where that would lead. "I don't think so. The Russians are here."

"You make it sound so Cold War." His hand touched her chin, lifting it. "Incoming."

C'mon, PJ, pull yourself together. "Really, Boone, you can't stay."

She was going to have to do better than that. There was a part, way deep inside her, that clucked with disgust.

"You know, I could say I'm here on official business. Protecting you."

"Protecting me?" PJ stared into his eyes, caught in their magnetic pull.

"If Jack didn't kill Hoffman, then there's a murderer out there."

Oh.

"*Oh!* You're right!" She ducked out from under his arm, and for a long moment he just stood there, as if a beat behind, trying to catch up. But she'd already paced away from him. "The murderer is still out there!"

Boone turned, and the porch light caught his wounded expression. "Peej, what does a guy need to do—"

"I'm serious! You need to be looking for him." She pointed to the great "out there," her breath quick in her chest.

"There's no murderer—"

"There is, and I'd start by looking at Ben Murphy and where he was on Monday morning!"

"You are *kidding* me! Have you completely lost your mind?" As he advanced on her, she ran to the porch steps. "Ben Murphy, our math teacher? Seriously?"

"Listen, the guy has a motive—Ernie was after his goat!"

The second she said it, the second the words left her mouth, she wanted to reach out and snatch them back, tuck them inside for another good perusal before she let that theory out into the light.

Boone stood a step below her, his eyes even with hers; all humor, all desire vanished from his face. "Really. You are something else."

PJ's throat thickened. "You used to say I was everything,"

she said, softly, too softly to cover the quiver in her voice. She tried for a smile.

Boone shook his head. "I'm not kidding, PJ. I don't care how much I've missed you. If you interfere, I'll haul you in faster than—"

"Your father did on prom night?"

His mouth opened and she clenched her jaw, not sure where that had come from, suddenly unable to look at the sting on his face. His face twitched, and he looked down at his sandaled feet. "You just don't want to forgive me, do you?"

PJ swallowed, looking past him, something gritty in her throat. "I . . ." She did want to forgive him—had already, long ago. Hadn't she?

"Someday you're going to get over the past and realize that we all make mistakes," Boone said quietly. Then he crossed the grass and disappeared into the dark fold of night.

PJ stood there on the step, the stonework cold on her bare feet, the heat of summer dissipating in the cool night. She wrapped her arms over her shoulders as she watched Boone's door open. For a moment, the light illuminated him—bronze hair, strong frame, the boy turned man she couldn't escape.

He drove away without looking at her.

She was turning to go into the house when she saw it, illuminated by Boone's passing headlights. A small white hatchback with a little red sign on the roof.

Pizza delivery.

The engine turned over and the car pulled out from the curb, the driver's cap low over his eyes.

PJ ran inside and locked the door behind her.

Chapter *ELEVEN*

Dear Ms. Nicholson,
Please forgive my recent outburst about the
missing library book—

Dear Fellows Director,
I know that attire sets an example for others,
and I apologize—

Dear Fellows Hall Monitor,
Okay, I can agree that maybe lateness is a
metaphor for disrespect, but I promise that
David is not the instigator—

PJ took the stationery, wadded it into a hard ball, and
threw it at the chrome basket in Connie's sleek office. It
ricocheted off the neat black credenza, the tall bookshelves

stacked with smart books, and landed on the white Berber carpet. She glared at the formal picture of Connie and Davy on the computer screen—Davy in a black three-piece suit, his wavy hair tamed into place, sitting up straight and grinning while his mother cupped his shoulder and offered a sweet, chaste smile.

All evidence of her deceased husband had vanished. An intimate photo of Sergei, standing bare-chested with a towel around his wide neck, grinning, perched in a five-by-seven frame next to the leather pencil holder.

PJ turned it facedown, feeling too much like an intruder. In the next room, Vera was trying to coax some sort of deep-fried bread into Davy's mouth while he pinned it shut and made noises like a wounded animal.

Boris sat outside in a Speedo, with his goat.

Dear Fellows Highbrows—
Math homework, in kindergarten?

Dear Connie,
I'm really sorry. But . . . seriously . . . Fellows?

PJ gathered up the debris of her thoughts, dumped the lot into the garbage, turned out the light to the office, and left. "Time for bed, Davy." She held out her hand.

To her surprise, he slid off the stool and took it. "Horton?"

"You got it, little man."

She read the story and two others before finally tucking him in. A light rain this evening had diluted the heavy summer heat and stirred the sweet syrup of flowers and fresh grass into the air. She'd left his window open, and now the crickets enriched the darkness with their song.

"Auntie PJ, can we go to church again?"

PJ brushed his hair from his face. "Do you and your mommy go to church?" The fact that he'd waged very little war this morning when she'd packed him up and brought him to the Kellogg Praise and Worship Center suggested he knew what he was doing. Then again, she'd slunk into the back and kept him supplied with a candy bar she dug out of her bag to keep him quiet.

"Grandma brings me to her church sometimes." He rolled over onto his side. "I saw Daniel and Felicia at church today. They want me to come over and play with them. Can I?"

PJ hadn't expected to see Maxine, nor to receive the hug that Trudi's friend gave her. How she appreciated the way Maxine steered the conversation wide around their friend's current pain. PJ had called Trudi that afternoon and been updated on her despair. Jack still sat in jail. They were still broke.

And PJ still believed that Jack was innocent. Despite the mounting evidence against him. She had to believe her instincts—they were about all she had left.

"Did you like church?" PJ gathered his dirty clothes and gave another cursory look for the library book, this time under the DVDs.

"It's loud," he murmured, his voice drowsy.

"Yeah." PJ kissed him on the forehead as he closed his eyes.

She took a bath, then put on her pajamas. From her window, she spied Boris limelighted by the outside spot, dressed in his scary blue nylon workout pants. He poured feed from a bag into a bucket. *Yeah, right, get a clue, pal.* Dora the Goat—Davy's choice of names—was going to be hiccuping gladiolas all night.

After cracking the window open, she turned off the light and climbed into bed, listening to the house groan in the darkness. The water from her empty claw-foot tub in the bathroom plinked, and the smell of the lilac bath oil she'd used scented her sister's white cotton sheets as PJ flopped back onto the pillows. Connie was going to take her head off when she saw the damage in the garden. Or when she found out Davy hadn't learned long division by the time she got home.

But . . . he had gotten his shoulders wet and learned to trust her, hadn't he? *Auntie PJ.* She could quickly fall in love with the singsong of her name in his little voice.

And what to do with the goat? Tomorrow she'd have to get serious about disposing—er, adopting it out. But what if Boris took it as a personal insult? Worse, would the consumption of Connie's gladiolas mean a rough start to her new married life?

Not to mention the fact that Jack still sat in the Kellogg lockup and that Trudi was losing her home and future right before her eyes.

Lord, a little help here?

Instead of a calming voice, she heard Boone's words from last night: *"You just don't want to forgive me, do you?"*

She *had* forgiven him, hadn't she?

She closed her eyes, seeing his broken, pained expression. She hated how it created the smallest ball of satisfaction inside her chest, how she clung to it. Even before she became a Christian, she knew that a person had to forgive to move on. It seemed pretty easy to forgive, or at least think she'd forgiven, when sitting in a pew surrounded by praise music. But in the real world, that's when forgiveness got gritty.

Maybe, despite the miles she'd put on her Bug, she hadn't left Kellogg at all.

PJ pulled the covers up to her chin, staring at the ceiling. Watching the fan whir in the shadows.

Okay, so she *hadn't* forgiven him. Because . . . then what?

Her unforgiveness lay like a boulder in the center of her stomach, heavy and taking up too much room. Maybe it *had* kept her tethered to Boone or at least to the past. Kept the blame on him for everything that had gone wrong in her life—from the night she left Kellogg, through all her travels, her job changes, her crazy whims that some might call mistakes, to a warm beach in Florida, throwing a shoe at Matthew. Maybe not forgiving Boone just made it easier to live with herself and her own failures.

PJ sat up, turned on one of the bedside lamps, and stared at herself in the mirror across from the bed (which, by the way, was a horrible place for a mirror). In this light she looked tired, her dark red hair hanging in long tangles around her head after her bath. She touched Boone's name on her shoulder. She probably could have turned it into flowers or something else long ago.

"You just don't want to forgive me, do you?"

No, she just didn't want to face the truth. That maybe the past ten years weren't Boone's fault at all. That once she made the decision to leave Kellogg and not look back, everything she did—every choice, every action, every mistake—had been hers alone. She was the only one responsible for the person she'd become today.

And frankly, she didn't know if she liked that person.

What might it feel like to be free of the stone inside? to forgive Boone? take back her life? start over, a true new creation?

The thought took her, filled her, pressed tears to her eyes. "I want to forgive him, Lord. Help me to forgive." She covered her eyes with the heels of her hands, listened to her breathing. "Help me to start over."

"Lord, help me understand the person I'm supposed to be here." The prayer she'd spoken in the shadowed hush of the sanctuary filled her mind now. She thought she was supposed to help Trudi . . . but maybe Boone was right; maybe she was just interfering. Except it had felt right, even good, to be doing something for someone else. To finally be the friend that Trudi deserved.

She got out of bed, the floor chilly to her bare feet, and dug around in her duffel for her Bible, then paged open to the verse from this week's sermon . . . 1 Peter 1, was it?

"To God's elect, strangers in the world . . . who have been chosen according to the foreknowledge of God the Father, through the sanctifying of work of the Spirit, for obedience to Jesus . . ."

Sanctifying work. The pastor today had suggested it might be more than just being a better person. That it meant becoming a servant for Christ. Someone different, set apart.

PJ knew all about being different, but maybe she could be set apart for God to use. The kind of person who stood up for the innocent. Stood up for those who couldn't find their voice.

Starting with Jack and Trudi.

She closed her Bible and tucked it next to her pillow, then turned off the light.

She had to get inside Hoffman's house. Maybe she could find some of those coins, sort out if they had something to do with his murder.

But how, exactly?

"I could use some help, Lord."

The sweet smell of evening and the sound of crickets harmonized her into sleep.

✳ ✳ ✳

She knew it was a dream, knew that she couldn't change a thing. Still, she tried—tried to change the wine-red dress she'd had tailor-made, with the empire waist, V-neck, spaghetti straps, and shirred front. Tried to change the look on Boone's face when he picked her up, scrutinizing her with those approving eyes.

PJ settled into the dream, feeling royal as she stepped from Boone's father's Cadillac, floating into prom on his tuxedoed arm. Roger Buckam stood near the door and nodded toward them. His eyes tight, he shook Boone's hand, his gold pinkie ring glinting under the light of the torches that lined the walkway.

Couples strolled the golf course just outside the halo of light pushing through the club windows. Boone winked at her, then ushered her into the dance.

She hadn't been much of a drinker even then, but when Trudi slipped her a taste of the liquid she'd poured into a medicine bottle in her purse, well, she hadn't been able to eat strawberries since without thinking of schnapps. She laughed too loud, danced hard, flirted well, and by midnight, Boone pulled her tight and offered an invitation that, even in her mood-heightened state, made her blush.

She'd agreed to meet him on the fourth tee, and he disappeared. *"Boone? Boone?"* She heard her voice, wondered if she spoke aloud, but then found herself at the pond, high heels swinging from her fingers. Overhead, the night sky played along with Boone's plans, stars winking at her, a slight breeze sullying a nearby willow, a golden near-full moon stealing her breath as well as any last remorse.

He loved her. Boone loved her.

And tonight, she'd love him back. A swirl of anticipation tightened inside her.

She heard laughter—Boone's, husky and deep—from the country club, and it lured her near enough to find him sitting on the back steps with his football cohort and Trudi's date, Greg Morris. Boone held the cigarette between his thumb and forefinger, and when he saw her standing barefoot in the shadows next to the dripping air conditioner, he looked up at her like a deer in the headlights.

Yes, that's right; she'd heard him.

She vaguely heard him tell Greg to get lost as she yanked the cigarette from him. He found his feet. "PJ—"

"Don't even try, Boone." She stared at the cigarette, her entire body shaking. "You totally cheapened our . . . wrecked—"

A group of boys walked by—football buddies—and Boone lifted his hand in greeting. They laughed, and one gave him a thumbs-up.

"Does the entire school know?" She had the urge to fling the cigarette to the ground, but she was barefoot and not about to put it out with her pedicure. "Here." She handed the smoke back to him. "That's the most 'fun' you're going to have tonight."

She turned away, sliding out of Boone's reach as he tried to catch her arm. Above her thundering heartbeat she barely heard the swish of her bare feet scuffing through the stubbly grass of the putting green. Even the trees seemed to want to hush her as she fought tears.

"PJ!"

He caught her on the tenth green, his hand on her arm. She whipped out of his grasp, slipped on the slick grass, and went down in a silky heap.

She felt ruined.

Boone knelt next to her. "I'm sorry."

He ran his thumb under her eyes, wiping her tears. "We weren't talking about you."

"Then who—"

But she never finished because he kissed her, softly, his eyes in hers as he drew away. "I love you, PJ. I always will."

When he kissed her again, her arms went around his wide shoulders. Her breath mixed with his, and she could taste the champagne he'd snuck into the prom. She lost herself inside his embrace, moving into his advances, barely aware of her shoulders bared, how he'd managed to woo her nearly out of her dress, wrap her in his jacket, how he himself had lost his tailored shirt.

Her heart had already said yes long before this night. It was only a matter of time before her body followed.

"Daniel Buckam, what in the—?"

Boone sprang away from her. PJ reached out to pull him back, but she'd already lost him as he found his feet, staring in horror at his father riding in a golf cart. Sitting beside him was Ben Murphy and, behind them, Ernie Hoffman.

PJ clutched Boone's jacket around herself, hot embarrassment wrenching away her breath.

"Dad—"

"Don't, Boone. Get in," Buckam said coldly.

Without a word Boone obeyed his father, sliding onto the back shelf of the cart.

PJ huddled in the wet grass, unsure what to do.

Then Director Buckam gave her a look that made her want to curl into the fetal position. "What are you waiting for?" he snapped.

Murphy crooked a finger at her. But Ernie smiled kindly, patted the seat beside him.

PJ turned her back to them and pulled her dress closed, shivering, shaking. Feeling naked even as she zipped herself back together.

And Boone didn't look at her.

She tried to find defense—wasn't prom night the perfect night? And it wasn't like it was a first for the country club or even, probably, this green. Still as she climbed on beside Ernie and they raced back to the clubhouse, she felt like a tramp.

And then she got it.

Smoke spiraled off one end of the country club. Near the restaurant. Where she'd taken the cigarette from Boone.

Thick and black, the smoke chewed up the night sky, devouring their prom.

She glanced at Boone. He'd gone pale.

When Buckam stopped the cart and got out, PJ expected him to address Boone. Instead he grabbed PJ by the arm and hauled her over to the chief of police, who gave her a look that cleared the final passion fog from her brain.

"Here's our little arsonist," Buckam said as smoke teared her eyes.

She looked over her shoulder and caught Boone's eyes. *What?* But Boone was the one with the cigarette—

He turned away, his hands in his pockets.

The memory of the smoke could still make her tear up, fill her lungs with acrid pitch. She coughed. Coughed again, her chest closing upon itself. Coughed again, so violently it woke her.

She sat up in bed, still feeling the bruise of her cough.

Smoke.

A thin veneer crept into the room in the early morning light, but because of her vast experience she recognized it in a second. As if in confirmation, the fire alarm went off, numbing nearly all thoughts save one.

"Davy!"

PJ launched from her bed and raced down the hall to Davy's room in zero point two seconds. Here, at the top of the stairs, the smoke thickened, a haze that stung her eyes. A quick sweep of his room revealed it empty. She hacked again, putting her hand to her mouth, and raced down the stairs. "Fire!"

She dove into the fog toward the kitchen and barely made out Vera, dressed in a rust-colored robe, her hair tied back in a scarf, fanning a towel below the alarm. Davy, seated at the counter with a stack of what looked like pancakes, clamped his hands over his ears.

"Turn off the stove!" PJ grabbed a wooden spoon and took

a swipe at the alarm, knocking it from its mount. It dangled, silenced, from a thin wire.

She turned her attention to the stove, where pancakes bubbled in a sea of sizzling oil from a smoking cast-iron pot probably hauled over from the motherland and formerly used to serve father Lenin.

"Blini," Vera said, as if explaining the food group.

PJ turned off the stove and squished past Vera, grabbing an oven mitt and then the pan. She expected it to combust at any moment. Muscling open the back door, she ran out onto the porch and tossed the smoking contents into the backyard, pancakes and all.

Dora looked up at her and stopped chewing a mouthful of hostas.

"Breakfast," PJ said.

"Shto tee dyelish?"

What was she doing? What did Vera think PJ was doing—watering the lawn? She rounded on the babushka standing on the porch. Vera seethed—PJ deduced that from the wild hand gestures, the rough-edged Russian that sounded like a curse upon their entire family. Which, PJ wanted to remind her, she was a part of now.

"Sorry," PJ said calmly, holding up a mittened hand in surrender. "I have this thing about fire."

"That oil's not good for the grass."

PJ whirled. Super, more criticism. Connie's lawn boy . . . er, man . . . in a green jumpsuit and brown cap knelt in her garden fertilizing the recently replanted, badly wounded bleeding heart. "When did you get here?"

"Maybe an hour ago. Sorry. Mrs. Morton expects me, so

I just come in and get started. I'm Anders, with the lawn service."

PJ looked at him, and while she had the vague understanding that she stood there in her jammies, what was providentially clear was that she'd found the answer to her problem.

She knew exactly how she'd get into Ernie Hoffman's house.

Marching inside past the angry Russian, she dropped the pan into the sink, opened a few windows, and sprinted upstairs. A glance in the mirror told her that she should be wincing. But she was too fueled by her plan to care. Sweeping her hair back into a ponytail, she whipped on a pair of jogging shorts and a T-shirt and pulled on her tennis shoes.

This wouldn't take long.

She took the stairs two at a time, swinging her keys.

Davy perched at the bottom, wearing a goatee of syrup.

PJ skidded to a stop. Oh yeah, *Davy*. She sank down hard onto the bottom step. Foiled again.

Vera materialized through the fog, wiping her hands. Her gaze ranged from PJ to Davy to PJ's keys. *"Ya smatroo za rebyonka."*

Hmm . . . PJ deciphered that as an offer to watch the fish. Which she dearly hoped meant Davy. Still, fish or not, he was a little guy who'd felt abandoned lately.

PJ crouched in front of him. "Little man, I gotta run out for a bit. Will you stay with uh . . . uh . . ."

"Baba Vera?"

PJ glanced at Vera; she was smiling at Davy. She focused on the smile and the way Baba Vera took Davy by the hand, leading him back to the kitchen, then perching him on a chair and patting his cheeks. It looked like the "fish" would be fine for a few minutes.

She tried to unstick herself from the syrup that had puddled under her tennis shoes.

Casting a final look toward Davy and his baba, PJ lit out for the front door.

She *did* have a plan, one that didn't include breaking too many laws. "Hey, Anders! I gotta move your truck, okay?" PJ peeked around the side of the house where he was watering the hostas. The spray rainbowed under the morning sun. He looked up, nodding.

She checked the back of the truck and yes, there hung an extra jumpsuit, a hat, and a plethora of gardening tools. She debated leaving a note, but judging by the amount of yard Connie had maintained, Anders would be busy for at least an hour.

She fully planned to be back before he noticed that she'd relocated his truck . . . to Hoffman's neighborhood.

Nobody noticed the lawn guy. Or the mailman or milkman.

She slid into the jumpsuit, zipped it up, and added the hat, pulling her hair through the back. As a former locksmith's apprentice, she was counting on her rudimentary knowledge of legal B and E to get her inside Hoffman's house. People often secreted a key outside their house. Seventy percent of their emergency calls had come from kids or the elderly who forgot where they hid their extra key. Maybe she wouldn't have to technically *break in*.

Regardless, she wasn't going to take anything. Just look around. Like a fly. And again, she was with the good guys.

Hoffman's house, which PJ had found from the address

listed in the paper and confirmed with the name on the mailbox, was a 1970s rambler with a long, low front porch overgrown with lilac bushes, purple viburnum, and two beautiful pink hydrangea plants. She put a hand inside the dying impatiens hanging near the front door and nearly tripped over the two huge frog planters guarding the stoop.

She was a lawn girl. So she filled the watering can from the outside spigot (no key box magnetized to the faucet) and watered some of the bushes and the impatiens. At the country club, they had always left the key to the pool house on top of the door.

PJ sidled up to the front door, ran her hand over the frame.

Nothing.

She lifted the welcome mat.

Nope.

She watered the geraniums in the frogs, picked out a couple weedy shoots, lifted and looked under one of the planters. Nothing but an outline of froggy.

A zippy red compact drove by. The driver waved, and PJ waved back with her watering can. Even criminals were friendly in Minnesota.

She moved to the next planter. When she lifted it, she heard something rattle inside, down deep in the froggy's throat.

Oh, she was so good at this. Or maybe that wasn't something she should be proud of?

PJ checked over her shoulder. Yes, she knew it made her look slightly guilty, but it could also come in handy if someone, say Boone or one of his henchmen, happened to be driving down the street.

Street was clear.

She entered Ernie's home.

A dead guy's house. Inside, stale air and the odor of rotting milk made her pause, and she tasted her heartbeat in her mouth. Closing the door behind her, she allowed her eyes to adjust and, for a moment, froze.

The place had been destroyed. Just from her vantage point looking into the family room, she could recognize Angry Search in the overturned cushions on the sofa, the pictures torn from the wall, the books strewn on the floor, a crushed trout ripped from its mount.

The mail had been scattered on the entry floor—newspapers, magazines, letters. She crouched and sifted through it: *AARP*, offers for credit cards, a history magazine. She accidentally stepped on a bubble envelope and heard it crunch. She winced and picked it up. Priority mail, with a green certified mail sticker.

PJ stared at the signature, the date.

Ernie had died sometime after getting his mail. After signing for it.

Strange that he hadn't opened it.

She put the mailer on the buffet table. Turning right, down the hall, she saw that the first bedroom had been dismantled—overturned mattress, a shattered mirror. Yeah, that made sense.

The next room down made her pause. A boy's bedroom, also destroyed. Even the wooden airplane that she guessed hung over the bed had been trampled into little balsa wood splinters. Hardy Boys books littered the floor, along with a torn *Men in Black* movie poster.

The room looked like it hadn't been updated since the mid-nineties. Her gaze lingered on a thick oil portrait of Ernie, Tucker, and Mrs. Hoffman. Tucker looked about ten, his grin betraying buck teeth PJ knew were later accessorized into submission. Ernie beamed, his hand on his only son's shoulder. PJ recalled Denise's words: *"You'd think a widower in his twilight years would want to spend time with his son and grandchildren."*

The next door led to the office. Curls of dust rimmed the tracings where the computer had sat, conspicuously absent next to the lonely monitor on Ernie's desk. She ran her finger along the bookshelf, taking in the volumes and volumes of books on ancient coins. She picked one up and was momentarily caught by a picture of a coin struck during the time of Constantine the Great, from the fourth century AD. She didn't even know there'd been a Great Constantine (although maybe Boris did). More importantly, what might such a coin be worth today?

A dusty guitar leaned on a stand in the corner, and through her mind swept the vague recollection of Mr. Hoffman playing "Elvira" during a talent night at the school. She plucked a string as she crouched next to it, paging through a photo album on the floor. In it she recognized a picture of Ernie jauntily dressed in shorts and hiking boots, posed in front of the ancient Parthenon in Athens. Another showed him at an archaeological dig in what looked like Italy.

She stood for a long time, looking at the blank monitor. She'd had a computer once, had spent long hours surfing the Net late into the night with a laptop on a pillow in her bed. Leaving the office, she found Hoffman's bedroom across the hall. She stood at the threshold, an invisible hand pressing against her chest. The covers had been torn from the bed, a puddle of brown cotton on the floor. Only the fitted sheet and the dust ruffle remained. A pile of books lay upended, tossed to the floor from his bedside stand. On the other side of the bed, a high school picture of his wife sat untarnished.

PJ tiptoed over the debris and sat down on the side of the bed. Dusty sunlight striped the green carpet through the venetian blinds, and a plant in the corner begged for water with its brown and curling leaves.

She should go.

But first . . . she fell to her knees and lifted the edge of the dust ruffle. And discovered that Ernie Hoffman and she had had one thing in common—they both kept their late-night surfing laptops under their beds.

More proof that it wasn't the cops who'd ransacked the house—since they'd taken Ernie's desktop, they would have also confiscated his laptop if they'd found it. But clearly whoever had tossed the place wasn't interested in Ernie's laptop. Which begged the question—what were they looking for?

She pulled the computer out and sat on the bed, booting it up.

For two months right after she started going to New Life Church and dating Matthew, the surfer-turned-pastor, she'd taken a job retrieving files from damaged computers. Yes, she used a software program provided by the owner and mostly just pushed Okay or Cancel. Still, she learned a few things, like how to search for files on a computer and access recently visited Web sites.

Ernie had file upon file of pictures, data, descriptions, and articles about coins, mostly centered around the time of Nero.

PJ remembered Nero. Like Buckam, he accused some perfectly innocent people of setting fire to something. In Nero's case, it had been Rome. She didn't particularly like Nero.

Thankfully Ernie still had his settings stored and she easily hooked up to his wireless connection. Going to his history file, she accessed his last few Web sites, starting at his account on Auction.com. The cookies still had him signed in under the name Antionias. Interesting. According to the site, his last auction had been of a Nero coin cast in AD 60.

She was googling that coin when a car door slammed outside.

PJ closed the laptop and hit her knees, peering over the sash just in time to see Boone standing in front of the lawn truck. He turned and stared at the house as if it might have come alive.

She tucked the computer under her arm, then keeping low, scampered through the house.

Surely there was a back door. Or a basement?

Or . . . the garage! From the kitchen, PJ spotted Boone striding by the picture window. She ducked under the counter and crawled, keeping her head down, toward what she prayed was the garage door and eased it open. Darkness and the pungency of oil, grass clippings, and cement sucked her into the muggy shadows.

PJ closed the door behind her, also closing her nose to the odor and the stifling air that pressed against her. The only light filtered through the grimy utility door window.

A shadow clipped the sunlight. Boone! She dodged a supply of rakes and shovels, leaped the lawn mower, and scooted behind the front end of the car. There she hid, sweat beading under the brown cap and dripping down the back of the jumpsuit, trying to swallow her heart back into her chest.

The shadow passed.

She hung on to the fender and breathed out, embracing the computer to her chest, gathering her feet under her to stand.

Something moved behind her—a scuff, a creak of bone.

PJ turned, but a hand clamped over her mouth just as a voice rasped, "Don't scream."

Yeah, right. Where was Boone when she needed him?

Chapter TWELVE

"Boone! Boone!" She didn't care that she'd spend the night in the slammer—better to be alive and booked in than murdered and stowed in Hoffman's greasy garage.

The hand over her mouth turned her screams more into "Moom! Moom!"

She kicked out at her attacker, her foot pinging off the fender.

"Shh. I promise I won't hurt you!"

Oh, that made a difference.

She levered her elbow hard and connected with a corrugation of rib. "Let go of me!" she tried to scream, finding flesh in the process and biting down.

The presence behind her sucked in a breath and yanked his hand away. "Calm down!"

She sprang out of his clutches, turned, and scuttled backward. Her breaths hammered on top of each other, fast, violent.

In the milky light, she made out her assailant. He wore a dark T-shirt and a baseball cap and seemed vaguely familiar.

A shiver ran down her back, but now freed and recalling how to use her self-defense techniques, she wasn't going to rush out into Boone's arms. Yet.

"Who are you?" she whispered, hating the shake in her voice.

"I'm just trying to help," the voice hissed.

"By attacking me?"

"I didn't attack you. I saved your skin."

"Saved my . . . You're confusing me."

"I'm not surprised. You confuse me too."

She blinked, trying to make him out. He resembled, in a way, Trudi's husband, Jack, except broader. More dangerous. "Who are you and what are you doing here?"

She scooted back on the gritty floor, her hand curling around a cool, smooth stick behind her. Maybe a bat.

"Same thing you are."

"I'm working on the lawn."

Even from here, she recognized a smirk. She brandished the stick. To her utter delight, she discovered it was a flashlight. "Hah!" She flicked it on.

He put up an arm, blinked, and recoiled.

"You're the pizza guy!" Even as she said it, her mouth dropped open and her breath slurped out of her. The pizza guy, here in Ernie's garage?

"Sorta." He smirked again, and she sensed a lie inside it. She didn't know what to think—she had to admit, it seemed like a friendly grin surrounded by a couple days of dark whiskers and brown eyes. He was crouching, and the muscles in his thick arms tightened his T-shirt. More than that, she made out confidence. Or perhaps arrogance.

"Who are you?"

He shook his head, put his finger to his lips.

She schooled her voice lower. "You owe me after that mini grope."

"I did not grope you. I saved your hide." His voice was solemn. "I'd never grope a lawn girl."

She glared at him.

Footsteps echoed outside on the pavement of the driveway. PJ flicked off the light. Pizza Guy held up his hand, some sort of sharp military move that should freeze her on the spot.

It was a weird kind of bonding moment as she crouched next to a Weed Eater with a could-be murderer while Boone sniffed around outside, possibly her last hope to save her from being brutalized and dumped under a bridge.

She became aware of her breath echoing like a buzz saw through the garage.

The footsteps moved away.

"He'll be back, and next time, he'll check out the garage," Pizza Guy whispered. "We gotta get outta here."

"We?"

He curled his hand around her arm lightly. "It's either me or the brig. And I'll buy your lunch."

"Let me guess. Pizza."

And boy, right now she needed a deep dish with extra cheese. But not with a guy she'd just met, who had danger radiating off him like a scent.

Besides, as much as she liked pizza, she couldn't be bought for a slice of cheese and pepperoni. Not even if he offered to add mushrooms. "Not today, pal. I gotta get home." And somehow return the truck.

They sneaked around to the back utility door. He eased it open, peeked out, then motioned for her to follow him as he leaped onto the open lawn of the backyard.

PJ flew after him, running like the wind toward freedom and the chain-link fence that separated Hoffman's yard from his neighbors. Pizza Guy took it with a vault. PJ tried to finagle the laptop, but it fell from her grip as she wrapped her hands around the bar.

"Leave it!" Pizza Guy said, and without a pause she threw a leg over. But her jumpsuit snagged, the crotch ever so inconveniently hanging around her knees.

"For crying out loud," Pizza Guy growled as he wrestled her off the top. PJ heard ripping as they dropped over to the other side in a tangle.

"Get off me." PJ pushed herself free.

He shook his head and took off.

She pounced to her feet, one step after Pizza Guy, feeling like she might be in familiar territory. At least in familiar company, because she passed a goat that looked at her with a mouthful of feed. It finished chewing, then let out a greeting.

"Try the hostas," she hollered as she ran by.

Oh, lucky her, it followed.

"Help!"

Laughter in her wake made her turn long enough to glimpse Pizza Guy doubled over, having lost his step.

Good grief. So much for their escape. Hopefully Mrs. Murphy wasn't watching her beloved Billie chase the service-people through the yard.

PJ reached the second fence and didn't care in the least that she ripped out the backside of the jumpsuit. She landed with another whump while the goat shoved his nose between the chain links, mawing. Good thing Billie filled up on Ernie's tulips or tomatoes or whatever, or she'd be goat fodder by now.

Pizza Guy landed beside her. "You have a fan club." He held out his hand to pull her up.

She swatted it away. "It's not funny. She could have eaten me."

"Oh yeah, goats are known predators. Right up there with mountain lions and wildebeests."

She turned to head back to the lawn truck. "I don't think wildebeests are pred—"

Pizza Guy snagged her arm. "He's already got the truck under surveillance. C'mon, I'm parked over here."

PJ pulled out of his grip. "I'm not going with you," she hissed. "For all I know, you murdered poor Mr. Hoffman and I'm your next victim."

He gave her a look. "If I were going to kill you, wouldn't I have done it in the garage and left you there to bloat?"

"That's nice. Way to lodge that image into my brain to terrify me in the middle of the night."

"I'm just saying, think about it. If I wanted to hurt you, I could have."

This time, all the tease had vanished from his face. And just like that, PJ believed him.

"Let's go," he said, as if the matter was settled.

She still wasn't going to let him tempt her with pizza like a little girl being offered candy. But she did follow his path, angling toward the front of the house and nearly running over him when he stopped to peer past the edge of Murphy's brick house and survey the neighborhood. She leaned over his shoulder. Nope, Boone hadn't left. He stood with his back to them on the front lawn, staring at the lawn truck.

"Still want to stick around? Or maybe introduce yourself to your cop friend over there?"

"No pizza, just a ride home, and for your information, I know tae kwon do."

"I'm shaking in my boots."

His white VW Rabbit was parked in the next driveway, still running. Speech left her as she glanced—obviously now fully committed to the furtive look—at Boone, then sprinted toward the hatchback, got in, and scrunched way, way down.

Pizza Guy sauntered over and adjusted his hat. PJ watched, her mouth unattractively gaping, as he stopped and lifted his hand in greeting. To Boone, of course.

Then he got in, backed up, and they passed the lawn truck as they pulled out of Hoffman's neighborhood.

PJ sat up, adjusting her cap. "This car doesn't smell in the least like pizza. Someone's living a lie here, and it's not me."

Well, not *only* her.

Pizza Guy looked at her with eyes that seemed too full of mischief.

What was her problem that she just couldn't escape trouble?

✳ ✳ ✳

"Are you sure you don't want pizza?"

"Just drive." PJ sat in Pizza Guy's car, trying not to get hit by the green fuzzy dice dangling from his rearview mirror, wondering what kind of guy had a Hawaiian girl deodorizer glued to his dash.

They wove through old neighborhoods with overgrown evergreens, stately oaks, old Colonials, and newer split-levels. She silently named houses, remembered parties, cataloged changes. "Are you sure you're not going to kill me and ditch my body somewhere?"

"Pretty sure."

Funny. She wrestled out of the ripped jumpsuit while Pizza Guy hummed and tapped his steering wheel as if they hadn't just raced a carnivorous goat and escaped incarceration. He touched the brakes just slightly as they passed Hal's. "Last chance."

"I have a fish at home I have to take care of." She smiled at him. Two could play the cryptic game.

They curved toward Chapel Hills. "So, I don't suppose you're going to tell me what you found on Hoffman's computer."

"Nope." She pointed toward her neighborhood when the road veered to the left, but he'd already turned that direction. For the first time, she realized he seemed to know where he was going.

"Who are you?" PJ said very slowly, trying to layer in threat to her voice.

He turned again, another road toward her house. "I'm Jack's cousin."

Her cousins would line up for a free peek to watch her burn at the stake. But this cousin cared enough to keep an eye out for possible felonies while delivering—or at least pretending to deliver—Italian pies?

"Do you have a name, Jack's cousin?"

"Jeremy. Kane. And you are . . . ?"

"PJ Sugar." She studied him, the way he gripped the wheel, those strong arms, his dark, whisker-stubbled jaw, now tight, and his dark eyes. There was more to this guy than just a by-the-hour deliveryman. "Do you deliver pizzas to this area?"

"Sometimes."

"Are you stalking me?"

He glanced at her, and although she expected defense, she could only peg his look as . . . concern? "What are you, a PI?"

Maybe. "No. Just seeing how convenient it was that you were outside Hoffman's house. What were you doing there?"

"Delivering pizzas?"

"Try again."

"Saving your life?"

She let out a harsh laugh. "Hardly."

"Listen, the truth is, I saw you sneak into Hoffman's house and was about to follow when I spied your cop friend pull up and thought I should warn you. So I snuck into the garage."

There was something in his easy telling of the story she didn't believe, but she couldn't seem to touch her finger to it.

He glanced at her. "Well?"

"Well what?"

"What was on Hoffman's computer?"

"Why should I tell you?"

One side of his mouth lifted up. "You know, you might even pull this thing off."

She eyed him. "What thing?"

"Proving Jack's innocence. That's what you're about, isn't it?" He gave her a look that said, *Don't bother trying to lie.* "Jack and I grew up together after my mom took off, and I know him. He's not a murderer. So . . . whatcha say? Can we work together? share information?"

She wanted to trust Jeremy. And not because of his smile or the fact that he had a sort of dangerous charisma. But because he too wanted to help Jack. Because although he might be just a pizza guy (and she doubted that greatly), he thought he could make a difference in the world, or at least in Jack and Trudi's life.

She narrowed her eyes at him. "You first. Who would want to kill Ernie?"

"I don't know, but Jack told me that Ernie had been doing some investing for him."

Okay, so maybe he was for real. "Have you ever heard of a numismatist? It's a coin guy. I think Hoffman collected or traded coins online. He had an entire bookshelf of reference books on the topic and recently sold a coin minted in the time of Nero."

Jeremy raised an eyebrow, as if impressed with her sleuthing. "I didn't know coins like that were around."

"And there's more. According to Denise, Ernie's daughter-in-law, the guy was broke. But he still hung out at the club and played golf with his cronies. I heard one of them say how he'll miss Ernie's art expertise."

Oops. That was a lot of information to just hand out to the pizza delivery guy. Even if he was Jack's cousin.

"Just how much digging have you done?"

"Some. This is my house."

He pulled up slowly, keeping his hands on the wheel. "And look at that. I didn't try to murder you once."

"Good thing for you," she said, but her gaze was on Anders the lawn guy, sitting on her front steps, a cell phone to his ear. He held his gloves in his hand, tapping them on his knee.

"Last chance on the pizza."

For a second, she gave it a serious debate. But she was done running from trouble. Even when she stirred it up. "No, I gotta handle this." She opened the door. "Thanks for the ride, Jeremy."

"See you round, partner."

Wait—but he was already pulling away.

She advanced up the walk.

Anders regarded her with cool eyes. "Where's my truck?"

"I can explain."

"I called the police."

She made a face. "You did say I could move it. . . ."

He narrowed his eyes at her.

Right. "Okay. I'm sorry. I know I shouldn't have taken it, and if you did call the police, I wouldn't blame you. But I didn't hurt it. I promise. And I'll take you to it." She handed over the jumpsuit. "However, I think I lost your hat."

He stood, took the jumpsuit. "Is this a joke?"

Oh, how she wanted to laugh. But alas, no. She hadn't meant to commit a felony. Why didn't she think beyond her so-called great ideas to the disastrous outcome?

"I'm really sorry."

Anders said nothing as he brushed past her toward her car.

She dearly hoped Boone wasn't waiting for her at Hoffman's.

Sadly, not only Boone but a couple of cruisers had joined the ponderings in Hoffman's front lawn. PJ pulled up at the mouth of the street, surveying the activity. "Maybe I'll let you off here."

Anders gave her a dark look.

"Listen, what if I told you that I'm not a thief? that I am trying to keep an innocent man out of jail, and borrowing your truck was really a good deed?"

His expression didn't change.

"And that Connie will have a big tip for you next time because of your gracious lending of your vehicle to help humanity?"

He pursed his lips and shook his head. But his expression softened. "You'd better get out of here." Then miraculously he winked. "See you in two weeks."

As she drove away, she saw Boone in the rearview mirror as he turned to watch her retreating Bug.

Chapter **THIRTEEN**

PJ had sorely misjudged Baba Vera. Not only did she return to find Vera in the backyard with Davy replanting gladiolas, but she was teaching him Russian and he was laughing.

She watched, feeling a strange curl of affection for Vera as the older woman guided Davy's hands, helping him grip the gladiola bulb and put it in the ground, then pat the dirt around it.

When Vera glanced up, PJ gave her a smile, a single nod.

Yes, she could watch the fish.

Boris had commandeered Connie's computer, so PJ grabbed her keys and headed for the library.

Housed next to a coffee shop in a shiny, modern concrete building with sleek lines, square pillars, and a fountain spilling over what looked like building blocks, the library contained a hush of quiet contemplation that made PJ feel like a felon, her mind too easily venturing back to the days behind the reference section, pressing both hands over her mouth to stop laughter from spilling out. Boone had been notorious for landing them both in detention, thanks to his stupid attempts at humor.

She took a chair in the computer section and began to google Nero and his madness.

"They're excavating an ancient palace in Italy that belonged to crazy Nero," said a voice in her ear, and she nearly flew out of her skin.

She turned, and there was the guy she couldn't seem to shake. Her new *partner*.

"They're keeping the coins in a museum in Venice."

"You *are* stalking me."

"Hey, I was here first. I've been here for an hour, at least."

"I think I would have noticed you when I came in." Oops, that was the wrong thing to say.

"Really," Jeremy said.

"I never agreed to help you."

"Yes you did. Our mutual sharing of information constitutes a tacit verbal agreement."

"Are you a lawyer now? I knew you didn't deliver pizzas."

"That's not a very nice thing to say," he said, pulling up a chair.

"Hey, I'm working here," PJ said, clicking on a link.

"Me too." Jeremy rolled his chair over to the neighboring computer and googled the site. "Did you know that ten years ago, a collection of recently excavated Nero-minted coins was stolen en route to Venice? Their collected value was a cool million."

"Listen, you do your sleuthing; I'll do mine."

He leaned back, his smile fading. "I really am on your side."

She had to admit he did seem genuine. "Fine. But don't lean over my shoulder."

Jeremy apparently shared the same lack of reverence for the posted quiet signs as Boone had, because in between surfing for information on ancient coins, he unearthed imperative information about how to dismantle a nuclear bomb, how to fly a Nighthawk, and how to make the best pizza.

PJ, meanwhile, rabbit-trailed down a conspiracy theory site. "The ancient coin world reads like a 007 novel. Here's a conspiracy site with bad guys named 'the Turk' and 'Dragonov.'" She pointed to the screen. "Just the look of the site has my skin crawling, let alone the stories. The credits say the designer's anonymous. Figures. This story should be made into a Robert Ludlum novel. According to this guy, a Bond-type from Scotland Yard went undercover a number of years ago as a black-market dealer and helped put a smuggler by the name of Rembrandt into prison—a French prison, no less."

Jeremy nodded.

"Rembrandt's been in prison for about eight years, and recently they convicted him for ten more years for attempted murder on the agent, whom they call the Doc. Apparently, even behind bars, a guy can hire an assassin, and said assassin botched the job."

"That's gotta hurt the old résumé."

"They say the Doc's in hiding. Hasn't been seen for years. But rumors are that the hit is still out, with a new assassin on the job. More than that, the Nero coins were never recovered."

"Aha! Your fast brain is thinking that Ernie is the Doc." Jeremy angled his head at her.

"Yes! I mean, what if, right under our noses, Ernie Hoffman was living a double life? By day, history teacher handing out Cs and chasing potheads through the halls . . . by weekend, he's the Doc, master sleuth, hunting down diabolical international thieves—"

Uh-oh. By the look on his face, clearly she'd misread his statement as agreement.

"I think you're the one living the double, diabolical life." Jeremy quirked one of his dark eyebrows. "Maybe *you're* the Doc."

PJ rubbed her hands together and manufactured her sinister look. "Maybe I'm the assassin, *heh heh heh.*"

He rolled his eyes. "I think you need a coffee."

She bit back a retort. But wow, she suddenly didn't want to look the fool in front of him. Perhaps she did need coffee. "You buying, Pizza Guy?"

"Coffee? For you, a grande double-shot macchiato. I'll even throw in a biscotti on the side."

He followed her out of the library to the adjoining coffee shop. She took a seat in one of the leather chairs near the fireplace while he ordered, letting the conspiracy theories run through her mind.

Yes, in the light of day, maybe she did need a strong dose of caffeine clarity.

"Miss me?" Jeremy said, returning.

PJ answered with an exaggerated eye roll.

"Here's your coffee." He repositioned next to her and handed her her order—a latte with a shot of vanilla and hazelnut.

"Where's my biscotti?"

"Sorry, they're clean out. But I got you a cookie." He handed over a chocolate chip cookie and she had no words.

"So, I think it's time to tell me the truth."

She nearly spit out her coffee, coughed, wiped her mouth. "The truth?"

"Yeah. About your name. Your real name. The one that shortens to *P* and *J*."

For a long moment she simply stared at him. She hated her full name. Always had, always would. It just didn't seem to grasp her . . . essence, for lack of a better term, an argument she'd been making with her parents since around the age of three. Since then, her father had indulged her, calling her PJ. She'd had it officially changed on her eighteenth birthday, two months before her infamous escape, and wild, starving goats couldn't chase it out of her.

"Peanut Butter and Jelly," she offered.

He narrowed his eyes. "Not telling?"

"Not in this lifetime. Especially to a pizza guy without pizza."

"I bought you coffee. *And* a cookie."

"It'll take a lot more than a grande latte to coax that secret out of me."

"What if I guess? Will you tell me?"

"Maybe."

"Patty Jane."

"Nope."

"Patricia James."

"That's the same as Patty."

"I just got chased by a goat. I'm not thinking clearly. How about Petunia Joyce?"

"Please."

"Penelope."

She shook her head.

"Portia, Paula, Polly, Pearl."

"Nada, nil, nyet." She couldn't stop her grin, and he matched it.

"Princess . . . Jacqueline."

"I like the Princess part."

He pursed his lips, shaking his head. "I'll get it, you know."

That's what she was starting to fear.

He'd ordered a cookie too and now broke it into pieces before eating them slowly. Up close and in good light, PJ saw that he had a small scar above his left eye. On his right arm, as his sleeve stretched up his shoulder, she made out a tattoo of what looked like some kind of Celtic symbol.

Jeremy chased his cookie with a sip of coffee. "Were you a PI in a former life or something?"

If only. "No. I'm just . . . well, I have a few hidden talents."

He wore a question on his face.

"Don't jump to any conclusions. I just have rather a long and varied résumé."

"Oh. Is lawn care on that list?"

Heat pressed her face. "No."

"How about librarian?"

"Used-book store clerk count?"

He nodded slowly, as if digesting that tidbit. "How long is that résumé?"

"Let's see. I worked for the San Diego Zoo feeding the animals."

"Seriously?"

"And I worked as a wrangler for a dude ranch."

"No, you didn't."

"I was a hot dog vendor, a pool lifeguard, a house painter, a locksmith's apprentice, a UPS girl. I made cotton candy and I worked as a clown, making balloon animals—mainly wiener dogs, but I was also really great at pirate hats. I've worked as a makeup assistant, learned how to do nails, and for two very exciting years, I worked as a stunt girl."

Jeremy had leaned back, his arms folded across his chest, his face stuck in a permanently openmouthed expression. PJ held up her hands, as if saying, *What's a gal to do?*

"You were not a stunt girl."

"Was. I started out answering the phone, and then they sent me to stunt school—"

"There's a stunt school?"

"Yes—it's a two-week intensive course. By the end of the year I was jumping off tall buildings, doing some fight scenes and even some high-speed driving."

"Like Supergirl."

PJ wrinkled her nose at him. "Yep, just like. That's me. Super. Girl."

He nodded, a terrible grin on his face. "I think you'd look really great in tights and a cape."

"Wow, thanks. I do have Superman pants."

"I should have guessed. Better than Lawn Girl, although that was an okay look."

"Please stop."

"Okay." He leaned forward, dark eyes on her. "So why so many jobs?"

PJ rubbed her arms, wondering if she could start the fireplace. "I was . . . well, I left home the night of graduation and never really found my groove."

Jeremy said nothing, his smile slowly dimming.

"What?"

"That's the shortest backstory for the longest résumé I've ever heard." He considered her for a moment. "I would love to spend about two weeks figuring out exactly what makes a pretty lady want to feed animals at the San Diego Zoo."

Pretty lady. Yes, she heard that. "I like gorillas. And new experiences. And I adapt well to . . . challenging situations."

He said nothing.

"Maybe I just wanted to see what else there was out there. I didn't want to forever be defined as a . . . stunt girl. Or a house painter. There was just so much more—"

"Of you."

She looked up. "I was going to say of life, but . . ." She lifted a shoulder. "Maybe I didn't want that to be all I was."

"I don't think you'll ever have that problem, Princess."

She looked away. "I take it back—I don't think you should call me that. Believe me, I'm not a princess."

He said nothing for a long time. Finally, "Okay, for now I'll buy your explanation. But no promises on the Princess."

She gave him a tight smile. "What about you, Pizza Guy, Jeremy Kane. Why aren't there any pizzas in the back of your car?"

"I delivered them all."

"Right. Have you always been a pizza guy?"

"I've done a few other things. Never found—how did you put it?—my groove."

"So pizza delivery is—"

"A short-term gig." He finished off his coffee. "Until I find what I'm looking for."

"Which is?"

He crumpled up the napkin, put it inside the cup, and peered at her with dark, even eyes. "I'll know it when I see it."

Oh.

"I should get home. I left my nephew with his Russian babushka, and you never know when she might start cooking pancakes."

"I don't follow," Jeremy said as he stood.

"Never mind. Thanks for the coffee."

He stuck his hands in his pockets. "It's been enlightening . . . Princess."

She glowered at him, not sure how she felt about the smile she hid as she left the shop.

PJ drove back to Connie's and was taking it as a good sign that the house still stood when she spotted the mailman pulling up. She hiked across the grass to the mailbox. "Thanks, Colin."

"You in some sort of trouble?"

He motioned with a nod of his head up the street.

Boone. Sitting in an unmarked car. Even from here, she could see his arms folded across his chest, lying in wait like a cheetah. The guy couldn't change his spots.

"Yeah." She nodded at Colin as he pulled away.

Boone got out and slammed the door. It echoed down the street. "PJ Sugar, you get back here."

She didn't stop her beeline for the house. "Go away, Boone. Don't you have a job to do?"

"I'm on the job."

Of course he was. Still, she didn't slow, and he caught up to her at the door just before she slammed it in his face.

"Davy?"

Boone grabbed her arm, turning her.

"Ow, Boone, knock it off." She twisted out of his grip and took a step back.

His blue eyes flashed. His shirt looked rumpled and sweaty, as if he'd been parked out front, staking out her house, for hours . . . perhaps all afternoon. His voice grated out between nearly clenched teeth. "PJ, did you steal a lawn truck?"

Steal was such a strong word. She'd . . . *moved* it . . . with permission, no less. "Did someone say it was stolen?"

"We found it. The guy said he'd forgotten where he parked it."

Good old Anders. Tips galore in his future.

Boone narrowed his eyes and leaned down, an inch from her face. She narrowed *her* eyes, lifted her chin.

"I've been at the library all afternoon," she said, smiling sweetly. She hollered again over her shoulder. "Davy!"

Footsteps pounded through the house. "Auntie PJ!"

She caught him as he flung himself into her arms; emotion exploded in her chest. He wrapped his legs around her waist and she squeezed tight, ignoring Boone. "Did you have a good day with Baba Vera?"

"We had fun! We planted flowers and played in the sand-box. And I petted the goat."

Oh no, they still had the goat.

"Goat?" Boone echoed, as if he might be an extension of her thoughts.

She put Davy down. "I'll be right out, pal. We'll run through the sprinkler."

He charged off to his magnificent backyard while PJ turned back to Boone. "Unless you have something to accuse me of, you'd better leave. Never know when my mother might show up." She let the bad girl inside have her smile.

His face twitched, but apparently he had no intention of letting her mother—or the threat of her mother—drive him off the scent. "I know you took the truck, PJ. And I know you were at Hoffman's house. And if I have to, I'll prove it. But for now, please, please, listen to me." His expression softened, and for a moment, guilt nudged away her smirk. "Stay away from this investigation."

"You still believe Jack killed Hoffman?"

He went silent, and in those blue eyes, she thought she saw exasperation.

"Why? Just last night you said that you believed me."

"I said that I would look into things."

"Why are you trying so hard to make Jack the killer?"

Boone shook his head. "Oh, PJ, I'm not trying to make him the killer." He sighed, turning away from her.

PJ studied his broad back, the way his shoulders had squared off, filled out.

"You remember when I beat up Gavin Barrett in tenth grade?"

"I remember you were really angry. You were covered in blood and it scared me."

"Do you know why we fought?"

She shook her head.

"Because he said that my mother slept around. That I was

just the son of the town tramp." His voice hit gravel as he spoke, and he didn't look at her.

"Boone—"

"No, PJ. You're not stupid. You know who my mother was, what she did every day."

PJ wanted to erase it all—the tirades that suddenly filled her ears, the smell of his mother, a martini in her hand, sloppy, her voice too bright as PJ asked for Boone at the door. "Yes."

"But you don't know the truth." He turned and met her eyes, and she saw the pain in his. "She married my dad because she was pregnant, and my dad was just stupid enough to love her, even if he didn't know if . . . the baby was his. He saw her money and her status, and Grandpa got him a job at the country club. But everyone knew. Ask your mom; she knew. She knew that Gavin was right. I don't belong with you . . . and I knew that from the very beginning."

"That's not—"

He raised a hand to silence her. "I have a lot more to prove in this town than you do, PJ. You might have been labeled a troublemaker, but I was labeled trash."

He let his breath run out of his lungs and stepped toward her, his hand touching her cheek, running down to her chin, lifting it. She recognized suddenly the boy she'd known—part football hero, part bad boy, desperate to find acceptance.

No wonder he hadn't stood up for her on prom night in front of the burning country club. He couldn't even stand up for himself.

"Boone, I never, ever thought you were trash."

He smiled, but it didn't reach his eyes. "No. You didn't, did you?" His hand slid down, ran a lazy finger around her tattoo. "I need to prove that I can protect this town. That I can do this job."

"Then find the real killer," PJ said softly, cupping her hand over his on her shoulder. "Be that guy who doesn't believe the worst in people."

He studied her. Finally his grim look morphed into that slow, one-sided smile. "Okay, I'll tell you what. I have the night shift on Friday. You go out with me Friday for an early supper and maybe I'll listen to your list of suspects and motives."

PJ wrinkled her nose at him. "Oh, you're smooth, aren't you?"

"You used to like that."

Maybe she still did. "What if my mother finds out?"

He tugged on one red lock of hair. "I promise to behave myself."

For Jack and Trudi's sake, she'd already buttered a woman's legs, humiliated herself on a golf course, and nearly been butted by a goat. She could probably sacrifice and spend a few hours with Boone. In the daylight. Only.

"All right. Friday, around three. But I have to be back by Davy's bedtime, okay?"

Boone grinned and her knees turned the appropriate texture of blubber. "See you Friday, Peej. And, please, try and stay out of trouble this week."

✳ ✳ ✳

"I think that's the last of it." Elizabeth handed PJ the roll of packing tape.

PJ took it and unrolled it over the last of the boxes, this one full of clothes, from her prom dress to her graduation gown.

"Are you sure you don't want to keep more of your old clothes?" her mother said, pulling out the vacuum cleaner from the hallway. "It seems that you're giving so many of them away."

"Where am I going to keep them?" PJ hauled the box into the hall, stacked it on three others. Besides, all this rummaging through and purging the past over the last two-plus days helped take her mind off crazy scenarios, like Tucker Hoffman breaking his father's neck in a fit of rage and ransacking his house or Ben Murphy appearing on Ernie's doorstep, as if to borrow sugar, and leaving his neighbor lying among the scattered mail. Did he toss the house in a desperate search for a measuring cup? Doubtful.

She was bright enough to see the holes in both those theories.

A good look at the facts pointed straight at Jack.

She was starting to hope that her crazy coin-conspiracy plot might be on target. Was it so far-fetched to think that Ernie lived a double life? He did know his history—and what was with those pictures of him in ancient locations? More than that, he'd been killed up close, his neck broken, as if by a professional. But did she really want to believe an assassin was running loose around Kellogg? Like Boone had suggested, if Jack didn't kill Ernie, then it could be that a killer still lurked somewhere in the city limits.

Much easier to reminisce about her old homecoming dress or the day she won the drama trophy.

Probably she could still win said trophy today.

"How's Davy doing?" her mother asked, now spritzing the window with ammonia, wiping it off with a paper towel.

PJ didn't look at her—couldn't. Not with the words *I got him kicked out of Fellows* sitting against her windpipe. She'd left him—happily, it seemed—with Baba Vera and the goat.

She still had time to plead her case with the director. Connie wasn't due back for a few more days.

"I'm no longer bruised, if that's what you're asking."

Elizabeth scrubbed the window until it squeaked. "Poor child. Never understood that it wasn't his fault his daddy died. He keeps walking around expecting people to abandon him."

PJ turned, just to confirm it was her mother speaking. Yep, she stood there in a pool of sunlight on the pink carpet, in her cleaning clothes—a pair of designer jeans, an embroidered shirt, pearls at her neck, and her hair up in a scarf.

"You can handle it, PJ. He's little. Just love him the way he is, and he'll come around."

"Love him the way he . . ." What about being a Sugar? toeing the line?

PJ wandered down the hall looking at the assembled pictures, a montage of their family before and after her father passed away. She peered at one of all four of them in front of a brown station wagon. She had wild, curly blonde hair—her perm days—and wore her shirt with the collar up, sitting on the hood of the car, "peacing" the camera. Connie, more sober-minded with her glasses and dark hair, her long shorts and button shirt, stood with her arms folded.

PJ ran a finger over her father's face. She could easily conjure up his hearty laugh when a joke found the right spot. "I miss Dad."

"Yes, well, he was a good man." Elizabeth set the window spray on the boxes and came over to stand beside her. "I remember how you were right after he died. So angry at the whole world. No one could talk to you. Sixteen is such a terrible age to lose a father. You were just trying to figure out how to sort out the voices around you, and you needed his. You wouldn't listen to mine, so I would creep into your room at night after you'd fallen asleep and tell you how much he loved you, how he missed you too. I don't know if you ever heard it, but I liked to think it helped."

"Subliminal parenting, huh?"

Elizabeth smoothed her pants. "Well, I hoped somewhere in there you'd hear the truth." She patted PJ's shoulder, then moved back to the bedroom and flicked on the vacuum. Its hum filled the hall.

PJ wasn't sure she'd ever heard the truth, but as she stared after her mother, she wasn't sure if she wanted to hear it either.

Heading downstairs, she took a right and opened her father's office door.

Her mother had clearly taken over. Strange, because in the two years PJ had lived here after that night when her father stumbled down the stairs, holding his chest, dying of a heart attack right before his family's eyes, Elizabeth had never touched the room.

Now, although it still bore the masculinity in the dark-paneled walls, the slatted venetian blinds, the mahogany desk, the awards and investment books on the shelves, her mother had also added a basket of note cards and a pile of novels next to the leather cigar chair. A knitted afghan wadded up on the chair suggested she sat here often.

Even her dad's smell, Old Spice and something she'd labeled as power, seemed diminished, filled instead with her mother's Chanel, the fragrance of culture.

PJ wasn't sure why she'd come in here. Maybe just to breathe in his presence one more time.

She turned to go and was startled by the two eleven-by-seventeen photos framed and hung on the wall opposite the chair.

The first showed Connie in her white angora sweater, leaning into the camera, her eyes soft, her lips red, looking elegant and adult.

PJ had hated that day. She'd arrived armed with her own outfit—her letter jacket. Just because PJ had lettered in football didn't mean that she didn't deserve it. She'd gone to every game and kept those stats clean and neat.

And of course, her sophomore year, football kept her close to Boone. Perhaps Elizabeth knew that too, because it seemed her mother had hated the jacket from the moment her father gave it to her on her sixteenth birthday.

"I'll allow two pictures, PJ. Two." Elizabeth stood out in the hall for them.

Elizabeth had insisted she take her "real" senior photos in pink angora. She had put the hideous angora picture in the paper, on the invitations, displayed it at their graduation party.

But here on the wall, instead of the pink sweater that cast PJ's skin red and blotchy, made her look comical, with her blonde hair long and flowy like she should be some sort of debutante, was the other photo of PJ, hands tucked into the pockets of her letter jacket, eyes sparkling, not a hint of demureness on her face, laughing into the camera.

"I liked that one better," her mother said from the doorway.

PJ waited for something to qualify her statement—maybe, *"Besides, the picture is in the office. No one can see it but me."*

But her mother just gave a nod. "I'm glad I told your father to buy that jacket. It's the real you."

PJ froze, replaying the words for herself. "What?"

But Elizabeth had turned away, leaving PJ to stand there alone.

She didn't know how her mother expected her to hear some subliminal voice of truth when she couldn't even figure out what she was saying out loud.

Chapter FOURTEEN

Boone motored up around three thirty in his restored Mustang, a Nirvana song blaring on the radio. Yanking PJ back in time to rev up their past.

Regretting that she'd thrown her floral sundress in the thrift store pile back in Florida, PJ had managed to dig out a mint green, scoop neck dress with bell sleeves and a pair of pink flip-flops. She scored a long, appreciative look from the man leaning against his red convertible, arms clasped over his chest.

"Where's David?" Boone asked.

"I dropped him off at my mother's."

"Oh, that's great."

"Calm down. Behave yourself and you'll come out unscathed."

"I think it's too late for that." He opened the door for her.

She put a hand on his arm. "She doesn't know. Just thinks

I have some errands to do. And for now, that's just fine." After yesterday's precarious conversation, she didn't know what to tell her mother.

Or what her mother might be trying to tell her.

He said nothing as he closed the door behind her and climbed into the front seat.

They stopped by Sunsets for an early supper. PJ spent the first hour lawyering for Jack's innocence, including hints at her conspiracy theory, and the possibility of an assassin right here in Kellogg, trying to hunt down the real Doc who had stolen the Nero coins from Rembrandt and finish the job.

It could happen, right?

Boone spent most of her tirade trying to balance the salt-shaker on its edge in a mound of salt.

But when they stepped outside into the humid air, he stayed silent, his only hint that she'd even been talking to flesh and blood being the way he reached down and wove his fingers through hers.

She'd never forgotten the feel of his hands—smooth, large, strong—holding hers. She dug her bare toes into the warm sand as they strolled the beach, then the boardwalk to where he'd parked his Mustang. Screams of joy and splashing lifted from the melee on the beach, and PJ could feel the pull toward yesterday.

Whatever magic Boone wielded, it still worked.

"I have something you'll like," he said, opening the door for her. He'd taken down the top.

PJ leaned back, closing her eyes, letting the sun have her face. "I can't believe you still have this old thing." How many times had she found him on a Saturday morning, greasy to his ears, the car jacked up, parts littering his parents' garage? Good thing he'd also had his motorcycle. "It spent more time in pieces and in the shop than we did driving around in it."

"She still has her clinks. Just put a new head gasket on a few weekends ago. And replaced the timing belt for the third time last year. Now I only drive her during the summers."

"Sounds like a lot of trouble for a car you don't get much enjoyment out of."

Boone gave a laugh that sounded more like a grunt. "Who says I don't get enjoyment out of her? I love her. Quirks and all. I'd never give up on this baby." He patted the dashboard. "No matter how many times she leaves me stranded on the side of road."

They pulled out of town, passing the high school and the local nursery stacked high at the entrance with pallets of bagged manure.

"Where are we going?"

"Just hold on, Sugar. We'll get there."

PJ smiled into the wind.

They turned in to the old drive-in, now gated with a long chain-link fence. A shiny security box sentried the door, and Boone keyed in a number.

"Where are we?"

Boone waited as the gate opened and then drove through. The gate closed behind them.

"Please tell me this isn't a prison or something." A shot rang out, and PJ jumped. "Boone!"

"Take it easy, PJ. They've turned the drive-in into a shooting range. Wanna learn how to shoot a gun?"

"A gun? I mean, I . . . maybe. I don't know what my stand is on guns."

"My stand is that they are weapons and shouldn't be on the streets. But used in a controlled environment like a shooting range, it's a fun sport."

PJ's stunt career had started with jumping from buildings, riding wild horses, rolling cars, and shooting blanks. It ended when the company she worked for wanted to set her afire.

She had history with fire.

However, the shooting fascination had stayed with her.

Another shot rang out, a pop that echoed against the far-off oak and poplar and a green fence that ringed the outer reaches of the forty-some-acre area. "Are we going to hit anyone?"

"I certainly hope not." Boone parked next to the only other car—a red Geo—and climbed out, retrieving what looked like a briefcase from the backseat. He stopped. "Maybe I should rethink this. . . . You are in that pretty dress. . . ."

"Just show me where to suit up, 007."

The old snack stand and picnic area had been revamped with shooting benches—T-shaped cement tables with seats. A long yellow line ran down the center, about a foot behind the shooting area. PJ walked it, one pink flip-flop over the other, as Boone signed them in and checked out two vests and ear protection. Another man, down toward the end, sat on the bench, sighting his gun toward a target a hundred yards out from the gallery.

"Ever shoot a gun?" Boone plunked down the equipment.

"Not one with real bullets."

He opened his briefcase. Nestled inside a grey cutout foam pillow lay a deadly arsenal—three very lethal-looking shiny guns. He picked up a small black one and handed it to her. Heavier than she expected, the power in its weight jolted her.

"It's a .22 Ruger. And this one is a Springfield P9, CZ-75." He pointed to a silver gun, worked it out of its nest, and pulled back the barrel. It rebounded into place. "It's called a double action, single action."

Boone seemed to be morphing before her eyes. His command of his weapons, his steady, low voice. The way his hands ran over the guns, knowing each part, an expert. This wasn't the same reckless Boone who lived to terrify her as he gunned his motorcycle. This was a different Boone. A Boone a girl might be able to trust.

He eased the .22 from her hands and traded it for a lighter gun. "This is a .40 cal handgun called a Glock."

She crouched in a cop show position, and Boone laughed. "It's not loaded."

"It's lighter than I imagined." She turned it over. "Where's the safety?"

"It's on the trigger. Don't put your finger on it."

"Oh, ha-ha."

Boone gave her a half grin as he took the gun and loaded in a handful of shells. He chose a stand in the middle, taking one side. She took the other, pulling on her vest.

He handed her the Glock again. "Don't put your bracing hand behind the other one or you're liable to break your thumb when the hammer pulls back. Brace it underneath."

She tried out that hand position, feeling like an action hero or a spy.

"Secure the handle into the web of your hand, as high as possible. That will control the recoil."

Okay, so he really intended for her to learn something here. He moved behind her, slipped her ear protection on, and pulled her close to his chest.

It felt so familiar that PJ relaxed and set her feet.

He reached out and braced his hands on her arms, right above her wrists. Firm. Unmoving. Steady. "Now, sight your target between the notches on the top of the gun, and then squeeze—don't jerk—the trigger."

She inhaled a deep breath, let it out, and squeezed.

The shot surprised her, and if Boone hadn't been holding her arms, she would have jerked back, hot with the adrenaline that surged through her. "I did it!"

"Not bad," Boone said. "I'm seeing a future in law enforcement."

She glanced at him, and he realized his words a second too late. "No, forget I said that. The last thing we need is you in police work."

But he chased his words with a smile.

She shot again. And again. And got better with each shot. Boone reloaded and she nailed her target. Which, she had to admit, was his look of admiration as he finally stood back, past the yellow line, and let her reload and shoot all by herself.

They finished the last set of rounds. As Boone began to pack up, PJ noticed a familiar face. "That's my mailman, Colin."

Or maybe not, because as PJ lifted her hand to wave, he stared at her without reaction. "Maybe he doesn't recognize me."

"Not in that dress," Boone said, snapping shut the briefcase. He raised an eyebrow, rich with suggestion.

"Boone, you promised—"

He held up his hands in surrender. "Your mother has probably got us centered in her opera glasses as we speak."

PJ laughed. "She just doesn't want a repeat performance."

His smile dimmed. He stepped close, running his hand down her bare arm, lighting it on fire. "Neither do I." Then, just like she feared—or hoped, perhaps—he leaned down and touched his lips to hers. Sweetly. So unlike the Boone she'd known that PJ stood there, unable to move, not sure she wanted to.

Maybe they didn't have to live in the past. Perhaps they could find a place, together, in today.

He raised his head, something tender, even unfamiliar, in his eyes. "Now I'm in real trouble, I guess."

"I told you to behave yourself." But her voice shook at the end.

"I have to turn in our equipment." He walked away from her and disappeared into the office while she tried to get her feet back under her.

Boone took her hand again as they walked to the Mustang. He tucked the gun case behind the seat, and PJ leaned back, letting the air cool her as Boone pulled out onto the highway.

"Where are you taking me now?"

"I want to show you something." Boone wore a secret in his expression, reminding her of those days when he'd pick her up after school, take her out to the lake or maybe on a ride on his motorcycle, and they'd end up making out at—

"We're not going to the hidden beach, are we? Boone? *Boone* . . ."

He slowed as he pulled into what had been the entrance to

an old fish market, now replaced with a sign that read Kellogg Park.

"You're kidding. Someone bought this?"

"The town bought it. Decided the kids used it for skinny-dipping way too long."

She didn't follow with any personal reminiscence. "I suppose knowing all the old hangouts works really well for you now as a cop."

"You suppose right."

"You gotta cut kids some slack. Remember, we were just having fun."

"Was it just fun, PJ?" He glanced at her.

She looked away, unsure what to do with this serious Boone.

They pulled into a manicured parking lot that rimmed the lake. Once a dirt lot with a trail leading to a hidden bay, now the place had been groomed and sodded, gracious elms and oaks trapping the shadows in their fragrant, dark leaves, picnic tables spaced wide apart next to dark grills. A family chased a Frisbee, a collie snatching it out of the air. The lake whispered against the shoreline. As Boone turned off the car, she saw a skateboarder push himself along the paved pathway.

"This is incredible."

"Massive, actually. The last of the Kellogg line died a few months ago—Aggie Kellogg—but about six years ago, she decided to unload a good portion of her estate and gave a huge grant to the city to clean up the park."

"Any reason why?" PJ got out of the car as Boone opened her door.

"Local buzz says there's some family secret attached to the

old fish dock, but who knows. We're just glad to have the park."

He took her hand and they strolled into the park, their feet swishing through the grass. A squirrel ran down a tree, stared at them, and darted away.

"Hey, there used to be a trail here from the drive-in, remember?"

He squeezed her hand.

"Isn't that dangerous—to have the shooting range so close?"

"They shoot in the opposite direction from the park. But the city looked at that, yes. There's an ordinance about when people can use the range—not on Sundays and not after dark."

"That's Kellogg for you. Nothing good happens after dark, and don't have too much fun on a Sunday."

"I think that was your mother, Peej."

She laughed. "My mother *is* Kellogg, Boone."

He swung their hands between them. Then he pulled her to a picnic table and sat down on the bench.

The sun hovered over the waters of Kellogg Lake, gilding the wrinkles with golden frost. Overhead, wispy clouds swirled against the canvas of deep blue.

PJ perched on the tabletop. "Pretty."

He took her hand again, traced a vein. "Okay, really now, why did it take you so long to come back?"

She'd known the question lingered out there, known it bothered him, known she owed him the truth. "Because I was afraid I wouldn't fit in. That I'd come back and see the truth—that I never belonged here. That the gap my leaving made was so small it simply closed up, and life went on as if I never existed."

"Listen, George Bailey, the world noticed. I noticed. You left a huge gap."

"Maybe for you—"

"For everyone. Your sister, your mom, the town papers—"

"Boone!"

He laughed. It sounded real and husky and seeped into her bones, warming her through.

"My sister maybe, but not my mom. I think my absence was a relief."

"Are you serious?" His laughter vanished.

"I never fit into her world. Never really was a Sugar. I was never enough to earn her approval. I tried, but it didn't work. So—" she lifted a shoulder—"I gave up."

"And went out with me."

She heard the unspoken words—*the town trash*—in his tone and wanted to cry. She saw him then, how he'd been as a boy, a wildness written in his eyes that seemed intoxicating. Now she saw him as he'd truly been—his own saboteur. Maybe he did have as much to prove. Maybe he too was a returning prodigal.

"Oh, I think I was trouble long before I met you. You just brought out the, uh, best in me," PJ said softly.

He pressed her hand to his, measuring it, then reached up and touched her hair again. "I just can't get used to it red. I always thought you'd have this long blonde hair—I loved it that way."

He met her eyes and then let his gaze trace her face, as if cataloging the changes. It finally landed on her mouth, and his hand slipped around her neck as he leaned close.

Her breath caught. "Boone—"

Her tone must have stopped him. He jerked back, frowning. "What's the matter?"

"There's a lot more than that that's changed." She curled her hand around his wrist, drawing his hand from behind her neck. "It's . . . I'm . . . Okay, Boone, listen. Just so we're straight. I'm not going to sleep with you. Or anyone else."

"Good grief, PJ, what kind of guy do you think I am?"

"Maybe I'm jumping to conclusions, but the last time we were out on a date . . ." She ended with a shrug that left room for memory.

He nodded slowly, looking away. "Okay, I might have that someplace in the back of my mind. But . . . I never forgot you. And seeing you brings it all back."

He caught her eyes with his, everything right there for her to see. She couldn't breathe. She closed her eyes. *Lord, I need You to give me words.*

"We can't be what we were, Boone." She opened her eyes, saw him still watching her, that same intensity in his blue eyes.

"Could we be something different? start over?"

"I . . . don't know. A lot has changed. I'm a Christian now."

"I go to church too, Sugar." He turned his hand so it meshed with hers.

"I'm not talking about going to church. I'm talking about being a different person—thinking differently and wanting different things than I did before. I'm not the girl I was when I left."

"So maybe we can start over."

She turned his hand over, traced the lines on his palm. "About three years ago in California, I decided I was tired of running and needed . . ." She'd needed so much. Forgiveness. A new beginning. Hope. "I needed someone to believe in me."

He pulled his hand away and rubbed it over his knee as if wiping something off. "And you found it in Jesus?"

"Well . . . yes."

He blew out a long breath. "If you're a Christian, how come you haven't forgiven me?"

She searched for the right words. Becoming a Christian didn't take away the desire to be wanted or the feelings of loneliness that might make a girl do things she shouldn't. It did, however, show her that she wouldn't find that answer in Boone's arms. "I'm working on that; I really am."

He was quiet for a long moment. "What does that mean exactly?"

"I guess what I'm saying is that whatever happens between us, you need to behave. *We* need to behave. I made that pledge when I became a Christian."

"Just tell me the rules, PJ. I can live by them."

The rules. "I'll let you know when I figure them out."

The afternoon had sunk toward the embrace of twilight, the sun low on the horizon.

"I'd better get you home before your mother comes looking for us."

She laughed. "Very funny. I think the last time you said that, we were sitting right here."

"Or something."

Boone stood and held out his hand. She took it, and they drove back to Connie's in silence.

The night was edging in, turning the air cool as they drove up to the house.

"Really, I can't come in?" He spoke into the windshield, as if trying out the words, the boy she'd known who'd been afraid to go home still reflected in his voice.

"Boone—"

Then the boy vanished, and instead, Boone the man turned and braced his hand on her seat, his bronze hair streaked with the fading sun, his glasses low on his nose. "Can't blame a guy for trying."

She got out, closing the door, but he'd already stepped out and was coming around the car. "Boone, really—"

"Just let me walk you to the door." He took her hand. "Unless that's against the rules."

"Not yet."

The shadows gathered on the porch prickled PJ's bare skin. She turned as she reached the door, looked up at Boone.

He hesitated, then leaned down.

A wail lifted from inside the house, sharp, tenebrous.

Boone jerked away from her, eyes wide. "What's that?"

"I don't know."

Again, the keening. It sounded more animal than human. *Animal.*

"Oh no, it's the goat!"

Boone peered into the house. "Goat? I thought I heard David mention that."

"Boris brought home a goat. He's probably eaten the rest of the hostas and has gas. I gotta check on it. I'm sorry."

Boone took a step back, then lifted his hands in surrender. "Babe, I have a shift in an hour. This is where I check out."

"What? Boone, I need you."

His mouth lifted in a half grin. "You have no idea how long I've been waiting to hear that."

"I'm serious. What if the goat is dying or something?"

"Okay, uh . . ." He held up a finger as if giving her a prognosis. "You're not allowed to bury an animal larger than a cat in your backyard. You'll have to take it to the vet." Then he pecked her on the cheek and shot off the porch.

The goat groaned, this time long and baneful.

"Have fun with that." Boone waved as he hopped in his car.

"You're such a hero!" PJ yelled to his retreating taillights.

Chapter *FIFTEEN*

The first time PJ had a pet, it had died in her cupped hands.

The last week of its sorry life, the white hamster spent most of its time racing around her room, PJ on its cute little pink heels while her mother hollered at her to put it back into its cage. So maybe she'd forgotten to feed it. Or water it. Or maybe it was that thirty-story fall from her dresser to the floor. Anyway, she returned home from church one Sunday to discover Fluffy a still ball of fur in the middle of his tube.

She'd tried mini CPR.

Since then, she'd had perish under her care a parrot, two guinea pigs, a turtle, a number of goldfish, and one sick puppy that she'd found shivering and wet on the beach. That one probably wasn't her fault.

She'd discovered a pattern. The larger they were, the better the chance for survival. Only, looking at the goat under the fading summer light, PJ wasn't so sure. Roped to a stake and surrounded by a bed of grass clippings (or maybe that was supper), Dora lay on her side, breathing hard. Her glassy eyes stared lifelessly at PJ, and every once in a while she emitted a *maa* howl that PJ thought just might make her cry.

She'd killed the goat. The gladiolas were gone, as were most of the hostas and Connie's roses. Perhaps, however, the source of Dora's demise could be CSI'ed to the grass—and the chemicals the lawn guy had sprayed on it to keep it green a few days ago. (Which said what for Davy's health as he romped barefoot on it?)

She crept forward, her voice low and soothing, "Nice goat."

Dora blinked. Moaned. PJ assumed a crawl position, aware that she was still wearing her dress, and reached out to pet it. "Good . . . Dora."

Dora's fur was spiny and not at all the softness PJ had anticipated. And her skull was hard, angular. Why would anyone want a goat?

There were probably plenty of goat lovers in the world. She just didn't happen to fit into that category. But she could be called a goat pitier.

The goat groaned again.

"You need help, don't you, honey?" PJ backed away, stood, dusted the grass clippings from her knees, and went inside, fishing out the yellow pages and searching for a twenty-four-hour goat service.

"Kellogg Vets," a cheery voice answered.

"I have a sick goat." Silence on the other end didn't bode well for their future. Kellogg Vets sent her to Large Animal Vets in Monticello. Nope, goats weren't their specialty. How about Animals Inc., specializing in rare and exotic pets?

She landed the answering machine and left a detailed message, pretty sure that if Dora died on her watch, it wouldn't bode well for the newlyweds.

She leaned over and touched her head to the counter, burying it under her arms, stretching out the screaming muscles in her neck.

"Is that some kind of yoga position?"

She looked up at the voice, and her pulse gave a crazy, unreasonable jig. "Jeremy!"

"The door was open—and I heard a funny noise. You okay, partner?"

Besides the fact that he'd nearly spooked her heart clear into North Dakota? Still, he was carrying a pizza in her time of need.

"What are you doing here?"

"I came to talk mystery. And I promised you a pizza." The goat emitted a cry that made Jeremy jump. "Seriously—what is that?"

"A Russian goat."

"You have a Russian goat in your backyard?"

"Don't ask me why. My mother thinks it's some sort of religious blessing for newlyweds." She lowered her voice. "I have to admit, I suspected something out of *The Godfather.*"

Jeremy's voice dropped an octave, added a Sicilian accent. "Never side against the family."

"We shouldn't joke. This is serious, Jeremy. She's sick."

"I'd say so. She sounds like she's dying."

"I was trying to find a vet in town. I don't know what to do."

Jeremy, quick guy that he was, glanced at the yellow pages

open to the veterinarian section, grabbed the book, and started running a finger down the page methodically, as if trying to solve her problems. Not that she particularly needed a guy to solve her problems, but the fact that he was trying to help found fertile soil.

Especially after Boone's fifty-yard dash off the porch.

"Did you try the Kellogg clinic?"

"Yes, and the large animal clinic in Monticello. I had just left a message at the exotic and rare animals clinic when you came in."

"Let's go." He tore the page out of the book, folded it, and crammed it into his pocket.

"Where?"

But he'd already cleared the back door, heading toward Dora. PJ grabbed a piece of pizza—okay, two!—and headed out behind him.

He already held the goat in his arms. "We can put her in my car."

PJ followed Jeremy to the car, eating fast.

Popping the hatch, he settled Dora inside. She barely moved. "Shh, old girl, we'll take care of you." He gave her the smallest of pats before closing the hatch and digging out the address. "The exotic animal clinic is in Farmington. That's over an hour away."

PJ's gaze went to Dora. "I'm not sure she'll last that long." More importantly, how long would the Russians be gone, and what would they do when they discovered the goat absent from her leash?

Would it be bad to hope they would go hunting for her . . . back to the old country?

Oh, PJ, be nice! Baba Vera did watch the fish.

She got into the passenger side. "Step on it."

They cruised through Kellogg and soon hit the highway into Minneapolis. Jeremy seemed to know where he was going.

"Where do you live, anyway?"

"Calhoun area." He tapped his fingers on the wheel to a country station, humming to Keith Urban. Who didn't hum to Keith Urban? But it stirred up a smile. Something about Jeremy just felt easy. Like they were already partners.

They passed an SUV, and she noticed a kid with his face pressed against the window, eyes wide. What? Did she have pizza on her dress?

Oh, wait, they had a goat in the back end. Which had been very quiet for the last ten minutes.

"Drive faster."

Jeremy turned south on Crosstown. "You know, I have some ideas."

"Do you think it's something she ate?"

"Oh, for sure, but I'm talking about Hoffman and the Nero coins. It turns out there's a reward for the coins. About a hundred thousand pounds. Put out by the insurer."

"That's about . . . how much?"

"About two hundred thousand dollars. I got to thinking about Ernie—"

"Do you know who killed him? I've been thinking more and more about his son, Tucker, and the fact that he needed money. Oh! Maybe he knew his father had the coins and wanted to find them—two hundred thousand dollars could sure get someone out of debt fast. So he had motive and opportunity—he was at his father's earlier that morning, and they had a fight. And—" she made a face—"I think he spent time in juvie as a kid."

"You didn't mention that."

"I didn't tell you about Denise and the butter?"

He glanced at her a second before he switched lanes. "I'm afraid you left that one out."

"Oh, well, see . . . Jack has an alibi. Only the lady claims she never made the appointment with him, and then I snuck into the spa, and Denise was there, and she told me all about Tucker and his financial problems, and pointing the finger at Tucker made sense at the time. Now I don't know."

"Who do you think did it?"

"Let's review. Ernie was killed on a Monday in his home. His neck was broken—"

"So someone had to get close to him and take him by surprise."

"Yes, and I went in; the place was destroyed—"

"As if someone might have been searching for something? like Nero coins?"

Aha! "Right."

"And our current list of suspects is . . ."

"Well, Jack of course, because of the money Ernie took from him, and Boone thinks he had means and opportunity."

"I'm impressed. Get that from *Monk*?"

She swatted him. Jeremy grinned.

"Then there's Ben—"

"Ben?"

"The neighbor with the hobby farm, who had motive and probably opportunity, although maybe not means."

"Motive?"

"Long goat story."

"I remember meeting the goat. Enough said."

"Then Tucker is number three. He had motive and probably means and opportunity. . . ."

"So did Tucker know his father had the coins?"

PJ scrolled back through her conversation with Denise. "Not that his wife knew or was saying. And we don't even know if Ernie did have the coins—or at least if the ones he bought at auction were the stolen ones."

"Denise could be protecting her husband."

"Right."

"Anyone else?"

"Uh . . ."

"How did you even find out about the coins?"

"Oh, the guys at the club were talking about it. A banker and three of his cronies. It was the foursome that went out before us, me . . . well, another long story."

"I'm not sure how many of your long stories I can handle before my brain turns into a giant mess of noodles."

"Try being me."

"Thank you, I'll just watch from afar." He gave her a wink.

She looked away, smoothing her dress.

"Okay, I think we need to know who that foursome was. Maybe one of them can give us a lead. Any ideas who they might be?"

PJ closed her eyes, trying to place them. "Not a clue, sorry."

"Then we need to get ahold of the golf list."

"How are we going to do that?"

Jeremy turned onto Cedar and 77, heading past the Mall of America without answering.

"I'm starting to get a bad feeling here."

"Oh, don't worry. Just trust me."

PJ studied him in the dashboard light, the dark eyes, close-cropped curly hair, wide shoulders. Something just didn't fit about the way he maneuvered through the facts, thought outside the box. "Are you really a pizza guy?"

"I brought you pizza, right?" He flashed her a lopsided grin.

Something inside her rose up, waving flags, warning her off. "It better not be illegal. Boone probably has my house staked out."

"Boone's your boyfriend." Jeremy said it more like a fact than a question, but she did hear inquiry in his tone.

"No. Just an old flame."

"No new sparks?"

Oh, there were sparks all right. "The thing is, I'm not the same girl I was when I left town. I've changed."

"Time does that to a person."

Time. Experience. Regret. "Yeah. But I also . . ." Wait. What exactly was she going to say? That she wasn't so much older but different, because she wasn't the person Boone had known? That hopefully every day, God was changing her, making her into a different, better person?

Yeah, right. Jeremy had met her while she was impersonating a lawn girl, sneaking into another man's house. Still, something inside her urged her on.

"I became a Christian three years ago. I guess I don't want to get sucked into old habits."

Jeremy fell silent. Then a slow smile broke across his face. "Really." He said nothing more as they turned off the exit into Farmington.

"I'm going to check on the goat." Unbuckling, she climbed into the back, leaned over the seat.

Oh no.

"Jeremy, we have a problem." She touched the goat to make sure, then recoiled fast and shuddered. "Turn around. We have a death in the family."

✳ ✳ ✳

"I don't know why you're so upset. You are not without options here."

"What makes you think I'm upset?"

From across the orange Formica table, Jeremy held up two fingers, shaking his head sadly. "Two pieces of pie? An Oreo *and* a French silk?"

So she was grieving her way through chocolate. Good thing the pie place stayed open for these emergencies. She kept her voice low, not wanting to alarm the two gray-haired ladies seated across the aisle. "Hey, emotional eating works for me, okay? Why do I have to deny it? So I have hips. I have it on good authority that men like hips. I was just born in the wrong era."

"I like hips. They work well with legs."

"See? Anyway, there are medicinal properties in chocolate, and right now, it's soothing my pain. And confusion." She finished off the Oreo, pulled over the French silk. "If you haven't noticed, there's a dead goat in the back of your car."

Jeremy nursed a cup of coffee, his brown eyes full of humor. "I have two suggestions for you."

"Really?" Her tone brightened, buoyed more by Jeremy's quirky smile than by any real hope of replacing the goat before the Russians discovered their loss and retaliated. "Fine. Option number one." She quirked an eyebrow.

"Take the goat back and tell the Russians that it died. Sorry."

"And find myself in a mini Cold War? Number two, please."

"I need some of that pie." He picked up a fork and stabbed at her plate. She yanked it away, but not before he scored a big chunk.

"That's not a suggestion!"

"So maybe you were just making me hungry. But I do have a suggestion about how to clear Jack."

"I'm listening."

"We need to break into the country club."

Her fork stopped midway to her mouth. If only for a second. "Uh . . . the country club? The *Kellogg* Country Club?"

"Yeah. Didn't you say you played golf there?"

"I . . . might have. But I can't break into the country club. . . . I . . . uh . . ."

"You broke into Hoffman's house." Jeremy took a sip of coffee.

"That was different."

"How?"

Because she wasn't banned for life from Hoffman's house. "The country club and I have a history. Like—"

"Yeah, I heard. You burned it down."

She put down her fork. "Not all the way down. Just the kitchen. And I didn't do it."

"That was then; this is now. You're not going to set any-thing on fire, and I promise, you won't get into trouble."

"What, do you have a get-out-of-jail-free card?" She couldn't finish her pie. *Thanks a lot, Jeremy.* She'd lost her appetite.

He smiled, took another sip of coffee, then pulled her plate over and picked up a fork. "How'd you get into Hoffman's place?"

"I found the key."

He made an *oh* face, and for a moment she was right back in the garage, tasting her fear as his hand closed over her mouth. How had Jeremy so quickly become her partner in crime?

"Hey, I have an idea." He signaled the waitress. "What about that goat in Hoffman's neighbor's yard?"

"Billie."

"The goat is a personal friend?"

"Another long story—"

He raised a hand to stop her.

She reached over and swiped the final bite of pie. "I think you're onto something."

* * *

Friendly lights illuminated the front porch of Ben's rambler, a duplicate of Hoffman's next door, and a recently watered pink geranium in a square planter indicated a loving touch. PJ hoped this boded well for the coming conversation.

Don't panic. Ben hadn't seen her—or at least hadn't recog-nized her—since the wedding. Still, her hand shook slightly as she knocked on the door.

Footsteps lodged her heart in her throat, and by the time the door opened, she could barely breathe.

Ben stood on the threshold in a pair of dress slacks, slippers, and a pullover golf sweater. "Hello?"

"Uh, hello, Mr. Murphy. Remember me, PJ Sugar? I saw you at Connie's wedding?" Was she breathing? She sounded like she was going to pass out.

Ben nodded. Was that a flare of recognition in his eyes? He glanced behind her at the six-foot-one guy who stood close enough to catch her when she went down in a heap.

PIs needed to be tougher than this. "I heard . . . through the grapevine, sorta . . . that you have a goat."

Ben's gaze came back to her, and he nodded warily.

"That you might be willing to . . . sell? give away?"

Ben sighed, then glanced over his shoulder. She knew a furtive look when she saw it, having employed it herself. He stepped out onto the porch, closing the door behind him. "I do have a goat. How much?"

So given the right incentive, he'd fork over his wife's prized beast. Interesting. PJ glanced at Jeremy. "How much?"

"It's your goat."

She grabbed Jeremy's collar and pulled him down, her mouth close to his ear. "I don't have any money."

"Oh, good grief." He stepped around her and faced Ben. "Thirty bucks."

Ben gave a disgusted snort and turned to go inside.

"Fifty."

He stopped, not looking at Jeremy. "A hundred."

"A hundred bucks for a goat? Does that come with or without a year's supply of hostas?" Whoops, maybe she wasn't supposed to speak.

Jeremy did his own bargaining snort and started to turn away.

"Seventy-five!" PJ added pleading into her eyes, layered it on thick to both Ben and Jeremy.

Ben exhaled, long and loud, clearly put out. "My wife loves that goat. It's been in the family for nearly five years. The grandkids will be disappointed."

"They can come and visit." PJ softened her voice. "It's for my nephew, Davy. He lives over in Chapel Hills. Your goat will be well loved and cared for."

"If she doesn't d—"

She poked Jeremy hard in the gut and he woofed out his last word.

"*Dream* of returning home. Which she won't because we will keep her oh so happy."

"It's a he."

Oh, *Billy*, not Billie. They might have a problem. But . . . it was either that or create an international incident.

"Is it a deal?" PJ stuck out her hand.

After a beat, Ben met her grip. "Deal." His hand wasn't as strong as she would have imagined, evaporating the Ben-as-a-murderer theory.

Jeremy fished out his wallet and peeled off seventy-five smackers to Ben. They went around back to retrieve Billy and loaded him into the hatchback. Thankfully, Ben stayed on the porch and didn't notice the expired goat in the backseat.

Billy didn't sit quite as quietly as Dora had. PJ sat with him, arms wrapped around his neck, as he tried to cram her into the tire well. "Drive fast."

They motored back to Connie's and unloaded Billy, dragging him around the house. While Jeremy tied him up, PJ raked all the smelly and probably poisonous grass clippings away from his reach. She picked up an already uprooted hosta plant and tossed it to him. "Welcome home."

As Jeremy collapsed next to her on the deck, the stars winking overhead, a summer breeze playing in the trees, it occurred to her that they still needed to bury the goat.

Er, goat number one.

"We need to take Dora to the vet."

Jeremy rubbed his hand down his face. "Isn't it a little late for that?"

PJ went inside and found an old sheet upstairs—although nothing Connie owned was technically old, besides the furniture, which meant that PJ owed her a sheet.

She wasn't sure that made them even, however.

Taking the sheet outside, she climbed back into the car, noticing a rank odor.

"The things I do for you, Princess." Jeremy picked up the goat and wrapped it in the sheet.

Under the circumstances, she let the nickname slide. "I won't forget this."

"Oh, neither will I."

The vet's office was closed, but they wrestled the goat out of the car and dragged it to the front step. Jeremy tucked a couple twenties into the door.

But PJ couldn't move. As she stood there, looking at the sheet-wrapped carcass, guilt wove into her chest. "Maybe I should take the goat home, explain that it died of natural causes."

Jeremy set a hand on her shoulder. "The truth shall set you free."

"Or it shall cause my sister's first big marital blowout." She hung her head. "I don't know what to do."

But Jeremy did apparently. "Leave the goat. It'll get a decent
. . . burial."

She sighed. "Should we say something?"

He didn't make a sound or break into "Amazing Grace" or
"In the Sweet By and By," so she just stood there in silence,
the wind shifting through the trees and raising the hair on
her arms.

"That's good," Jeremy finally muttered, as if closing the
moment.

They climbed back into the car, but Jeremy didn't turn into
the Chapel Hills neighborhood. "Where're we going?"

"We have unfinished business at the Kellogg Country
Club."

"Seriously, Jeremy."

But he reached over, patting her arm. "Relax, PJ."

How exactly were they going to get into the country club
without setting off alarms? And what would Boone do if he
found out?

She saw herself on the turnpike back to South Dakota
before morning.

Chapter **SIXTEEN**

"You seem a little tense."

PJ could barely make Jeremy out through the jagged shadows cutting through the viburnum bushes ringing the country club. They'd parked up the hill and special-forced their way through the golf course, sticking to the trees and avoiding, for the most part, the sprinklers.

Now they crouched just beyond the clubhouse outside the pool, in a cubby of darkness that, if she had her way, would suck them in forever, whisk her away to a place where she couldn't be talked into crazy schemes. She'd lost her mind for sure.

"A little *tense*? I'm about to relive the worst night of my life, the night that derailed every dream, every romance, every hope for a reasonable future, and you think I'm *tense*?"

"Shh, not so loud. There might be a security guard."

"You mean you haven't cased the joint?"

"What do you think I am, a professional burglar? You're the one who brought up the golfing foursome."

"I don't know what you are!"

"Shh! You're going to get us caught."

"This is the worst idea—"

His hand on her arm, tightening, made her stop. She heard footsteps scuffing against cement and ducked down, trying to make herself the size of a flea.

The steps moved away, dissipating into the night.

"Who was that?" she hissed.

"Looked like someone in charge. He wasn't wearing a uniform but held a ring of keys."

Perfect. Probably Director Buckam. Wouldn't that be poetic? To catch her breaking the law at the country club. Again. Could a girl be banned for life twice? "Tell me one more time why we have to do this?"

Jeremy's voice was close to her ear. "How many suspects do you have?"

Well, there was Ben, but not so much anymore, and then Tucker, although that, too, didn't make sense. . . . "Okay, fine. I'm short on suspects."

"And long on instinct."

She was relishing the compliment when he moved away and took another peek at the club.

"Besides," he whispered, "we're not stealing anything. We're just taking a look at names. People you, as a member, should know."

"I'm not a member."

She felt more than saw his movement in the dark.

"You said you went golfing."

Okay, see, this was why she'd never make a great PI. Because she couldn't keep her stories lined up. "I was . . . let's just say, not myself."

He was silent, only the breeze intercepting his thoughts, rushing through the poky bushes protecting her. Then, "You scare me."

"Let's just do this. My mother probably thinks I've abandoned Davy and made a run for the border."

Jeremy took her hand in his. "Stay with me."

"Where else am I going, Tahiti?"

He held up his other hand, a fist, like she should freeze or something. So she did.

"Okay, now!"

He nearly yanked her arm from its socket. She gulped in a yelp but took off after him to the back of the building, around the first tee, and up to the entrance to the pro shop, her feet slapping in the wet grass.

"Get down!" He backed her into the shadows as he crouched before the locked door. She crouched behind him and tried to disappear.

Seconds later Jeremy held the door open and motioned her inside. She scampered behind the registration desk and slumped onto the floor, holding her heart inside her chest with her hand. "What kind of guy jimmies open a locked door that fast?"

Jeremy was all work, no play as he produced a flashlight, clamped it in his teeth, and started opening doors. "Whaf hay hid you go gofing?"

She stared at him and for the first time placed it, that thing that made her take him seriously when he said run, that feeling of danger despite his teasing.

He had military written all over him. And not just any military, but the sneak-and-peek kind, the carry-guns-and-set-explosives kind. The kind that knew how to break a man's neck with a quick twist.

What was she thinking, sneaking out into the night—into a building—with someone she barely knew, regardless of the pizza and even his help with Dora? Maybe she did want Director Buckam after all. What were a couple hours in the slammer—?

"PJ?" Jeremy had taken the flashlight out of his mouth and now crouched before her. From the dim light shining in the shop from the outside lamps, she could see his face, his expression. His . . . concern?

He obviously knew the gig was up. "You okay?"

She didn't know what to say. Or, rather, couldn't speak. "I, uh . . ." She looked away.

"What?"

She reached deep for some foothold on indignation or righteous anger or something that would drive out this crazy, unfounded fear. "You're some sort of special ops guy or something, aren't you?"

He smiled slowly. It touched his eyes. "Maybe."

"Maybe?"

"Shh!"

Sure enough, more footsteps, this time across the floor upstairs, creaking it. Jeremy clamped his hand over her mouth, pulled her tight to his chest. She could feel his heart—not such a tough guy underneath, huh?—hammering against his rib cage.

She pulled his hand from her mouth and drew away, noting how he now held the flashlight like a club. As if . . . protecting her?

She listened until the footsteps died away.

"Let's get out of here. What day were you here?" Jeremy asked again. "There's a notebook in the drawer. Let's hope they handwrite their tee times. I really don't want to have to boot up this computer."

He started to get up, but she turned and grabbed his arm. "Not until you tell me—"

"SEALs. I was with the Navy SEALs. Until a year ago when I blew out my knee. I got a medical discharge." There was something else in his eyes, but he hooded that away so fast she thought she might get windburn.

"Saturday. In the morning, ten o'clock or so," she whispered.

He opened the drawer and pulled out a leather-bound book. Trust Buckam to keep up the old ways, to relish anything archaic, but she recognized the book.

Jeremy opened the cover. Ran the flashlight over the page. Turned it, ran the light again, once more turned the page. "Here. Ten o'clock. But I don't see your—"

"Constance Sukharov."

"Ah. Yep, got 'em." He reached above him without looking and grabbed a notepad. She had already unearthed a pen.

He scribbled the names down, closed the book, and shoved it into the drawer.

They were just rising when a light flickered in the hallway leading to the upstairs.

PJ froze.

"Let's go!"

But her legs wouldn't work. Simply wouldn't move . . .

Jeremy picked her up and carried her to the supply room behind the counter, tucking her in the darkness behind a tower of boxes near the back. He hovered at their edge, his flashlight-club at the ready.

PJ closed her eyes and listened to her heartbeat swish in her ears. Why, oh why, did she do stupid things? They seemed like good ideas at the time. Like motocross. Fun until a girl panicked and forgot how to stop. Then there was pain and screaming and blood.

Please.

Footsteps descended the stairs.

PJ drew up her knees, tucked her head into them, trying to be invisible.

The footsteps clomped across the thinly carpeted floor. Stopped. She saw light come on under the supply room door. She heard humming, then drawers opening, closing, and finally Director Buckam's voice. "I knew it."

She would probably look up and see Buckam standing over her. *"I knew it—you'll never change, PJ Sugar."*

But she did change, could change, had changed. She didn't want to be the troublemaker. Didn't want to find herself hiding from her past in dark corners.

The footsteps exited up the stairs; the light flickered off. Jeremy pulled her to her feet. Her legs felt like fire, melting fast.

"On my tail."

She had no quips for him. Just a crisp nod.

They made it out of the building, across the lawn—she didn't even flinch when a sprinkler bulleted her with spray—and to Jeremy's VW Rabbit.

They drove home in silence, PJ shivering in her soaked dress. She didn't ask him how a guy—a Navy SEAL—became a pizza deliveryman/burglar/bodyguard.

Tonight, she just didn't want to know.

"Long day," Jeremy said. "Sorry about the goat."

PJ stared at him, mouth open, not sure how to respond.

Jeremy pulled up to the house, but as she reached for the door, he said, "What I don't get is how Boone connected Jack to Hoffman's death in the first place."

"Jack gave Hoffman money to invest—in the ancient coin market. Apparently Hoffman took money out of Jack's account, or maybe Jack just got panicky. Either way, Boone thinks that's motive enough to kill him." She tugged on the handle of the door, opening it.

"And who tossed Hoffman's place? I've been rolling that over in my mind. If Jack is innocent, it wasn't him. So who did it? And why?"

She shook her head. She just wanted bed. Her bed. Connie's bed. Whatever.

The dome light illuminated Jeremy's face. He wasn't smiling; his face wore more of a pained grimace. He put his hand on the passenger seat and leaned toward her, as if trying to figure out what to say. Then finally he sighed and leaned away. "See ya round, Princess."

PJ didn't have the energy to correct him. Only later after she stepped into the shower did she realize that he'd taken her list of new suspects with him.

✳ ✳ ✳

"Please tell me that you are not just now getting in." PJ's mother pulled her reading glasses off her nose and set them on the table, looking up from her Saturday morning crossword.

The other sections of the paper were scattered along the length of the table, which could still seat eight.

A pitcher of orange juice and a basket of muffins lured PJ in to her mom's kitchen. She took a muffin and put it on a napkin. "No. What do you think, Mom? That I'm still in high school?"

She felt like it. Felt like she'd snuck out of the house and was trying to cover for it. Only she'd lost her skills. Her hand shook and she clenched it in her lap.

It didn't help that the touch of Jeremy's hand wrapped around hers, guiding her to safety, lingered on her skin. Like an itch, it bothered her. And his revelation of being a SEAL stirred up more questions, and frankly, unnerved her. She knew in her bones that there was more behind Jeremy's smoky, hooded eyes. Maybe it was better to stay as clear of him as she could.

Her mother looked back at the crossword. "I'm glad I stopped by the house and picked up Davy's pajamas."

Was that before or after Dora lay dying in the backyard?

"Did you have a good time on your date?"

PJ broke open the muffin and spice drifted out. "You knew it was a date?"

Elizabeth penned in an answer to the crossword. "Please be careful." She sighed, as if the next words greatly perplexed her. She had been doing crosswords so long she probably dreamed in crosswordspeak. "I just don't understand what you see in that boy."

Something about her tone brought back Boone's own label. *Trash.*

PJ poured herself a glass of juice. "Did you know the stories about Boone's mom? that she was an alcoholic?"

Elizabeth looked up, plucked eyebrows raised, as if waiting

for PJ to finish her sentence, elaborate. Finally she said, "Yes, I knew about Boone's mother. The entire town knew about Boone's mother."

"That's why you didn't like him, right? That's why you hated us being together—"

"No." Elizabeth set down her pen and folded her hands on the paper. "Boone and you were like two sides of the same coin, PJ, but . . . he couldn't see all that you were. All you could be. You had a light inside you, and I was afraid he'd snuff it out or eclipse it with his own. Which is one of the reasons, I admit, why I wanted you to leave. Not for ten years, of course, but maybe enough to get Boone out of your system. I didn't want you to end up pregnant . . ."

PJ looked down at her crumbling muffin. "Like my biological mother?"

Her mother sighed. "I just wanted you to have a future that wasn't influenced by Boone."

"I didn't know that."

"You wouldn't have left, would you?"

Perhaps her mother understood her better than she realized.

"But my actions had nothing to do with Boone's parents or even the rumors in town. The mistakes of the parents don't have to be the legacy of the child." Her mother picked up her crossword, contemplating it again. "What's a four-letter word for 'a polite interruption sound'?"

"*Ahem.*"

"What?" She looked up, her eyes sharp. "I just think a person is who they make of themselves. Like you." She reached over and patted PJ's arm. "You never let expectations get in your way."

"I was actually answering your question. A polite interruption sound. *A-h-e-m. Ahem.*"

"Oh, right." She picked up her pen and pressed the letters into the boxes.

PJ worked on her muffin, washing it down with the juice.

"Auntie PJ!" Davy came flying through the kitchen in his Spider-Man jammies.

PJ had to scoot out and react fast to catch him. "Hey there, little man!"

He flung his arms around her, then pushed back and scrambled onto her lap. "Mommy called!" He reached for a muffin.

PJ looked at her mother.

"Last night. She was concerned because no one was home at her house. I let her talk to Davy. Can you believe it's already been two weeks? . . . What's 'an expression of surprise'?"

How could the weeks have passed so quickly? PJ wasn't ready. She didn't have a job or a place to live. And what about Jack and Trudi and her investigation? Who would watch over the goat and make sure Boris didn't offend the neighbors with his sunbathing? And most of all, who would teach Davy to swim?

She'd accomplished nothing of what she'd hoped. She was still jobless and, after last night, just a fingerprint analysis away from jail, considering Boone's threats. And so much for earning her mother's respect.

No, she never let expectations get in the way, because, well, why bother?

But she did know she didn't want to be the girl hiding in the storage closet under the cover of darkness, waiting to be discovered, forever labeled trouble.

No more supersleuthing for her.

Her mother wore a strange look. "PJ? Did you hear what I said?"

"Hah."

"It's not a joke, PJ. I'm serious. I don't think she's going to want to see a goat in her backyard. And it's a good thing it's Saturday, or Davy would be missing school."

Davy looked up and, before PJ could stop him, spilled the beans . . . or muffin, as it were. "I don't go to school. I stay home with Baba!" He slid off PJ's lap, and it took everything inside PJ not to run away with him. She swallowed and looked down at the last of her muffin.

"He doesn't go to school?"

"Listen, Mom, don't you think it's a little *stressful* for a four-year-old to go to summer preschool?"

"Not if he wants to get into—"

"The best colleges, I know."

"I was going to say private kindergarten, but yes, Connie intends for him to have the best start he can under the circumstances." She sighed and shook her head. "Oh, PJ—"

"What have I done, I know." She stood. "I'm sorry, Mom. I didn't mean to make a mess of things. It just happened. I think Connie can probably get him back into Fellows—at least I hope so. Until then, Davy and I have an appointment at the beach."

She moved to follow him from the room, turned back, and tapped the crossword. *"Hah.* A three-letter word for an expression of surprise."

Her mother looked down. "I thought it was *aha.*"

PJ shook her head. "No, that would be a three-letter word for 'I knew you'd mess this up.'"

Her mother said nothing as she left the room.

✳ ✳ ✳

They didn't end up at the beach. PJ wasn't sure why, but she couldn't go there, despite the sun trumpeting above, announcing a day created for swimming and sand castles.

Instead she and Davy drove into the city to the Mall of America, parking in the cool cement structure, aware that she had about seven dollars to her name. But she didn't have to buy anything—just wander.

Davy slid out of the backseat. "LEGO land!"

So he'd been here before. They found the entrance, and the cool air whisked off the morning's heat. She realized as she watched neatly attired, buggy-pushing mothers that she'd come dressed in her yoga pants, a T-shirt, and flip-flops, but with Davy pulling her toward the sound of waterfalls and rides and the lure of ice cream and chocolate cookies, she didn't have to watch their expressions.

Not that she thought she might live up to any expectations anyway.

Davy ran to the edge of the second-floor balcony and stood on tiptoe, poking his nose over the rail. "Wow. It's big."

She wasn't sure if he meant the park or the Ferris wheel or the roller coaster, all contained in the center of a three-story mall, but she came up behind him and lifted him for a better view. "Yep."

"Can I get a cookie?"

They both needed a cookie.

PJ fished around in her purse and discovered two extra dollars in change. She bought them a chocolate chip cookie each and a carton of milk for Davy, cutting her dollar supply down to change. They sat and watched moms and dads load their children onto kiddie rides.

"I'm sorry I don't have enough money to put you on a ride, kiddo."

Chocolate piled in the corners of Davy's mouth and he wore a milk mustache. "That's okay. I got sick last time." He grinned at her, and she resisted the urge to wipe his face.

"PJ!"

She heard her name but couldn't believe it when she turned and spied Maxine Hudson, gripping tight to a twin with each hand as they dragged her toward their bench. She finally let them go, and Daniel and Felicia scampered to Davy.

"So you decided to join us. How are you doing?" Maxine sat down next to PJ on the bench.

Maxine didn't really want an answer to that, did she?

How PJ wanted to figure out how to help Jack or sort out anything on her list of messes, but she'd run out of ideas. And time.

Davy had finished his cookie, so PJ grabbed a napkin and wrestled him clean.

Maxine pulled out a ride ticket. "Do you guys want to ride the kiddie coaster?"

Davy began to jump, clapping along with Daniel and Felicia.

"Oh, Maxine, we don't have a ticket—"

"I have plenty of ride points."

PJ glanced at Davy, remembering his comment about getting sick. Maybe he'd been exaggerating. "How fast does the coaster go?"

Maxine was already halfway there, her children streaking ahead. "Not fast. It's for kids."

Right. PJ followed behind, watching the crew climb aboard. Davy strapped in and waved, beaming.

Thankfully, Felicia and Daniel were sitting behind him.

Or maybe that was worse.

"Keep your mouth closed!" she hollered and then saw parents glance at her. She shrugged. "He . . . screams pretty loud."

Maxine came over to join her. "Trudi and Jack were in court yesterday for his arraignment."

"I know." She'd called Trudi this morning before the flogging at her mother's house and gotten a speedy, tense update.

"Jack didn't confess, did he?" Maxine asked.

"No. But they can't get the process of not guilty going until they indict him."

"What would make Jack kill someone?"

PJ gave her a sharp look. Maxine was shaking her head, looking at the kids, waving at them as the ride swished past. "You don't think it's true, do you?" PJ asked.

"I don't know. But they don't have anyone else in custody."

PJ leaned her hip against the rough-hewn wooden rail, arms folded. "I've hunted down a few leads, but they all seem to dead-end." She didn't mention that she'd gone so far as to break the law. "But I can't escape the voice inside that tells me he's innocent."

"Not every voice is one you should listen to—uh-oh!"

PJ turned. "Oh! Davy, no!"

The crowd around her moaned as Davy unloaded his snack on the floor of the ride.

Maybe there were some voices she *should* listen to.

Maxine was a trouper, and they camped out in the ladies' bathroom while PJ washed Davy's shorts and top in the sink with some sanitizer gel she had in her purse, then blew them dry. Maxine even bought Davy a 7UP to calm his stomach.

PJ ducked her head when a couple fellow mothers came in and cast them a dark look.

Maxine held up her hands in a sort of surrender. "Cookies, ladies. The kid tossed his cookies."

PJ laughed.

"So, how did you like our church?" Maxine held Felicia on her lap and they paged through a picture book she'd dug out of her purse. PJ made a mental note to add Horton to her wannabe mommy bag.

Except she wasn't going to be "Mommy" for much longer. She looked at Davy, and something inside her weighed heavy.

"I liked the praise and worship, and your pastor seems down-to-earth. Gotta like a guy who preaches in jeans and a polo shirt."

Maxine turned the page, leaning over to read, glancing up at PJ to nod. "We've been going there for about five years."

PJ tested the shirt—it felt dry enough. She wiggled it over Davy's head. He was already wearing his dry shorts. "I liked the sermon. I can relate to Peter. He was a mess, had more passion than brains, and still managed to become something with God."

Maxine finished the story, letting her daughter page through the book. "He had brains, just needed direction. I think that's one reason Christ gave him a different name. We'll be studying Peter all summer long. Come back to tomorrow's services— Davy can come home with us for that playdate after church, and maybe we can even make it an overnighter."

PJ washed her hands one more time, touched by Maxine's offer, and followed her out of the bathroom. Maxine's kids begged for another round of rides, but PJ gave Davy a quick shake of her head before he could suggest anything. Fat tears rimmed his eyes.

PJ crouched next to him. "I'm sorry, pal. That's just the way it is. You'll get sick."

Maxine took out her ride card, looked at the points, then leaned down, putting her hands on her knees. "Your auntie loves you. You need to trust that when she says no, it's for your good, Davy. Not everyone can ride the roller coaster. But I'll bet you could ride that Ferris wheel." She handed PJ her ticket. "Finish this one off. We'll get another."

"No—really." PJ made to hand it back, still hearing Maxine's words: *"Your auntie loves you."*

She did love Davy. It took her breath away, really, how much she wanted him to be whole and happy and at peace. To shake free of his fears and nightmares, the terror inside that had made him kick her instead of accept her hug.

"No, really," Maxine said, closing PJ's hand around it. "Being a good parent—or aunt—isn't about being perfect. It's about making him know you love him, protecting him, and seeing in him more than what he sees."

PJ looked at Davy now, rumpled in his bathroom-dried clothes, climbing a bench, jumping from it. Reckless, head-strong, sometimes afraid. Armed with his own dreams and now ready to love her back if she just opened her arms.

Maybe she already knew this child. Maybe she saw him in the mirror every day.

"By the way—" Maxine snared her twins one by one—

"I hope Jack is innocent. Maybe he just needs someone to believe in him, to keep looking harder and with a different perspective. Someone who won't give up." She glanced at Davy, then winked at PJ and pulled her kids over to the bumper cars.

Chapter *SEVENTEEN*

Thwump!

PJ heard her own gasp of pain and doubled over as she clawed her way out of sleep.

Thwump! "Auntie PJ, wake up!"

She covered her head, then her stomach, not sure which was more vulnerable as she focused on her attacker. Sunlight streamed in like fingers through the shuttered windows, reaching into her day. Davy stood at the edge of the bed, his dark hair sticking straight up from the bath she'd given him last night, hands on his hips, grinning.

Better than an alarm clock.

"Are we going to go to church?"

Church.

She sat up. Glanced at the clock.

A smile found her, despite the early cast of morning as Davy climbed on the bed and bounced on the covers. "I wanna go to church."

She scrolled back to last week, wondering at his fascination, and remembered that he'd scored a candy bar from the storehouse in her bag. Yeah, she'd go to church for a candy bar too.

She sank back into the pillow. "Are you sure, little man?"

"Daniel and Felicia will be there."

Oh yeah. And Maxine. And most importantly, it was probably the one right thing she could do for Davy.

"Get dressed, pal."

She climbed out of bed and peered out the window, her spirit rising at the sight of Billy on his feet in the yard. However, the smell that drifted toward her watered her eyes.

Connie, and probably all her neighbors, would ban her from the city limits.

Boris moved into her view, bringing the goat a bucket of grain, petting it, cooing. PJ wanted to pump the air with victory. She'd fooled him.

She should probably be ashamed of that, but she couldn't help it. In fact, maybe she would ride the winning streak and today attempt to fit together the pieces of the puzzle surrounding Ernie's murder. The truth felt just beyond her fingers.

If only she could get her hands on that list Jeremy had scored from the country club break-in. But she hadn't a clue how to track down Jeremy.

She tossed through her clothes and pulled out a pair of jeans and a pink tee. If the pastor could wear jeans, so could she.

She showered, dabbed on some makeup, and met Davy downstairs.

He wore the suit that Connie had purchased for the wedding. A regular dapper young man. "Want some breakfast?"

"I ate."

On closer inspection, she spied the trail of chocolate Pop-Tart down his white shirt. She wiped his mouth with a paper towel and raced him out to the Bug.

Music streamed from the open doors of the praise and worship center as they parked. Davy jumped out and charged the doors. She caught Maxine waving from across the parking lot.

"Davy's sure looking happy today." Inside, her son intercepted Davy in a headlock and they tussled, scattering conversations in front of the welcome booth. "Recovered from yesterday?"

"Just a little." Seeing Davy laugh and wrestle nudged PJ's spirit further upward. She snagged him and grabbed a bulletin from one of the ushers.

"Sit with us, PJ." Maxine wound her way through the crowd to a dark-skinned man waving to them from a wheelchair near the front. "My husband comes early for prayer," she said, as if explaining why they weren't together.

Her husband was in a wheelchair? He seemed older, despite his dark brown hair and obviously strong arms. Suddenly it came back to her—Maxine's contemplative, even distant, look at the beach. Did she struggle with her husband's disability? She seemed such a refined, relaxed picture of a put-together woman.

Then again, PJ more than most knew that what you see isn't always what you get.

"Ethan, this is PJ, Trudi's friend. PJ, my husband, Ethan." Maxine held the twins back for PJ to scoot in.

He greeted PJ with a smile and a handshake. "Glad to meet you." She hid her surprise at his British accent.

She slid into the pew, bookended Davy, the twins, then Maxine and Ethan. Praise songs had already begun and worshipers filtered in, some clapping, others chatting. The fresh music found her frayed ends, and before long, she could sense the not-so-absent PJ, the one she seemed to have forgotten during the last week, rising again to the surface.

Maybe she wasn't lost. Just buried under a habitual sense of shame.

She raised her arms and sang, almost losing herself in praise, when she noticed someone else ahead of her doing the same. A man with curly dark hair, strong arms, dressed in khakis and a white polo, just a hint of a bright red and blue Celtic tattoo showing, all cleaned up and cultured.

Jeremy.

Shame ran to her cheeks when she realized by the time the sermon started, she'd practically memorized the back of Jeremy's head, wondering how long he had before his hair thinned completely. And what his tattoo meant, and if he'd seen hers—how could he, and would she want him to, and wouldn't that bring up a lot of questions that maybe she didn't want to discuss—and if he'd surprise her with another pizza today, and most of all, if he still had that list of suspects on him.

She made such a fine Christian. She flipped her Bible open and tried to catch up.

"Where are we?" she mouthed to Maxine.

Maxine smiled and showed her the Bible. "Same one as last week. First Peter."

She ran her finger down the passage. Oh yes, the bit about being chosen by God and changed by Him. The one that made her believe that she might even be able to help people. Do some *good* in Kellogg.

She wondered if it was safe to listen to the sermon.

The pastor was warming into his preaching. "I always liked Peter, the rough disciple, the one who always got it wrong. The guy who chopped off the soldier's ear, who panicked and offered to make a tent for Jesus when he saw Him trans-figured. I probably would have done the same thing. I relate to his fear when he told Jesus he'd never leave Him, then hours later denied he knew Him. Peter was so desperate for Jesus' love, His attention. I wonder if it was hard to see it so easily fall upon John, to hear Jesus call him the Beloved One."

No, not safe at all. The pastor's words had the power to scour up old wounds. She swallowed the emotions away.

"Peter just had to accept who he was to Jesus. Not the beloved. But the rabble-rouser."

PJ looked down at her Bible, wishing she could slink out of the pew.

"Yet to Peter, the troublemaker, Jesus gave the responsibility of feeding the sheep, taking care of the people of the church. While John saw visions of glory, Peter fought for the truth at home among his Jewish friends, neighbors, and relatives."

PJ glanced up just in time to see the pastor come out from behind the pulpit. Was he looking at her?

"He might have denied Christ, but that day when Jesus offered him forgiveness, Peter finally heard the truth—that Jesus loved him despite his flaws. That God would do great things through him, if he was obedient. All Peter had to do was surrender. He gave everything completely to God—his future and his reputation and his dreams. And that's when God took over and did amazing things in Peter's life. And He'll do that in your life."

Surrender. She was never very good at that word. It felt mostly like defeat. Still, she gulped those words in and held them like her breath, hoping they would seep into her soul.

A half hour later, PJ cut through the crowd, dodging blockers like a fullback, zeroing in on Jeremy, who held a cup of coffee while reading the list of activities on the bulletin board. PJ had Davy by the paw; he was working on a lollipop Maxine had passed down the pew during the sermon.

"Are you stalking me?"

Jeremy seemed genuinely surprised to see her. "Why, should I be?"

There he went again, being mysterious. And maybe even impressive—who would have thought Jeremy Kane attended church?

He directed his gaze at Davy. "Hey there, pal. That looks good."

"Grape." Davy held up the dripping sucker. His hand was permanently glued to the stick.

"Yum." Jeremy said, sounding halfway believable. "And to answer your question, PJ, no, I'm not stalking you. I saw the church on one of my deliveries and thought I'd check it out. I'm glad I ran into you. I went by your house yesterday."

Really? While she was moping at the Mall of America?

"I was relieved to see the goat still lived."

"Shh!" PJ shot her gaze to Davy, then gave Jeremy the hush-or-I'll-have-to-hurt-you look.

"The secrets you keep."

"I'm trying to save lives here."

"Of course. Well, I checked out our list of suspects and wanted to report in."

Perhaps she'd forgive him for making her feel like a burglar. Well, maybe not so soon. "So? What did you find out?"

"They all have airtight alibis. Your banker was at a meeting—confirmed. The three others—an accountant, a CEO, and a pharmacist—again, all confirmed alibis."

"How did you—?"

"I have my ways."

That was all, accompanied by a sharp tone. Clearly he had no intention of letting her in on his methods. She just hoped that none of them included something dark and sinister. "Well, you're a regular PI, aren't you?"

He still didn't share; instead his eyes twinkled. "I don't suppose you'd like to go on a picnic with me today, would you? It'd be a great day to swim." He put a hand on Davy's head. "We can bring Drippy here with us."

Drippy. She would reluctantly admit that was sorta cute. "Actually, Davy is invited to the Hudsons' for lunch and an afternoon of play."

Jeremy's smile was slow and sweet. "That's perfect."

Uh-oh. It was?

Her face must have commented, for he followed with "It can just be you and me."

"You and me?"

He looked over his shoulder—a furtive look by her standards. "The crime-fighting duo."

She wanted to smile, to laugh, but her recent failures felt too fresh, tasted too sour. She managed a wry expression. "Yeah. Maybe that's not a good idea. I'm kind of tired of causing trouble."

He considered her a long moment. "It's way too late for that. Come out with me. We'll keep our conversation limited to murder and mayhem."

It was the way he cocked his head, raised his eyebrows at her, as if he meant it, as if it wasn't at all horrible to be causing him a little trouble, that made her say yes. Either that or again her mouth had ventured out on its own, without a care to consequences.

PJ found Maxine standing next to Ethan, one hand on his shoulder as they talked to the pastor.

Maxine broke away from the conversation. "What a great sermon, huh?" She took hold of Davy's nonsticky hand. "I love the idea of God doing something through me. Despite my flaws."

Yes. Because more than anything, PJ longed for some sort of hope that at the end of all this, there would be a better, stronger PJ, a registered difference that showed from taking the road less traveled.

"Ready, Davy?"

PJ gave Davy a hug. "Have fun, little man. I'll pick you up tonight."

To her shock, Davy popped her a kiss.

"Thanks, Maxine. Don't forget he's allergic to peanuts, okay?" Hah! She remembered.

"We'll be fine. Take your time."

PJ searched briefly for Jeremy, then headed out to the parking lot. He leaned against her VW, ankles crossed, wearing a pair of black sunglasses, watching her. She couldn't place his look, and the fact that he knew what car she drove niggled inside her.

Still, she couldn't help but appreciate the way he stood out, the sun upon him like a halo. "I'm gathering that you want to take my car."

"We can take the pizzamobile if you want."

"Hop in."

She rolled down the window and headed toward Connie's so she could change. The grill from Sunsets tempted her as they drove by, and she cast a longing look at Hal's Pizzeria, to Jeremy's laughter.

"Let's pick up some chicken from the deli," he suggested.

They breezed into the Red Owl Grocery Store and loaded up on fried chicken, potato salad, crusty French bread, and Concord grapes, as well as bottled root beer. PJ picked up some ice while Jeremy loaded the lot into her trunk.

At the house, PJ located a picnic blanket in Connie's garage, a cooler, and a basket. Nothing like outfitting her own date. While she changed into shorts, Jeremy packed the basket, cooling the root beers.

She couldn't dismiss the feeling that he'd already moved into her life. Nor the chaser that said maybe she liked it.

They drove through Kellogg, out to the highway, and toward the new park.

Jeremy hung his elbow out the window, the wind running through his short dark hair. "Today's sermon made me think of you."

It did? "What part?"

"The alien part."

"Oh, that's nice, Jeremy. Are you trying to win friends and influence people?" Never mind that she'd always sort of thought of herself as an alien. She didn't need Jeremy pointing it out.

"Calm down, Princess—"

"Ixnay on the Princess. Especially when I'm driving."

"Fine. But I liked what the pastor said about sanctification working out in life what is already true inside us."

"Which is?"

"That we're not the same people we were. We're completely new. But so many of us walk around with the same perspective as we did when we were lost. Wondering where we fit in. What a new creation looks like."

PJ couldn't look at him. Somehow, he'd climbed inside her soul and done some poking around. "But how does that remind you of me?"

"I think that's the reason you keep changing jobs. You said you don't know what skin you belong in, what identity you are. But maybe it's a little bit of all of them. One second you're Lawn Girl; the next you're Goat Procurer; to me you're Princess—" Seeing her glare, he quickly added, "Just as an example. To Drippy you're Auntie PJ. But the thing is, only God knows who you really are and who you're becoming in Him. Maybe you just need to live on the outside who you are on the inside."

Her throat tightened. Jeremy spoke like a man acquainted with his own words. But more importantly, those were the words she'd been trying to say to herself for two weeks.

"And who are you really, Pizza Guy? Are you living on the outside who *you* are on the inside?" PJ attempted to keep her voice light, but it emerged pitiful and way too high.

Jeremy looked at her through those dark glasses and said nothing.

"What are you doing at my church anyway?"

"I told you," he said softly. "I saw it on a delivery." He peered out the passenger window, his gesture pregnant with what he wasn't telling her.

"So, what do you do when you're not delivering pizzas and solving murder mysteries?"

"Ride my motorcycle, fish, read a good book. Sometimes I go salsa dancing."

She saw his grin out of the corner of her eye. "Funny."

"Really. I'm very light on my feet."

"They teach you that in the SEALs?"

"Nope." Jeremy stretched out his legs and propped the seat back, reposing as they drove. She wished his eyes weren't hidden.

"Did you grow up in Minneapolis?"

"Nope."

"St. Paul?"

"Nope."

PJ glared at him. He smiled, white teeth showing.

"How'd you get that tattoo?"

The smile vanished. Aha, a soft place.

He sighed. "It's sort of an identity too." He shifted his seat back up. "All done with the bright lights?"

"Hardly. We have so much left to cover."

He turned toward her, his shoulder against the seat. "Let's talk about you. Like, how long did you and Boone date?"

Now that was an interesting starting point. "Two years, with lots of flirting before that."

"Is he the reason you left town?"

Susan May Warren

Hmm. "Not anymore."

"And the reason you returned?"

His question turned her silent. Yes, she may have had Boone on the brain when she motored back into town. But in truth, perhaps she'd been searching for more than the what-could-have-beens. Maybe she'd longed for the what-could-bes—a taste of acceptance, of redemption.

But all that information at once might make her bleed out right here in the car. "I came back to right old wrongs. To rewrite the headlines."

Jeremy's posture changed, and he considered her for a long, inscrutable moment. "Are you sticking around?"

Wow, he had the precision of a sniper with his questions. Again, she didn't know. Maybe she wanted to.

No, it was more than a maybe. With everything inside her, PJ wanted to dig a hole and plant roots, be a part of Davy's life, and perhaps figure out just what her mother might really be saying. "I . . . don't know. Maybe."

"Don't run away too fast. . . . You should know that I'm not quitting until I figure out what the *P* and *J* stand for." Jeremy reached over and pushed a strand of her flying-about-her-face hair behind her ear.

She nearly shot past the entrance to the park and smashed the brakes hard as they turned. Jeremy rocketed forward into the dash, barely catching himself. She said nothing as she screeched to a halt before a speed bump.

"In a hurry?"

No, not at all, but her heart had inconveniently decided to stand up, pay attention, and compare Jeremy to Boone. She wasn't sure how to interpret the results.

They drove around the lake to the public parking lot, and by the time she found a shady spot, she'd finally dislodged her heart from her throat. The sun drew a hazy circle in the sky, and the faint aroma of grilling burgers laced the air. Birds serenaded the day as the lake caressed the shoreline.

She tried to push the memories from her mind. Memories as recent as Friday night.

Jeremy said nothing as he got out of the car.

PJ took a deep, heated breath. Boone she could handle. She'd already left him once and survived, if poorly. And while he still had his dangerous allure, she understood it.

Jeremy, however, became more seductively mysterious with every meeting, and his edging toward her heart felt sweetly terrifying.

"What keeps bothering me," Jeremy said as she opened the trunk hatch and handed him the basket, "is how the killer got into Hoffman's house. It had to be someone Ernie knew."

"Now that you're done with a deep analysis of my life we're suddenly going to talk mystery and mayhem?"

"It's just been bugging me."

She eyed him as he lugged out the picnic basket and set it on the ground. "If it wasn't Jack, it had to be someone else he expected."

Jeremy returned for the cooler, handling it with ease. "And another thing—we still don't have a motive."

"Oh yeah? How about the Nero coins?"

He wore the smile that said she had a large and overactive imagination. "I know I suggested that, but it's probably something much simpler. Like betrayal or revenge. Most crimes are ones of passion, not calculation."

She reached into her trunk and grabbed the blanket. It was then she noticed the gun. Nestled under the blanket, it lay there like a Frisbee or a softball or another addition to the picnic. She picked it up, her heart thumping. It looked similar to the gun she shot with Boone, the black one.

Had he put it in her car? Why?

She fit the gun into her hand just like Boone taught her, with the handle tight into the web of her palm. Curled her finger around the trigger. It had a hard pull, so that it wouldn't go off by accident, but she heard Boone's voice in her head, telling her to keep her finger off the trigger if she didn't want to shoot. Yes, *that* made sense.

She glanced at Jeremy. He'd turned away from her and walked out onto the lawn, staring out across the lake, his hands on his hips. She could make out the Navy SEAL in his posture, tall and confident.

Maybe it was Jeremy's gun.

Maybe . . . if he, unlike Boone, thought Hoffman's killer still roamed the streets of Kellogg. "Jeremy!" she hollered, lifting the gun toward him. He turned at her voice. "Is this—?"

A shot cracked the air, splintered her words. She ducked, her hands over her head.

Jeremy fell, adding a cry of pain that parted her breath. He sprawled on his back, holding on to a gash in his arm.

She ran toward him, her head ducked a little like some sniper might take it off. "Jeremy!"

Blood pooled between his fingers, and his shocked expression wavered from the gun in her hands to her face and back again. "You shot me!"

She looked at the gun, felt its weight, and unhanded it into the grass.

Jeremy morphed right before her, back into the soldier she'd seen at the pro shop, dark and very, very dangerous. Even his eyes seemed to be on fire, scorching her as he climbed to his feet and strode toward her. She shrank back.

"Maybe I should be asking *you*, PJ Sugar, where you were the day Ernie Hoffman was murdered."

Chapter EIGHTEEN

"Boone, I swear, I didn't shoot him."

"Save it." Boone didn't look at her, shaking his head as he penned something on his clipboard. He'd been working on his car again, evidenced by a smudge of grease behind his ear, as if he'd scratched his neck, perplexed. Still, he'd donned a clean button-down shirt to apprehend public enemy number one.

Behind him, paramedics bandaged Jeremy's arm as he perched on the open end of an ambulance. They'd attracted a crowd with the whirling lights and the sirens. A cluster of horrified mothers clutched their precious children, wide-eyed, leering at her as if she were a serial killer. Overhead, the beautiful day mocked her with its pristine, cloudless sky, gentle breezes, the lure of lunch in the air.

"C'mon, Boone, he's not even hurt . . . much."

"I'm telling you, PJ, for your own good, stop talking." Boone's tone bore something beyond anger, edging close to panic.

Okay, now he was scaring her. "I didn't shoot him!"

Boone put down the clipboard, backed her up to his police cruiser, and lowered his voice to a gravelly whisper. "In my book, shooting a PI is close to shooting a cop. It's serious, Peej."

"PI?" Suddenly everything lined up. She could nearly hear the clicking in her brain as she watched Jeremy sitting in the ambulance, stone-faced, cold eyes on her.

Her mind went back to the shadows in the garage, saw Jeremy hiding from Boone, remembered how he knew exactly where she lived, considered his covert supersleuthing of their list of suspects. Of course he was a PI.

And apparently she was too. A Perfect Idiot.

"How did you get my gun?" Boone had taken a step back, and the look on his face made her want to, uh, shoot him.

"I *didn't* take your gun!"

"It's mine. And it went missing the night we went shooting together."

"I didn't take it."

"I keep running it over in my mind—it was when I went to turn in our equipment, wasn't it? You slipped it out of the case into that black-hole purse of yours—"

"Why would I steal your gun?"

"Where's the other one?"

"You're kidding me, right? *Two* guns are missing?"

Boone paced away from her, said something nasty under his breath, then rounded. "Do I look like I'm kidding?"

No, and in that second the final vestiges of the boy he'd been vanished, replaced by a man she didn't know, one with wrinkles framing his darkening blue eyes and a solid, angry set to his mouth and tense, ropy shoulders that carried what he must consider to be his biggest mistake.

Trusting her.

"I didn't think to check until last night, and even then, I never considered you, PJ. I don't know why I didn't."

She sucked wind. "I didn't take your guns, and I didn't shoot Jeremy. And I can't believe you don't believe me."

He held up his hand, palm out, as if to push her words away. "Please, just stop talking."

Another cop walked over, this one thin and younger than Boone, holding the gun in a cloth, as if there were any question her fingerprints were all over it. "If we find the bullet, we'll be able to match it to the gun." He gestured to the two detectives that roamed the picnic area.

Boone took the gun and dropped it into an evidence bag. He didn't look at her when he said, "It's clear that it's been recently shot, and there's a bullet missing from the magazine. We can test your hands for residue. If it's clear, you're off the hook."

"Please. I watch *CSI*. I know that it takes more than two days for gun residue to wear off. If you'll recall, I went shooting with you less than forty-eight hours ago."

"I also recall teaching you to load and shoot a gun. Don't go anywhere." Boone walked over to Jeremy.

Like where? South Dakota? She sighed.

Across the parking lot, Jeremy pushed the paramedics away, arguing with them as he got up and approached her. He still wore the unfriendly tint in his dark eyes, and her stomach gave a curl of pain.

Why did she care? He'd lied to her.

"I have to say, you surprise me more than anyone I know." Venom now infected his normally teasing, warm voice.

"I didn't shoot you, Jeremy. I promise."

Boone looked up from where he conferred with his fellow cops and met eyes with Jeremy.

PJ saw it, and her mouth fell open. "You're in cahoots, aren't you? How do you know him?" She turned to Jeremy, heat rising in her voice.

"Boone and I work together occasionally. He asked me to keep an eye on you, try and keep you out of trouble."

She locked eyes with Jeremy, hoping to turn him to ash. "Two lies. You told me you were Jack's cousin."

"I am. *And* a PI. And I *was* trying to find out who framed Jack."

"While babysitting me." She shook her head. "I don't need babysitting."

Jeremy gave a nasty snort.

"Did you lie about being a Christian too?"

His eyes narrowed. "Hey—"

"Don't even talk to me."

No wonder he hadn't been afraid of them getting in trouble at the country club. She'd endured a night noosing herself in her bedsheets for nothing.

Boone came over. "I'm taking you in for questioning."

"I didn't do anything."

"You shot me," Jeremy said, like she'd forgotten.

She ignored his tone and glanced at his bandaged arm. "How bad is it?"

"It's bad enough." Jeremy turned away, as if washing his hands of her.

Boone grabbed her arm but she twisted out of his grasp. "Don't touch me."

"I can cuff you."

"Don't even think it."

Options ran through Boone's expression, all twisted in a look of frustration. Finally he opened the back door of the cruiser. "Please?"

"This isn't fair," she said, climbing inside. "I'm innocent and you know it. Again."

He flinched, a gesture that gave her not nearly enough satisfaction as he closed the door.

Jeremy was climbing into the ambulance as they pulled away. And behind that, a tow truck began hitching up the wheels of her Bug.

Boone got into the front seat, his face blank.

PJ leaned back against the seat, remembering too easily the haunting, oily smell of the backseat of a police cruiser, wondering if her mother would post bail.

✳ ✳ ✳

"Local Girl Shoots PI."

The headline lasered into her brain as Boone led her through the station to the cells in the basement.

She couldn't believe she'd been formally arrested.

With each step she took, past the desk attendant Rosie, downstairs and into the holding cell area, then past a collection of other Kellogg truants, the truth drilled farther into her soul.

She'd never escape trouble.

Boone opened the cell door. An overhead light fractured the darkness inside the clean yet barren, solitary, cement-and-metal cell. At the end of the hall, a barred and dirty window tried to barricade even the gaunt sunlight.

She stumbled into the dungeon, her legs numb.

"I'm sorry, Peej."

"Go away."

He sighed and looked like he might cry or maybe send his fist through something. "I want you to know that I . . . I'm not sure you shot Jeremy. It's just that right now we don't have a better explanation."

"Sorta like you blamed Jack because he was the most logical suspect?" She let her voice drive that point home. "Old habits are hard to break, I guess."

His face hardened. "Do you want me to call your mother?"

"Oh yes, please. She'll be thrilled to hear from you. Don't forget to include the part where I stole your guns while we were on a date, and how you arrested me despite the fact that I'm innocent. She'll be glad to know I'm in really good hands." She forced every bit of rancor she could into her voice, needing to hold on to her anger. Otherwise she just might crawl under the metal bed, roll into a ball, and scream.

"Fine then. You can do the calling." He sounded defeated, his voice without heat.

She hated the tears that burned her eyes.

He didn't move, however. Didn't close the cell, didn't reach out to her. Just stood there as if unable to move, as if his world lay on the floor in jagged pieces. "I wish I could get you out of this."

"Then why don't you?"

He winced. "Because . . ."

Oh. Because if he didn't bring her in, then the voices would return, the ones from his childhood that told him he was trash. After all these years, he too was caught in time, watching her with tortured eyes as the cops dragged the girl he loved away. Still trapped between honor and his future. *I forgive you, Boone.* The thought rushed through her and pushed her hand to her mouth, wrenched her breath from her chest. *I forgive you.*

The years of anger, the blame, the regret, suddenly loosened from her. She reached out for the bed, sat hard on it, and hung her head in her hands, shaking.

"Peej?" Boone crouched before her, touched her knee.

"You're right, Boone. It's not your fault my life is a mess. I screwed it up all on my own."

"I'm right? Did I ever say that it's your fault? I—if anyone is to blame, it's me for betraying you."

"Maybe you didn't betray me as much as I betrayed myself. Maybe I've been hoping all these years that someone would stand up for me. That someone would believe in me. And when that didn't happen, I ran. Kept running. But that's my fault. I should have stood up to my mother and to your dad— to the entire town. But I didn't believe in my ability to stand alone."

He closed his eyes. Lowered his head to touch her knee. "And I only made that worse." His voice was so soft she could barely hear it. When he looked up, even in the dimmed light, she saw tears in his eyes. "I believe in you, PJ. I always have. And I should have stood beside you. That's what killed me when you left." He touched her face lightly, as if seeing it for the first time after years of absence. "And why I thought my

297

life might have started over when you returned. Something about you just makes me think everything is going to be okay. It gives me strength to be a better man than I know I am. You've always been the light in my world."

Oh, Boone. When would she escape his hold on her?

"It's time I figure out who I am and how to stand up for myself. Alone, if I have to." PJ framed his face in her hands.

"Boone?" The male voice echoed down the hall.

"I'll be right there." He removed her hands from his face but held them a moment before he shook his head, rose, and walked out.

The click of the cell door resounded like a trigger.

Chill seeped into her. She drew up her legs and folded her arms around them, as fetal position as she could get.

She hadn't shot Jeremy. She knew they'd eventually figure that out, so she turned to the bigger questions: who stole Boone's gun, and why would the thief put it in the trunk of her car?

And why would someone make an appointment for Jack that they didn't intend to keep?

The truth landed like a fist in her chest.

To frame Jack.

PJ got to her feet, pacing to keep warm. Who would set Jack up for a crime?

Footsteps scuffed down the hall. She stepped back as Jeremy appeared. He looked grim, with a bandage around his upper arm and eyes that held no humor.

"Ten stitches."

"I did mention that I didn't do it, right?"

He nodded to someone down the hall, and her door slid

open. After Jeremy walked in, it closed behind him. He pressed his lips together as he sat down on the bed.

"Not afraid to be alone with me? I might strangle you with a shoelace."

"You're wearing flip-flops."

"I'll—I don't know—do something villainous." She let her tone bite despite her lack of appropriate threat. How she longed to be dark and dangerous just once.

"Stop." He ran his hand over his head, sighing. "I'm not supposed to be visiting you, but I thought I'd let you tell me in your own words why you did it."

"Did what? Shoot you?"

He considered her with a look that should have scared her. But it couldn't penetrate her righteous anger. "I finally figured it out while I was sitting in the waiting room. I can't believe I let you fool me like you did."

"Huh?"

"You roll into town after being gone for ten years, and within two days, one of the men who blamed you for burning down the clubhouse is dead—your history teacher, if I get my facts right. What, did seeing him at the club on Sunday dredge up too many painful memories?"

Her mouth opened but no sound emerged. Jeremy hadn't just been babysitting—he'd been investigating *her.*

"Did he plead for his life, PJ? Maybe offer you money? this Nero coin collection? After you killed him, did you start to wonder if it was true? Maybe you went back to his house to look again, tore it apart. Good thing Boone drove up or you'd have gotten away with it."

"Gotten away . . ." She found disbelief but no words.

"Then, to throw me off the track, you dragged me to the library and fed me a tall tale, all the time planning to kill everyone who wronged you."

"Can you hear yourself?"

"And then, when you realized I'd figured it out, you tried to kill me. I guess my interrogation touched a few nerves, huh? Like when I suggested it was a crime of passion, even revenge. I have to say, PJ Sugar, you're good. I guess I should be thankful you don't have better aim."

Oh, she had spot-on aim. Except apparently when it came to trusting the men in her life. "Have you lost your mind? Did they give you painkillers? Because I think you might be having an allergic reaction."

He grabbed her wrist.

She stepped back, snapped it out of his grasp. "You're serious. Even in your delirium. You actually think that—what, I'm a *murderer*? That I came back, like Carrie, to enact my prom night revenge? Oh yes, I have kung fu written all over me. The goat—it's really a killer Doberman in disguise. I meant to take you out in the car, but dear old Fido died on his watch."

Jeremy's eyes tightened into small angry bullets. "You yourself said you had learned every trade in the book. Certainly in there you learned how to break a man's neck."

"Yeah, they taught that in my manicurist's class. Why would I do that?"

"Like I said. Betrayal. Revenge."

"I'm not here to kill anyone! I just want to hang out at the beach with Davy, get a tan."

But that wasn't entirely true either. She'd wanted more—

to maybe murder her lingering reputation as a troublemaker. Find a new one as a rescuer. "Why would I set up Jack?"

"To hurt Trudi."

"I love Trudi. She's my best friend."

"But didn't she blame you too? I read the police reports. She testified that she saw you with the cigarette that started the fire."

"Trudi wasn't even there—" But her boyfriend Greg had been. And he'd also known the truth. PJ closed her eyes, pressed her thumb and forefinger to her temples. "I didn't know that."

"You purposely brought Boone out to the shooting range so that you'd have residue on your hands."

She opened her eyes, wanting with everything inside her to shake his crazy words out of her brain. "I can't believe you're actually saying this to me. That you think . . . I didn't kill Hoffman. Just like I didn't shoot you. Someone's setting me up, just like Jack. Someone who wants me out of the way—"

"Stop. It's time to confess the truth, PJ."

A coldness pressed through her and she ran her eyes over him, saw the strong arms, lethal hands, face chiseled with the grim truth. Jeremy Kane, former SEAL, could probably kill a man with his bare hands.

"Boone!" She ran to the cell bars, framed her face with them. "Boone!"

What, was he on a coffee break?

Jeremy closed his mouth, and she thought she saw real confusion on his face. In her mind she saw everything they'd gone through over the past few days, from the garage to the pizza to the goat, from the B and E at the country club to the moment in the car only hours ago when he'd looked right into her soul and spoken words of truth.

"What are you doing?"

She turned, gripping the bars behind her, measuring Jeremy, wondering if she could resurrect any of those fight scenes she'd learned as a stunt girl. "Boone!"

No Boone to her rescue. But the image of her mangled body in the middle of the cold, undecorated cell dissipated as Jeremy held up his hands as if horrified by her tone. "Calm down, PJ!"

"I'm not going to stay here and let you kill me!"

He recoiled as if she had slapped him, his mouth open. "What—?"

"I'm not stupid. This is just so . . . predictable. Blame it on me, and then come in here—what, were you going to tell Boone I attacked you? that you had to defend yourself?"

Jeremy wrapped his hands around her upper arms. "Stop it. I'm not going to hurt you!"

She launched out with the palm of her hand, connecting with his chin. His head snapped back and she ducked under his arm and leaped onto the bed. "Stay away."

Jeremy pressed his hand to his chin but kept his distance. "Get ahold of yourself. I'm not going to hurt you." He shook his head, as if she'd really rung his bell.

Good. She balled her fists. "Yeah, there's more where that came from, pal." So what if her voice shook. And she was probably lying, because, well, she could do the math, and he had a good fifty pounds on her, not to mention a killer set of muscles. But she was quick. And a little bravado went a long way.

He ran his hands through his hair, and the anger deflated from his expression, matching his voice. "Put 'em down, slugger. I can concede that maybe I overreacted. It's just that as I sat in the ER, it made sense."

"I told you it was the drugs talking." Her voice wobbled and adrenaline made her light-headed. She stepped off the bed, bracing her arm on the wall. "A dozen people saw me at the shooting range with Boone on Friday, even my mailman. What if one of those people is the real killer, and they're trying to get everyone to look at me? Or maybe they were trying to take you out and make me run—"

Jeremy folded his arms, eyes on her.

"I'm just saying there are other options. You out of everyone, Mr. PI, should understand that."

She could tell she had his attention now, if not his confidence, by the way he sighed and scrubbed a hand down his face. "I guess, with your history, that's not so far-fetched."

"Yeah, and what if Hoffman wasn't the Doc, like we thought, but maybe the Doc lives somewhere here in Kellogg, and the assassin tracked him through the Internet? And because Hoffman was selling Nero coins, he thought Hoffman was the Doc, only he got it wrong and—"

Uh-oh, she was losing him.

"We're back to that?"

"—and now he's going to get the real Doc while we sit here and argue, and Jack and I are going to go to prison for crimes we didn't commit."

Jeremy looked away. She could see him struggling. About time someone listened to her.

"I wish I could believe you, PJ. But it's too . . . tall a tale.

Or like you said, a Robert Ludlum novel." He pursed his lips, swallowed. "Good try." He got up and rapped on the door. "I'm done here." It opened.

Had they been deaf to her cries for help? Sure, let the town pariah get murdered in her cell; that'll solve problems.

"Jeremy, think about it. It could be true!"

She stepped aside as the door closed, his form blurry through her tears.

"Sorry, PJ." Jeremy held on to the bars, not looking at her. "I'm really, really sorry." Then he turned and walked down the corridor and probably out of her life.

* * *

So much for her lofty hopes of changing history, of making the world believe in her.

But even she had to admit her story sounded far-fetched in the light of day. Jeremy's sounded much more plausible.

More probable cause in a court of law.

"Oh, PJ, what have you done?" The words scalded her brain as she waited for Boone or someone to return. Ten years old, the words still stung on open wounds as she slunk back to the metal bed and stared at the ceiling. She ran a hand over her cheek, making a fist to trap the moisture inside.

She heard the words as she took the blanket the warden offered, rejected the meal, and laid her head upon her hands in the cell, realizing that Boone wouldn't be returning.

She knew Boone did have probable cause to hold her, but why hadn't he even questioned her? Maybe he realized it wouldn't do any good.

Jeremy had probably confirmed that she'd lost her marbles, anyway. Maybe she was under a twenty-four-hour crazy watch.

And what about Davy? He would be safe with Maxine, but he'd feel abandoned again. Just when she was getting him to trust her.

She wiped her soggy cheeks, breath shuddering, and bruised herself tossing the night away on the hard metal, finally falling into an exhausted, spent slumber in the wee hours of the morning.

She woke up too soon, with a start, in a rush of panic, blinking against the dim fluorescence at one end of the hall, the gray press of sunlight at the other. Her stomach pinged, empty and roiling, and she needed to use the facilities, but she'd die before she stepped near the commode. She sat up and scrubbed her hands over her face, tasting her teeth, feeling wrung out.

Apparently she wasn't getting a phone call, a lawyer, or even a trial. Just lock her away and forget about her.

Forgive me, Trudi. PJ leaned her head back against the cement. Because the minute her mother showed up—if it came to that—to spring her, she intended to pack her Bug and floor it as far away from Kellogg as a half tank of gas and seven dollars could get her.

No wonder she reminded Jeremy of an alien. At the moment, she didn't even recognize herself.

"To God's elect, strangers in the world . . . who have been chosen according to the foreknowledge of God the Father, through the sanctifying work of the Spirit, for obedience to Jesus . . ."

Of course, now God chose to send that verse into her brain.

"While John saw visions of glory, Peter fought for the truth at home among his Jewish friends, neighbors, and relatives," the pastor had said.

Just like she fought for truth. Couldn't anyone see that?

Apparently her friends, neighbors, and relatives saw only the tainted PJ. How long did it take for Peter's family, his town, to see that he'd been changed by his relationship with the Savior? that he wasn't the same flawed guy who used to stink like fish? Or maybe he carried that smell with him forever . . . blending in with the guys at the dock because he could.

"One second you're Lawn Girl; the next you're Goat Procurer; to me you're Princess . . . to Drippy you're Auntie PJ. But only God knows who you really are and who you're becoming in Him."

Who exactly was that?

Trouble.

So maybe that was partly true. She'd always be the girl who poked her nose in, tried to help. Couldn't leave well enough alone. Like with Jack. Or Davy.

"He keeps walking around expecting people to abandon him." Her mother's words slipped in like a thief and stole her breath.

Poor Davy thought it was his fault he'd been left behind by his father.

His fault he'd been abandoned.

His fault he'd been put up for adoption—oh, wait . . . no . . . She pushed the heels of her hands into her eyes. It wasn't her fault. But it had felt like it over and over, as she tried to be a Sugar. Tried to be like Connie. Unflawed. Beloved.

She leaned back against the cold wall as a knife went through her chest. She could see it all—the ballet classes, the Sunday morning outfits: her disheveled skirt over a pair of tube socks and tennis shoes. Connie's outfit beautiful and unsullied.

She could see her mother's thinly veiled disappointment.

Flawed. Flawed. Flawed.

"He might have denied Christ, but that day when Jesus offered him forgiveness, he finally heard the truth—that Jesus loved him despite his flaws."

"Please, God, help me to hear the truth like You told Peter." PJ closed her eyes, hearing her breathing, her heartbeat.

"Sometimes, someone just needs a champion."

"I knew you had it in you. Just needed someone to hold your hand."

"I'm glad I told your father to buy that jacket. It's the real you."

She wasn't sure why she'd expected to hear a male voice. But her mother's words splashed over her like rain, into her heart, her soul, spilling down her cheeks.

Maybe she, like Davy, just expected the worst. Maybe she'd blocked out the truth. She'd been living with the belief that she wasn't what God wanted. But the very fact that Christ died for her said that God liked her.

The truth pressed against her chest, burning.

He liked her before and after she'd become a Christian. With or without flaws.

God believed in her.

And she could probably surrender to someone who liked her enough to die for her.

"He gave everything completely to God—his future and his reputation and his dreams. And that's when God took over and did amazing things in Peter's life. And He'll do that in your life."

Just like God did with Peter.

PJ caught a tear on her hand, swiped her fingers across her face. "Okay." Her voice was tiny against the cement ceiling. "Okay. I don't know what's going on here, but You do. And right now, I'm going to trust You." Footsteps in the hall cut her voice to a whisper. "Please, save Jack, save Trudi. Save . . . me. I'm handing it all over to You."

Boone appeared at the cell door. "You talking to me?"

She shook her head.

Wearing a tired expression, he unlocked the door.

"What's this? Breakfast?"

"I'm sorry you had to spend the night. We couldn't find the bullet, and yes, your prints were on the gun."

"Big surprise there."

He opened the door. "You're free to go."

She wasn't sure if that last line was a joke or not. "I don't understand."

"We don't have enough evidence to hold you for attempted murder." Boone managed a sad smile.

Free to go. Wow, that was quick, even for God.

She straightened her shirt and walked past Boone on cramped legs.

"Not so fast." He grabbed her arm and lowered his voice. "Please, Peej, don't leave town."

Oh no. This time she was sticking around until the bitter end.

Chapter *NINETEEN*

Freedom. PJ expected—no, deserved—sunshine and blue skies on her first day out of the clink. But a chill seeped through the building, cold and angry from the drizzle outside as PJ collected her keys, her bag.

She didn't look at Boone as she left, just pushed open the doors and stood under the awning, watching the rain run off the sides into a muddy puddle framing the stoop. Her car was parked a block away at the impound lot. She calculated the rain and puddle, did a cursory search for an umbrella—hello, certainly she had an umbrella in the black pit of her bag?—and realized that she'd be an otter by the time she got home.

No, not home. To Maxine's to get Davy, who was probably already a mess by now. She wasn't sure how she was going to explain her absence to a four-year-old. She raised her eyes to heaven, shaking her head. "I could use someone on my side here."

Behind her, the door opened, bumping her, and she tripped out from under the awning into the sniper line of rainwater. It doused her, dripping off her hair, down her shirt. "Oh!"

"PJ, get out of the rain!" Boone grabbed her arm, pulled her back.

She shook out of his grip. "It's your fault—you pushed me off the step."

He looked as wrung out as she felt. "Need a ride to your car?"

It didn't take a mind reader to see the apology in his eyes, even if he couldn't muster the words. "Just this once."

He touched her elbow. "Stay here. I'll pick you up."

Sometimes she just didn't understand men. Where did chivalry fit in with unfounded accusation?

Boone splashed out into the rain and a moment later pulled up in his black F-150 pickup. She covered her head, letting her purse take the punishment, dodged the puddles, and slipped into the cab. "Where'd you get this?"

"The Mustang is just for special events."

Like what, breaking her heart?

He drove her to the impound lot in silence, stopped at the gate, and even pulled out his wallet to pay her fine.

She let him, turning away from his actions, reminding herself that she'd already forgiven him once. Maybe she could someday forgive him twice.

He drove to her Bug and reached out to touch her arm before she could slide out of the cab. "Peej—"

"There's nothing to say, Boone. I'll see you round." She closed the door on his words.

✳ ✳ ✳

Ethan and Maxine lived in Lion Heights, a development of suburbia just north of Kellogg. With split-levels and updated ranches, the houses looked straight out of *The Brady Bunch*, each yard perfectly groomed, not a blade out of place, bright impatiens hanging from the narrow porches near the doors being jostled by the wind and rain.

She drove slowly, deciphering house numbers, not sure what she would do after she picked up Davy. Or how to explain to him that she hadn't abandoned him.

The Hudsons lived in a long ranch on a cul-de-sac; PJ took in the handicap access ramp as she pulled up. It struck her that from the outside looking in, no one realized how different life was for someone in a wheelchair.

She pressed the bell and waited, shifting her weight on the steps, stifling the urge to race back to her Bug and call her mother to pick Davy up. She could probably just leave her duffel and clothes at Connie's. They could donate it all to charity—

No. She would stay. Needed to stay. For Davy. At least until Connie got home.

Emptiness shook her as she looked at the black void beyond that.

Maxine opened the door, her smile warm against the brisk, wet air. "Hey! You okay?" She held a towel and wiped her hands. "We're having pancakes. Want some?"

PJ wanted to fling herself into Maxine's arms. "That's okay. But I'd take some of the coffee I smell."

"Coming right up." She turned toward the kitchen, and PJ

followed her past the expansive tiled entry with a gilded mirror that captured a blue and white vase filled with fresh lilies on the sideboard underneath. The perfect, refreshing escape out of the chaos of the world.

"Jeremy called. Said you were tied up with the investigation, asked if we could keep Davy overnight," Maxine said over her shoulder.

He did? PJ didn't have time to sort that out, however, because Davy spied her and jumped off the stool, launching himself at her.

PJ caught him and swung him around, squeezing tight. "You okay, little man?"

He pushed back, his hands on her shoulders. "I had a sleepover!"

Not a hint of shadow in his beautiful blue eyes. PJ pressed a kiss to his forehead and pulled him close again, breathing the smell of his skin, fresh and innocent. "I missed you."

"Me too," Davy said, although he didn't put as much gusto into it as she would have liked as he untangled himself from her arms and hit the floor. He climbed back up on his high stool. "More pancakes, please."

Maxine stood at the griddle on the counter, holding a pancake turner. "Coming right up, kiddo."

Daniel and Felicia were steering their pancakes through a sea of syrup as Maxine poured PJ a cup of coffee and set it in front of her. "Have a seat."

Maxine's kitchen and family room connected into one long room with no carpet, probably so wheels could roll easier. PJ stared out the large picture window that overlooked the neighbor's backyard. Beside the window, brown velvet drapes framed French doors. No keeping secrets in this house. Maybe no need, either.

"Is Ethan around?" PJ sank onto a microfiber brown sofa in the family room and picked up what looked like a photo album.

"He's working on his Web site."

PJ opened the book.

"Those are from our early years," Maxine said, "so no laughing. Hey, c'mere, you." She caught one of the twins making a break from the counter. "Let me wipe your face."

PJ paged through the pictures. "I've never seen such a put-together scrapbook."

"I love to scrapbook. It's a wonderful legacy for the children."

She flipped back in time to pictures of just Maxine and Ethan posing at a tall gate. "Is this Buckingham Palace?" She recognized the red uniform, the bearskin busby of the soldier.

Maxine leaned over the back of the sofa. "Yeah. Ethan used to work just down the street. We would watch the changing of the guard on his lunch break."

"You used to live in London?" She turned another page. "The Eiffel Tower." Again, they stood together, arms around each other.

PJ was about to turn the page. "Wait, he's standing in these."

"Oh, sure. That was a long time ago. Before Ethan's . . . accident."

PJ's curiosity meter flickered into the red, but she couldn't stop herself. "How was he hurt? Car accident?"

Maxine went quiet behind her.

PJ turned and looked up at her. "I'm sorry; I shouldn't have—"

"No." Her voice pitched low. PJ wasn't sure if it was for the kids or if rehashing their loss brought the pain fresh to the surface. "He was shot."

"Shot?" PJ wasn't sure if she spoke or just mouthed the word.

"In Germany—Berlin, actually." Maxine wrapped her hands around the edge of the sofa. "They never caught the assailant. We were walking home from the Brandenburg Gate when Ethan just crumpled beside me. I didn't even hear the shot. We didn't think he'd live, but he pulled through miraculously. We moved to America for rehabilitation and finally to Minneapolis because of Courage Center."

"I'm sorry." And because it felt right, however foreign, PJ cupped her hand over Maxine's.

Maxine smiled at the gesture. "The good news is we were finally able to have children because of it. I'd never been able to get pregnant before. We had to do things the newfangled way—in vitro—but we got Felicia and Daniel out of it." She glanced at her twins. "Who would have thought out of the darkness might come a new future for us? We just consider each day a gift from God."

PJ couldn't speak, didn't know how to follow those words. She could learn a lot from Maxine.

Maxine slid her hand from PJ's as Ethan motored out of a room just off the family room. He smiled at PJ. "I didn't hear you come in."

"Thanks for keeping Davy." She cleared her throat. "We should get going."

"Any pancakes left, Maxine?" Ethan snagged his wife's hand as she walked by and pulled her down for a kiss.

PJ turned away before she got soggy again. She kept thumbing through their past. "Is this the Louvre?"

Ethan wheeled over to her. "Yes. Art used to be a passion of mine. I was a professor of art history at Oxford a long time ago."

PJ turned another page.

"That's at an archaeological dig in Italy." Ethan pointed to a picture of himself in a pair of Bermuda shorts, a handkerchief around his head.

"Did you know that in Italy, they're digging up a palace that belonged to Nero?" PJ said, proud of that piece of trivia.

"Yes, I did. They've been excavating for a couple decades."

"I read online that they unearthed a number of rare coins from the dig. But they were stolen." PJ looked at Ethan and gave a short burst of incredulous laughter. "You're not going to believe this, but for a while in the last two weeks, I actually thought that Ernie Hoffman had been killed because he was collecting those coins."

Now she was the prime suspect. Right next to Jack. Her smile faded.

Ethan had also lost all expression on his face. In the kitchen, Maxine's spoon dropped to the floor with a wild clatter.

"What?" PJ glanced at her as she crouched to pick it up.

Ethan was shaking his head.

Something low and repugnant started in PJ's stomach, that same feeling she'd had ten years ago, when she smelled smoke from the country club, or when she watched the goat go hooves up, and especially when Boone hauled Jack away for murder.

She just might need to put her head between her knees.

"Davy, time to go." She didn't want to know if Ethan was who her brain screamed he was. She just wanted to leave. Because paramount in this situation was the fact that if she was right—and for the first time she longed to be definitely, horribly wrong—an assassin still stalked the neighborhoods of Kellogg.

Where was Boone—or even Jeremy for that matter—when she needed him? She couldn't meet Maxine's eyes. "Thanks so much for taking care of him." She strode over to Davy, wiping his face. "I'll call."

She would. Right after she barricaded herself and Davy inside her house. Or maybe she'd call Boone first.

Because the truth was as deafening as the doorbell buzzing through her head. Whoever had killed Ernie had also fired on Jeremy. Or maybe her . . .

"C'mon, Davy." She took his hand.

The doorbell rang again. PJ stepped back as Maxine crossed to open the door.

Oh, whew, it was just the mailman. A breath of relief passed through her.

Colin stood there with an envelope in his hands. "I'm looking for Mr. Ethan Hudson?"

"That's me," Ethan said, rolling up.

Wait—what was *her* mailman doing on this side of town? She couldn't even get pizza delivery in her neighborhood. No way the mail route extended this far.

PJ couldn't move as she stared at the envelope with the little green sticker on the front.

Someone Ernie knew.

Someone Ernie trusted. Someone no one would notice. Someone like the mailman.

Colin extended the clipboard to Ethan.

PJ's breaths came fast, one after another, and she clamped her mouth shut. Davy squirmed next to her.

"Excuse me, PJ," Ethan said.

But PJ couldn't tear her eyes off Colin. He looked back at her then, a little surprised, as if he only now recognized her. His smile vanished.

She dropped Davy's hand and gave him a nudge. "Go play with Daniel and Felicia." *Go.*

Maxine frowned. Ethan took the clipboard.

As Ethan signed, Colin stepped inside and closed the door with a soft click. "Hi," he said to PJ.

PJ lifted a hand, gave a timid, unarmed wave.

Then, from behind him, Colin pulled out a gun. And of course, she recognized it as the heavy .22 Ruger Boone had introduced her to.

Colin, aka the mailman, aka Rembrandt's assassin, turned his attention to Ethan. "You're hard to track down, Doc."

Why, oh why, didn't anyone listen to her?

Chapter *TWENTY*

PJ liked being right, but she preferred to do it from a safe and painless distance.

In another life, or perhaps later in this one, she was a spy. A steely-eyed, roundhouse-kicking secret agent who could flatten Colin with a punch.

In this life, however, she was only a pathetic, slightly tanned, underdressed, hungry, and tired aunt to a four-year-old covered in syrup.

She raised her hands along with Maxine and Ethan.

"Please," Ethan said, his voice quiet, not quite to pleading yet.

Think, PJ. She tore her eyes from the gun and over to Ethan, then to Maxine, who had shuffled toward her husband.

Silence.

"Run!" PJ channeled all of her stunt-girl experience into a front kick at the gun.

She'd expected an explosion of activity, sort of chaos accompanied by chase music. Last in her mind was the way Maxine looked at her, wide-eyed, while Colin dodged her kick, grabbed her leg, and sent her spinning to the floor.

"Ow!"

"Stay down."

She crumpled onto the tile, blinking up at Ethan, who gave her a pursed-lipped shake of his head. What? She'd tried, at least. That should count.

"Don't do that again," Colin snapped.

"Or you'll *shoot* me?" She threw Ethan and Maxine a daggered look. What had happened to them?

If she had superpowers, Maxine might have been able to kill her with her narrow-eyed glare.

Maybe PJ could distract Colin long enough for Maxine to catch on and get away. "You can't do this," she said to him. "You can't just come in here and shoot these people."

"Shut up."

"You're the assassin, aren't you? the one hired by Rembrandt? You're here to finish the job, the one you started on Hoffman. Hurts to get the wrong guy, huh?"

Obviously this wasn't one of those scenes where the bad guy told everything. But she deserved some answers to questions like "Were you the one who shot Jeremy?"

"Shut up."

"What, you knew I'd figure it out, were to trying to make me look guilt—?" She sucked in her realization. "You *followed* me here!"

PJ noticed that Ethan had taken this opportunity to roll his chair away from Colin, pocketing his wife behind him.

"Stop your babbling!"

"I don't babble."

"Shut up!" Colin lunged toward her.

PJ rolled into a ball and braced her hands over her head.

Behind Ethan, glass shattered. Maxine screamed. A gun exploded, a shot that separated PJ from her self-control. She joined Maxine in the screaming.

A body fell against her. She pushed away from it, opening her eyes.

Colin lay on the tile, bleeding from the chest, making a noise much like a goat.

"Get down!" someone yelled.

She was down; she was down! PJ clamped her hands tighter over her head as the door slammed open.

Another body landed on Colin, who hollered. This one flipped him onto his stomach.

Then hands jerked her off the floor and into a hard, shocking embrace. "Are you okay?"

Was she okay? She wasn't sure—she couldn't feel anything and only after a moment became aware of how she had her hands fisted into the cloth of a shirt, clinging to safety.

She looked up.

Jeremy.

And he was just about squeezing the life out of her. She unhinged her hands from his shirt and wrapped her arms around his waist, laying her head on his chest, listening to his heart jackhammer. She'd yell at him later.

Now she just tightened her grip.

"You okay?" he asked again.

She nodded, but another voice answered.

"Yeah."

Ethan. Maxine sat on his lap, her face hidden in his chest, her shoulders shaking.

And on the floor at everyone's feet, subduing the assassin, was Boone, wearing body armor and looking fierce.

She wanted to hug him too.

Boone looked up at her just as Jeremy put her at arm's length. She glanced at Colin. Boone had him cuffed and rolled onto his back and now applied pressure to the wound in his chest—upper left shoulder, not life threatening. He was surrounded by chunks of Maxine's vase in a puddle of rank water and wounded lilies.

"What happened?"

"I shot him," Jeremy said.

She leaned away from him and for the first time noticed that he held a gun. "Where did you come from?"

Jeremy nodded toward the back French doors, now hanging open and blowing the rain in past the velvet draperies. Glass from one pane littered the floor like ice. "Nice kick. And by the way, you do babble."

"I don't." She raised her chin.

"PJ, without your babbling, we'd have carnage and lots more blood. Probably yours."

She warmed at the concern in his eyes. She'd probably have to consider forgiving him too. "Where'd the vase come from?"

"I hit him," Maxine said, lifting her head, her smile shaky.

"Where's Davy?" PJ stepped past Colin and Boone and ran down the hall. "Davy?" She found him in the bedroom with Daniel and Felicia, watching a Disney movie at a decibel level that had probably saved them years of trauma counseling, not to mention their lives. "Are you okay?"

"I don't wanna go." He sat back, chin jutted out, and she could have swooped him up and hugged the breath out of him for his headstrong, rebellious ways that had directed him to toys and movies and away from danger.

"Okay. Just stay put." She returned him to his movie, then closed the door and hung on the doorknob a moment, in case her knees gave out.

"He's okay." Jeremy came up behind her.

She couldn't reply.

Jeremy glanced back at Boone, who was turning over his paramedic job to the real guys now rushing in with a stretcher. "How badly is he injured?"

"I think he'll be fine. I hope so—we'll need him to testify against Rembrandt."

She had no words. Not one. She just stared at both of them, shaking her head. "You . . . you . . . I cannot believe you both let me believe that you thought I was nuts!"

She turned to Jeremy, and he stepped away.

"Yeah, you'd better run."

"Sorry, Princess. But after we talked, I also got this gut feeling that someone was setting you up. I just didn't know who."

"You have a lot of penance to pay, *partner*. Cough it up. How did you know Colin wasn't just the mailman?"

"It was something you said about how easy Hoffman let his killer into his house. I thought about the people we trust, like the newspaperman and the lawn guy and—"

"Pizza guys?"

He grinned. "Yes, and especially the mailman. You said your mailman had seen you at the shooting range, and Boone gave us a rough sketch of the only person he could remember. I ran a check on your mailman with a buddy of mine in the FBI, and his stated identity didn't match the description of the guy Boone saw."

Boone stepped away from the paramedics. "Obviously we had a case of stolen identity. That's when we started thinking there might be something to your theory."

"You mean my *tall tale*?"

They both looked sufficiently chagrined.

"I knew it."

"And then I got to thinking, how better to find a man in hiding but follow his sales and purchases? Especially a collector of ancient coins." Jeremy looked smug, like he'd solved the entire thing.

"Except Colin found the wrong man," PJ said, her gaze landing on Ethan, who still held Maxine's hand. "Maybe Colin never knew what the Doc really looked like, and when he saw all the registered packages from coin dealers around the world, he must have assumed that Hoffman was his target."

Boone and Jeremy looked at her with a sort of confusion.

"The registered mail. As soon as I saw the little green slip, I knew Colin was the assassin." She walked to the envelope now lying on the floor, half-covered with Colin's blood, and picked it up by one edge. "Ernie had one of these on his floor by the door, unopened."

Jeremy's smile came slow and sweet. "Of course."

"Except . . . why Hoffman?" Boone asked.

"Like she said—he got the wrong man," Jeremy said.

Like she said. She smiled at the unbelievers.

"So why did he search the house?" Boone asked, mostly to PJ. The girl with all the answers. The girl he should have believed in.

"I got into Ernie's laptop and saw some of his auctions online," PJ confessed. "He'd sold a few of the Nero coins, but not all of them. Colin must've been looking for the rest."

"He was also looking for this," Ethan cut into their conversation. He wheeled over to the hutch by the door, opened a panel, withdrew a safe box, and opened it. "It's an Athenian dekadrachm, one of fifteen like it in the world. It's worth millions. I took it off Rembrandt in Italy along with the Nero coins, and Rembrandt knows I have it." He took the coin out of the case and closed his hand around it. "This whole thing isn't about revenge. Well, not entirely. It's about money."

Ethan handed the coin to Boone. "Here. Give it to Scotland Yard. At the time I thought it was insurance—if Rembrandt killed me, he'd never know where I'd stashed it. But it's just brought me heartache." He glanced at Maxine, who took his hand despite the whitened hue to her face.

"The truth is, this is all my fault. The Nero coins were probably how our killer found Ernie. I stole the coins from Rembrandt while I was working undercover for the art squad. I knew I shouldn't have, but I wasn't a Christian at the time, and I let my greed get ahold of me. I've regretted it ever since. Jack admired them one day, and I thought he'd like a souvenir from Europe, so I gave him the coins. I never thought he'd sell them, that he even knew their value. And I just wanted to be rid of them and their hold on me."

Maxine had wrapped her arms around her waist and was

looking at the floor. PJ walked over to her, put an arm around her.

"If I had known, I would have never put Jack in danger by giving him the coins. I'm sure that as soon as they hit the market, Rembrandt's men flagged them and came after Hoffman."

"Then why was Hoffman broke, if the coins were worth so much money?" PJ took the coin from Boone, running her thumb over the ornate silver head of an ancient warrior.

"He was probably reinvesting. It's easy to catch the bug."

"Using Jack's money to do it. That's why Jack went after him at the pool. He needed his money back." PJ remembered Ernie's shock, the way Jack had tackled him. "Ernie probably figured he'd give Jack a cut of the profits."

"And in the meantime, his activities flagged Rembrandt's attention or at least Colin's," Ethan said.

"So are you still working for Scotland Yard?" Boone asked Ethan as PJ dropped the coin back into his hand.

"Yes. On the art squad. I still consult for them as an appraiser. Which is why I receive certified mail." Ethan's gaze settled on PJ.

She shrugged. "With the assassin acting as the mailman, it probably wasn't hard to get Ernie's bank information, connect him with Jack, and then pin the blame on Jack. I wouldn't be surprised if he emptied out Jack's bank account before the murder, just to cement the blame.

"In fact . . . hey—" PJ walked over to Colin, who lay writhing in pain, an IV snaking from his arm. "I saw you that day in front of Hoffman's house, in your little red Geo. You *waved* to me. And then when you saw me at the shooting range, you thought I'd figure it out. You knew—" she sucked in another breath of disbelief—"and you saw Jeremy at Hoffman's too. Who exactly were you aiming for at the park, me or Jeremy?"

Colin looked away.

"Or both." Jeremy came up, curled his hand around her elbow. "PJ, let's get out of here."

Boone's face was full of the remorse she'd longed for ten years to see. "So . . ." He looked away and cleared his throat, and when his eyes found PJ again, the expression was gone. "You did steal the lawn truck."

PJ didn't know what to say. Thankfully he didn't know about the country club. Yet. She didn't answer.

"And you . . ." He cut off Jeremy. "You were there too?"

Jeremy shrugged, stepped around him.

PJ went back to the bedroom and scooped up Davy, hiding his eyes from the blood as they moved toward the door. As she glanced back, she saw Boone staring after her, something forlorn again on his face.

The rain had stopped, only a haze of humidity in the air, the sky clearing to a crisp blue. Police cruisers flashed red lights across the houses, and a news crew had arrived, probably listening to the scanner. PJ moved over to the driveway, Jeremy beside her as Ethan rolled out, followed by Maxine and the twins. Boone directed his deputies to tape off the house while he pulled out his cell phone. PJ watched his eyes train on Ethan. Clearly a conversation with Scotland Yard was in Boone and Ethan's near future.

"Nana!" Davy wiggled out of her arms and hit the pavement running. PJ turned in time to see her mother stalking toward her, a hard look on her unmade-up face. She took Davy's hand and kept coming, like the Terminator. She looked like she'd thrown on an old pair of jeans and one of her husband's ragged sweatshirts. PJ barely recognized her.

PJ had begun to edge behind Jeremy when her mother flung an arm around her neck.

Tight.

Can't breathe . . . Mom.

But Elizabeth didn't let go. "I was so worried about you. The phone rang off the hook this morning. People said that you shot Boone yesterday at the park—"

"I didn't shoot Boo—"

"And then when I went by the house, you weren't there, and I couldn't believe that you'd shoot—"

"I didn't shoot anyone!"

"So I went to the station, and the fiasco came over the radio, and, PJ, are you okay?"

PJ pushed away from her, held her at arm's length. Her mother looked old. Worry etched into the lines of her naked face. She wasn't even wearing lipstick. "Mom?"

Elizabeth blinked; a tear winked out and trailed down her cheek. She didn't even bother to wipe it away as her voice fell to just above a groan. Or maybe a prayer. "I couldn't bear it if anything happened to you. Not now, when I have you back."

PJ opened her mouth, but only a hiccup of breath emerged.

Her mother touched her face, holding her hand there a long time. Finally the smile—even, calm, Sugarized—took its place. She patted PJ's cheek. "I'm so glad you're okay."

PJ nodded.

"She's more than okay. She stopped an assassin from killing

her and the entire Hudson family." Jeremy put a hand on her back. PJ didn't bother to move away. For now.

"Well, of course she did." Elizabeth smiled. "PJ can do anything."

Someone had stolen her mother.

Or maybe PJ had finally discovered her.

The static of police radios competed with the murmur of neighbors clumping in curiosity behind them. Jeremy moved his hand onto PJ's shoulder.

Brakes screeching on the wet pavement parted the crowd, and PJ saw Trudi tumble out of her car.

She ran to PJ. "Are you okay? The police dispatcher just called."

"Yes—now. We're all okay."

Trudi swallowed her in a clench. "Thank you for standing by us."

"Well, it's about time. I'm really sorry I left town all those years ago and didn't stand by you then."

Trudi pulled away, wiped her eyes. "You're here now."

Yeah, she was.

"Oh, by the way—" Trudi reached into her purse, one nearly as big as PJ's—"I found this in Chip's diaper bag. I think it was from when Davy read it to him on the beach that day. So cute." She handed her a book.

The Little Rabbit Who Wanted Red Wings. PJ flipped open the front cover. Of course, there it was: "Property of Fellows Academy Library" printed next to an IPC coded label.

"Thanks, Trude."

Trudi gave her another squeeze before she ran to Maxine and her family.

PJ turned to watch as the paramedics loaded Colin into the truck. Boone stood in the sweep of red lights, looking grim. He shot her a glance, his gaze flickering to Jeremy and back to PJ. Then he turned away.

"Wonder if he'll pull through," PJ said, nearly under her breath.

"It wasn't much more than a flesh wound," Jeremy said, but she wasn't exactly thinking of Colin. "You did a good thing here, PJ. If it weren't for you and your nosiness, Jack would be in prison, Trudi would be broke, and Ethan and Maxine would still be living a lie with a price on their heads." Jeremy directed her gaze to Maxine and Ethan with Trudi and the twins.

Yeah, well, it wasn't all her. In fact, maybe it wasn't her at all. But, like Peter, it was just being the person God made her, letting Him do amazing things as she . . . surrendered.

Surrendered her reputation. Her future. Boone.

She glanced back at Boone. As much as she missed him, she wasn't sure she could be with Boone and love God at the same time.

Boone must have felt her gaze on him for he met her eyes. She lifted her hand in a wave. His mouth tipped, just a little.

"So, I'm wondering if you want a job."

Huh? PJ looked at Jeremy. "As a pizza delivery girl?"

"No, as my assistant." He pulled out a business card from his wallet and handed it to her. *Kane Investigations.*

She flicked it between her fingers. "I don't know; I was kinda looking forward to free pizza."

"I'll write it into your benefits package." His eyes laughed, clear of anything dark and mysterious. "That is, if you're sticking around town. Boone says you do this run thing."

She glanced over his shoulder at Boone folding himself into his cruiser. "There's more to that story."

Jeremy followed her gaze. "He says you're nothing but trouble," he said, more in his voice than she was prepared to address.

"He's probably right."

Chapter **TWENTY-ONE**

Dear Constance Sukharov,
It's come to our attention that while under
the supervision of your sister, PJ Sugar,
your son, David Morton, was expelled from
Fellows Academy. We're pleased to inform
you that the circumstances under which he
was expelled have been rectified. Accordingly,
we'd like to reoffer a position for David at
Fellows Academy. Our deepest apologies for
any inconvenience this may have caused you.
Thank you for your desire to give David the
best educational experience available to him.

Regards,
Priscilla Nicholson
Director, Fellows Early Education Academy

LOCAL WOMAN SAVES LIVES,
Captures International Assassin
by Macey Harrison

PJ Sugar, of the Kellogg Sugars, helped apprehend an international assassin Monday morning at the home of Ethan and Maxine Hudson, 138 Lion Drive. The assassin entered the Hudson home shortly after 9 a.m., holding the family at gunpoint. Sugar, who had previously alerted officials, was at the residence and assisted in the assailant's capture. Jeremy Kane, a private investigator employed by Trudi and Jack Wilkes, who had been indicted for the murder of Ernie Hoffman, also assisted in the apprehension.

"Although evidence pointed to Jack's involvement in Hoffman's murder, evidence surfaced by Sugar and Kane proved to clear Wilkes of all charges," Lt. Daniel Buckam of the Kellogg Police Department stated in a press conference early Tuesday morning.

Following a confession, the suspect, Colin Butcher, has been charged with one count of first degree murder of Ernie Hoffman and seven counts of attempted murder, including an attempt made on Jeremy Kane at Kellogg City Park. The suspect's employer, a French smuggler known as Rembrandt, has also been charged with accessory to murder.

Butcher lived in the Kellogg community for six months, posing as a mailman. He gained access to the postal service through a stolen identity, the postal service confirmed in a statement.

Sugar left town ten years ago after being suspected of setting fire to the Kellogg Country Club.

"I only returned to Kellogg to watch my nephew while my sister went on her honeymoon," Sugar said. "But when my friend's husband was arrested, I knew that there was more to the story."

She has recently been cleared of arson charges, and her membership to the club restored.

"I'm just hoping to start over," Sugar said. "This time with a clean slate. But I know how it feels to be falsely accused. I didn't want Jack and Trudi to live with that stigma."

In a related event, Sugar led a search of Ernie Hoffman's home. "As a teenager, I plastered my walls with cute teen stars. So when I saw the picture of the Hoffman family hanging in Tucker's room, I knew it had to be hiding something. No teenage boy is going to put up an oil painting of his family in his room."

Behind the picture, Kellogg Police and Scotland Yard's art squad discovered a stash of first-century Nero coins, whose worth is estimated at $1.5 million. Officials suspect that Hoffman, a registered numismatist, had been tracking down the coins in hopes of receiving the international reward posted by the insurer. A check was issued to Tucker and Denise Hoffman, beneficiaries of Hoffman's estate. Jack and Trudi Wilkes also received an undisclosed amount for the recovery of the lost coins.

PUBLIC NOTICE:

I, Daniel "Boone" Buckam, declare, in the matter of the incident at the Kellogg Country Club on prom night ten years ago, that PJ Sugar is innocent of all involvement in the accidental fire that consumed the KCC kitchen facilities.

PJ folded the paper, set it on the sand next to her, and leaned back onto her hands, lifting her face, her eyes closed. The sun boiled her bare shoulders; the sand, moistened by the occasional motorboat-riled wave, cooled her feet as she tunneled her toes into it. She counted the blue sky as God's reward for having helped her mother box the rest of her possessions this week since Connie's return.

For now, she'd negotiated space in the garage. Next to her father's golf clubs.

Behind her, Connie and Elizabeth argued over the condition of the steaks on the hibachi, the smell of garlic and fat dripping on coals carving into her hunger. Davy and Sergei threw a Frisbee in the grass beyond the picnic tables, overlorded by Vera, who shouted what sounded like military commands in Russian.

Boris lay ten feet away, sunbathing. At least here he could get away with his Speedo.

PJ avoided looking in his general direction.

The only family member missing from their Saturday afternoon picnic was Dora, safely anchored in the backyard a secure chewing distance from the hostas. Who would have guessed that he'd become part of the family? Or that Sergei had asked his parents to buy Davy the same type of pet he'd had growing up?

"Did you invite Boone?" Elizabeth came padding over, flicking sand out of her white sandals. She'd recovered from her stint out into society as a real person and had resumed her tailored Sugar persona, pearls included.

She peered at PJ through dark glasses.

It was probably a good thing PJ couldn't read her eyes.

"No." PJ turned to see Boone swaggering across the beach. Off duty, or perhaps on duty, depending on his job description. He took off his sunglasses and grinned at her.

Perhaps he'd had a sort of aneurysm, forgotten that he'd arrested her a week ago and left her to freeze to death in a cell the temperature of Siberia. Or he thought the ad he'd put in the paper bought him grace.

She got up and brushed off her legs, feigning nonchalance.

"Be careful," her mother muttered. She ignored Boone as she passed him.

"Did you feel that arctic blast?"

"You're still standing. Be grateful."

He twirled his sunglasses between his fingers. "Thought I'd find you here on such a beautiful day. Looks like you're having a barbecue."

"A welcome-home bash."

"For you?"

That was sweet. "For Connie and Sergei." And, yes, maybe her. Because so far, she still had an address in Kellogg. "Saw the ad. Thanks."

The smile he gave her resonated with chagrin. "I owed you. Still do, probably."

"Yep." But she added a wink. "I'll let you know when I need to collect."

"How about now?" Before she could react, maybe step away, he touched her shoulder. "I like that you still have the tattoo."

Of course he did. "It should read *Trouble*."

He dropped his hand. "Not ready yet, huh?"

She didn't know how to answer. Mostly because she didn't have an answer yet.

They stood there on the beach, the hot sand seeping into her feet, the sun's eyes on her, burning. Her mother made no attempt to hide her scrutiny of their conversation, one hand holding a spatula, the other on her hip.

"Jeremy says you're going to work for him."

"Yeah."

A job. A real job with real money. She'd been churning that over in her brain for a week now. Finally decided to hop on and see where the ride took her.

She wasn't making anyone any promises. Especially herself. However, the yes she'd given Jeremy resonated in her like a victory cry, bathed her in something that she could only name as hope.

"I don't know if I like the idea of you working for him.

Going undercover, causing havoc." But in Boone's pretty blue eyes she saw something unfamiliar that, together with the hard edge of his jaw as he looked away . . .

"Are you jealous?"

"Of what? Is there something to be jealous of?" He put on his glasses, hiding those eyes. "I just don't want you to get hurt."

"I won't get into trouble."

He gave a huff that sounded so old Boone, so arrogantly challenging, that she half expected him to follow it up with *"PJ, you're nothing but trouble."*

Instead he just shook his head. But the smile stayed. "We'll see."

She gave him her best look of indignation. However, in the wake of his laughter, she'd already become a liar. Because over his shoulder, in the lot behind him next to his shiny red Mustang, a motorcycle pulled up, a red and yellow Harley.

The biker stopped at the curb and lifted his glasses. His gaze ranged from her to Boone, then back.

"Hey, Princess. Want to go for a ride?" Jeremy chased his request with a wide, white, reckless grin.

Oh, boy.

PJ, what have you done?

Author's Note

Sometimes, do you feel like you just don't fit in? You look around you and think that if anyone knew how difficult it was just to put yourself together, to smile when you feel completely overwhelmed, to even figure out what you were making for supper, they'd know what a mess you were. Maybe you totally relate to those words in 1 Peter—"God's elect, *strangers* in the world." Do you feel like when you look in the rearview mirror, all you see are your mistakes?

Maybe not. But if so, then PJ is your gal. I wanted to write a story about the person in so many of us who just wants to get it right . . . but can't seem to stay out of trouble. My friend and I have what we call the "stupid mouth" club . . . and we report our weekly foibles (usually on Monday, after Sunday church!). PJ is our charter member. She's the girl that changes her mind, always hopes for the best, is always discovering that she is just a little different from everyone else. PJ is us.

And that's good news. Because God loves PJ. He loves her messiness and her impulsiveness, her heart bent toward others, the hope that fuels her actions. And He has a plan for PJ—one that includes her weaknesses as well as her strengths.

Yep, I need to hear that—need to hear that I don't have to be perfect for God to love me, use me, sing over me. Need to hear that although I don't fit in, I'm not supposed to. . . . In fact, I'm supposed to be a little . . . alien.

So, to all the PJs out there—and anyone who knows a PJ—this book is for you. Thank you for reading PJ's adventures—I hope you come back for her continuing craziness with Boone and Jeremy and her PI dreams in the next book: *Double Trouble*. And meanwhile, may you live with joy on the outside the unique and delightful person God has created on the inside.

IN HIS GRACE,
Susan May Warren

About the Author

Susan May Warren is a former missionary to Russia, the mother of four children, and the wife of a guy who wooed her onto the back of his motorcycle for the adventure of a lifetime. The award-winning author of over twenty books, Susan loves to write and teach writing. She speaks at women's events around the country about God's amazing grace in our lives. Susan is active in her church and small community and makes her home on the north shore of Minnesota where her husband runs a hotel.

Visit her Web site at **www.susanmaywarren.com.**

More great fiction from

SUSAN MAY WARREN

THE NOBLE LEGACY SERIES

After their father dies, three siblings reunite on the family ranch to try to preserve the Noble legacy. If only family secrets—and unsuspected enemies—didn't threaten to destroy everything they've worked so hard to build.

X